STITCHES

An Ale Ferretti Novel

SANDY J HARGRAVES

 FriesenPress

Suite 300 - 990 Fort St
Victoria, BC, V8V 3K2
Canada

www.friesenpress.com

ISBN
978-1-03-911360-2 (Hardcover)
978-1-03-911359-6 (Paperback)
978-1-03-911361-9 (eBook)

1. FICTION, CONTEMPORARY WOMEN

Distributed to the trade by The Ingram Book Company

This book is dedicated to my Italian friends
and to two of my English teachers,
Allan Nelson and Edward Poley.

She survived the pandemic as an ER Nurse in Los Angeles,
so why are people trying to kidnap and kill her??

CHAPTER 1
Happy New Year!

Hallelujah! It's 2023 and we finally have a handle on the COVID-19 pandemic. Those who chose to be vaccinated have received it, the sickness and deaths have slowed, if not ceased, and life is back to almost normal. Whatever that is.

Ale (pronounced "Alley") Ferretti is a twenty-nine year old ER nurse for Good Samaritan Hospital in Los Angeles, California. Tonight, is New Year's Eve, normally Ale would be in the Bahamas with her girlfriends, staying at her uncle Tony's beach house, enjoying some well-deserved vacation time. With the pandemic over and people back vacationing and travelling, the islands are saturated with visitors. The hospitality industry is slowly getting back on its feet and people are feeling safe to travel.

Instead of being in Bahamas with her friends, Ale is in LA, helping her caterer friend Leslie Butler. The party circuit is in high gear, especially at New Year's and she is overwhelmed and understaffed. Everyone is celebrating and spending money like crazy. On her days off, Ale always helps Leslie out. It's great extra income and it allows her to mingle in social circles that she rarely frequents.

Tonight, they are catering a VIP party at the Wayfarer Hotel. VIPs in Los Angeles can mean anything from actors, politicians, music leaders, glorified celebrities, TV personalities, you name it. The job is to wear a uniform, be impeccably groomed, avoid eye contact, and avoid conversation, except to respond to requests and circulate incredible hors d'oeuvres and champagne. A majority of VIPs barely look at you or realize you are there and that suits Ale fine. Some waitstaff want to catch the eye of certain people to get ahead in career or life, but Ale is not one of them. Unfortunately, being an ER nurse, she has seen the outcome of some of those scenarios, so she makes it her mission to be invisible. The upside of catering VIP parties is the generous tips!

Leslie Butler is a well-known and respected caterer in LA. Her catering business almost died because of COVID, however she turned it into a food-delivery service and managed to keep the lights on. Tonight's party is very important to her, as they all are; it will set the pace for what is to be a fabulous party year. Everyone wants to be socializing, eating, and drinking again.

All VIP parties have security, and it's everywhere. Leslie hired the team for this party. She pays the security company for its services, and she bills it back to her clients. It allows her to keep eyes on her staff and ensure they are safe. VIPs can be assholes and even rapists. She's experienced that the hard way. Tonight, she's using a company named StrikeForce. All in black suits, earpieces, and barely noticeable. Just the way Leslie wanted it. If you work enough of her parties, you start to recognize some of the regulars, but tonight they all looked new, probably because businesses were just getting back on their feet and staff were newly hired.

Tonight, Ale's uniform is a fitted black sheath dress that goes down to the knee. It has short sleeves and a round neck, not showing cleavage, not that she has any. Her very, very curly blonde hair is in a tight bun on top of her head, makeup is minimal, and jewellery consists of stud earrings. Black pumps complete the school marm look. It's all business.

As Ale walked from the kitchen, dropping off dirty glasses and plates, she decided to take a different route to the roof top terrace, get some air, and see if any dirty dishes needed to be gathered. The view was incredible from there; it made her want to just sit in one of the comfy chairs and relax. It was a clear night, and you could see all the way to the Pacific Ocean. The city was alive, in a good way, with people laughing, live music playing, and people dancing. Everyone enjoying themselves without having to social distance or have the fear of Covid. It was a beautiful sight.

Duty calls. Most of the guests were moving on to other parties, so the terrace was bare. The exception being a strikingly handsome Latino man, dressed all in black. He had an earpiece in, so Ale's assumption was that he was security. He smiled and nodded. She returned the nod while keeping her eyes straight ahead. He wasn't a guest, he was security, maybe the rules don't apply? She turned to look at him, thinking that she might check him out. He also turned his head, and she did the one thing she was NOT supposed to do and looked into his eyes. OK, wow. Nipple alert. She immediately turned her head back, just in time to avoid walking into a large pillar. Ale quickly refocused and gathered up glasses and dishes, then headed back down to the kitchen.

The staff continued with the clean up, rarely speaking to each other, keeping it professional. Once all the guests were gone, Ale looked at her Fitbit; it was 3 a.m. *Jeezus.* How did that happen? Most of the female wait staff were taking off their heels, except for Ale. She was raised by an Italian mother; heels were a part of her upbringing *AND* she was an ER nurse, so being on her feet for twelve-hour shifts was her normal.

Leslie was in the kitchen looking happy and handing out little envelopes of cash to everyone, thanking them and telling those who wanted drives home that the security company would be downstairs waiting. Another thing Ale loved about Leslie was that she really cared about her people. Safety was everything.

Ale was certain most of the young, beautiful ladies who were serving tonight received business cards and numbers to meet up with some of the VIPs and would be stupid enough to agree to it. Leslie could not control that. She could only control what happened when they were under her care. Some would learn from the experience and others may not even make it out alive. Sad, but true. The pandemic had put a big squash on people hooking up for random sex, so everyone was super horny. Not Ale; just the rest of the world

Time to go home! Sometimes Ale brought a change of clothes to go home in, but tonight she just wanted to get home and sleep. She had an adorable apartment near Korea town in a well-maintained building, a clean one-bedroom with balcony. It was close to her work so she could take the bus and not have to worry about LA traffic. Convenient and inexpensive.

Ale said good night to Leslie and hugged her, accepted her envelope, grabbed her coat, and rode the elevator to the lobby with the others. The hotel was still packed with drunks and partiers. It made Ale happy she wasn't working the ER tonight.

The security team was directing them to their vehicles, which were all black, of course. They held the doors open, Ale piled into a Land Rover SUV, and gave the driver with the StrikeForce jacket her address. He looked into the rear-view mirror and those same dark eyes looked back at her. Her driver was the Latino guy she had met on the terrace. Interesting. Ale smiled and checked her phone. Oh great, nothing but photos from her friends who had gone to the Bahamas, Happy New Year greetings from family and friends, the usual. She smiled, scrolling through the messages, replying, and leaning her head against the window. Man, she was tired. Maybe working tonight wasn't the best idea, but she didn't like to disappoint her friends. Actually, she didn't like to disappoint anyone.

When they arrived at her apartment building, Ale rummaged through her small cross-body bag to find cash to give the driver a tip. He got out, walked around the vehicle, and opened her door to help her out. Ale put the money in his hand.

He smiled and said, "That's not necessary. Please let me walk you to your apartment and make sure you get in safely; Leslie would want that."

Ale was hesitant. She didn't want some stranger knowing her apartment number, so she declined. He said goodnight and waited until she was in the building lobby and drove off. *Hmm.* Somehow the whole experience made her edgy, not in a scared way, but in a way that heightened her senses.

Ale unlocked her apartment, turned on the lights and smiled. She loved having her own place: no roommates, no family, all hers. She hung up her coat, kicked off her heels, and headed for the bathroom. She showered, conditioned her hair, moisturized, and collapsed into a deep sleep. *Thank God 2022 was over.*

CHAPTER 2
Momma's House

Most people spend New Years Day taking care of hangovers, swimming, sunbathing—all the fun things you can do in Bahamas. Only problem is, Ale was still in LA. She woke up around noon, showered again to wake up, dressed, and headed over to her momma's via the bus, as momma would be serving lunch and Ale was starving! Before she zipped up her little purse, she remembered the envelope from last night was in there. She opened it and counted out the bills. *Jeezus*, $2,000. Unbelievable! She grabbed a few bills and put the rest in her safe with all her other bundles of cash. Yeah, she has a cash problem. We will talk about that a bit later.

With names like Maria and Vito Ferretti, it's no surprise her momma and papa were old-school Italian. They're actually her adoptive parents, who took her in when she was seven, bringing her to their California home from New Brunswick, Canada. She inherited an older brother named Gio who is hard-core Italian. Her papa is one of the most renowned tailors in California. He also owns a family restaurant called Vito's Pizzeria in downtown LA. Her zio Luigi (papa's brother) runs it, along with a slew of cousins and aunts. Best Italian food you will ever taste. Their little family tailor shop is on West Sixth Street; it's been there for decades. Her parents still have the large home that she and Gio grew up in when they were kids, but they actually live in the nice-sized apartment above the tailor shop. They want to be close to the business and each other. Now, they mostly just use the house for large family gatherings.

Lunch at momma's is like a buffet at the Hilton. Ale opened the door downstairs from the back. Her papa wasn't working as it was a holiday. She took the elevator up because she was too lazy to take the stairs and her momma greeted her like a Labrador retriever.

"Alessandra, oh baby, you must be exhausted. Come sit, eat, *mangiare*."

Sometimes she spoke in Italian. Ale adjusted to this, as she was fluent in French, Italian, Spanish, English, some Portuguese, and some Arabic. More about that later. She kissed her momma and allowed her to pet her up and down, then went over to hug and kiss her papa, who was already at the table. Papa was a man of few words. When he smiled, it was always with his eyes. Ale always felt loved when he looked at her. He was quiet for an Italian male, which is unusual, and he looked like Robert DeNiro. When he spoke, they all listened.

Ale's momma, Maria Ferretti, was stunning, and everyone thought she should have been a model or actress. Momma only wanted to be Vito's wife and their momma. She was from Southern Italy, with ginger hair, big Root Beer-coloured eyes, gorgeous pale perfect skin, and a set of boobs that made all Ale's boyfriends wonder what happened to hers. Well, technically Maria wasn't her real mom, so she didn't have any of her beautiful genes. Maria was a stunner, she was lovely, she could cook, and she had a great marriage. Goals!

As they waited for others to arrive, Ale filled her family in on the party. She knew exactly when her brother Gio and sister-in-law Sophia had arrived. Gio was the unquiet Italian; you could hear him coming for miles. He had a mouth like a sailor, a heart of pure gold, was always the life of the party, outgoing, and hilarious. Sophia was blonde, tiny, and quiet. She adored Gio and all she wanted was babies. Unfortunately, that wasn't going so well. She looked stressed. It is almost a cardinal sin when an Italian cannot conceive, and it is always the woman's fault. Ale's momma could not have any more babies after Gio—adopting Ale was a life saver. At least that is what she tells everyone.

Gio managed most of the family "business." There was always

speculation that their Italian family was linked to the mob but Ale didn't see any of that, nor did she ask. Their zio Tony who owned a jewellery store and other businesses seemed shady, but he was married to momma's sister Connie. Zia Connie was the female version of Gio and she was Ale's favourite zia. They loved each other like crazy. While momma was a bit reserved and appropriate, zia was neither. They bonded over that.

Lunch was loud, noisy, and happy with everyone talking over each other and groaning from the taste of the delicious meal. Momma smiling. Having everyone at her table was heaven.

"Who was at the party?" asked Gio while piling more prosciutto on his plate and filling up his wine glass.

"No idea," Ale replied dryly. "Have you ever used StrikeForce Security for anything?"

"Yeah, all the time. Good bunch; I know the owner well."

"Everyone knows the owner," said Sophia, smiling.

They all looked at her. She rarely spoke. Vito smiled, Gio frowned. Momma and Ale both looked confused.

"Who's the owner?" they asked in unison.

"Striker," Gio replied. "Good guy." Ale looked at Sophia and Sophia fanned herself. *OK, thought Ale, she's getting it.*

"Striker? What kind of name is that?" Ale asked.

"It's a nickname he had from the military. His real name is Carlos Montoya."

"They did the security last night," said Ale.

Sophia caught Ale's eye and mouthed "*Lucky you.*"

Hmm, Ale thought.

Gio was shoving food into his mouth. "We've used them a few times; they do security systems as well. He's a customer of papa's."

She looked at her papa, he nodded while putting more bread in his mouth.

"Why are you asking, Ale?" said momma, who was still in the dark.

"Oh, just curious. They did a great job. Not sure I worked with them before," Ale lied. She was certain the guy who drove her home wasn't the owner, but she was a bit curious as to who he was. Maybe

Gio could find that out for her.

Sophia spoke up. "Striker is a total player. Women throw themselves at him and yet he is always very polite and respectful."

How are you a player and polite and respectful? Ale thought.

Gio turned and looked at Sophia. "How the hell do you know this?"

Ale smiled. Seriously, Sophia was quiet and a good listener, but she knew everything that was going on, she just didn't talk about it.

"Everybody knows this, well, at least all the women in LA county," she replied, then chewing politely, and smiling. Gio gave her a dirty look.

"I didn't know," both momma and Ale said, again in unison. Then again, how would they? They both tried to stay out of the limelight and away from drama.

Gio shrugged. "He's a good-looking guy, fit, has a dark past, and apparently the ladies love him." Gio chewed. "He's just like most Latino guys in LA."

Ale looked at Sophia—she was shaking her head. OK, so she needed a lunch with Sophia to get the real scoop.

"Anyways," Ale said, putting a piece of fresh mozzarella in her mouth. "The tips were good and there were no incidents, Leslie was happy, it was a success." Hopefully changing the subject. *Why was it so hot in here?*

They continued to talk about everything from family drama to business to politics, which is when Ale decided it was time to leave. After helping to clean up, she kissed her parents, goodbye, and Gio and Sophia gave her a drive home. The entire ride, Ale was thinking, *Who was Striker?* and was he, in fact, the man who had driven her home?

CHAPTER 3
Mystery Man

As soon as Ale was home, she changed into her comfy clothes and looked at the two sewing machines in her bedroom. She should do some sewing. Maybe tomorrow. She sewed regularly for her papa. His delivery guy, Danny, who was like another brother to her, drops off the pieces in plastic bins and Ale measures, pins, cuts and sews them. When they are ready, Danny picks them up and they rinse and repeat. She loved sewing. As early as she can remember, her papa would put her on his knee, and they would sew together for hours. She also made most of her own clothes, clothes for others, whatever she wanted. She found it very therapeutic, and her papa pays her in cash. We will talk about the cash later.

Ale opted not to sew and instead went to her leather couch and grabbed her tablet. She searched for Carlos Montoya/Striker and almost dropped the tablet on the floor. *Holy shit, are you kidding me?* It *was* Striker who had driven her home. *Holy fuck! She had even tried to tip him!* Oh Alessandra! She could just hear her momma.

How could she live here all this time and NOT know about this guy? Wow. OK, he did get around. He was linked to a lot of women. Of course, it doesn't mean the information is true. After all, it's the internet, but still. His company provided private security. Oh, she bet he did. OK, but why was he driving waitstaff home? He was the owner! Maybe he was desperate because of the pandemic?

The photos did not do this man justice. He was perfectly made: fit, muscled body, all alpha; smooth, mocha-coloured skin; dark-black hair; and the darkest eyes she had ever seen.

Gosh, why was it so hot in here?

According to the internet, he was Cuban-born, joined the military, and his family immigrated to Miami. No other personal information available, which was not surprising. After all, he is in security. He probably is a master at hiding information and or finding it. He wasn't flashy and almost every photo showed him not smiling, and yet he smiled at HER. Probably his signature move. But seriously, Ale thought, he could be with anyone, he wasn't flirting with her, so maybe he was just doing his job and being polite. Why did it matter so much?

The photos showed him with a beautiful woman on his arm at various parties, some looked like crazy horny housewives; maybe he did security for them? There were photos of him frequently going in and out of Miguel's Restaurant. Gawd, she loved that place: best prickly pear margarita and burritos in the world. She'd been there a million times and never once saw or heard of him. Of course, she didn't have social media because it's the root of all evil, so that didn't help either. Ale sighed. Maybe she should call Leslie.

Ale's curiosity was giving her a headache and she decided to bake to help take stress away. Her momma and zia taught her to be a good baker and a good cook. She just didn't have the boobs. She heard it all the time, *Girl—you live in LA; get the fake ones*. NOPE. She was a nurse and saw the dark side of implants and she refused to look like every other blonde in LA. Gawd, they wouldn't even recognize themselves if they removed all the fillers and implants. This town thrived on fake and Ale preferred to stay natural, even if she never got laid again.

CHAPTER 4
Who Is the Blonde?

StrikeForce headquarters in downtown LA was not impressive looking. In fact, you wouldn't know anybody worked or lived there at all. That's the way Striker wanted it. After all, his business was about security. He had a past, a dangerous one, and he had enemies. Blending in was necessary.

It was an older square ten-storey building with bulletproof windows and underground parking. The top floor had a balcony that faced the back; that is where Striker lived. He crashed there and found it efficient to live and work in the same building. He had a beautiful big house with a pool in one of LA's upscale gated communities however he rarely stayed there. Sometimes he used it as a safe house.

Carlos sat at his desk at StrikeForce headquarters obsessed with finding out who the blonde was he met on New Year's Eve and why he cared. She wasn't his usual type, but something happened when she smiled at him, and he hadn't been able to shake it. He was Striker, nickname from the military. He'd strike and leave. No relationships, no drama, just sex. He loved women—all of them. He loved making love to them, and they loved having him. He made it a rule to never go back for seconds. He made the rules clear, and the women still lined up wanting time with him. He wasn't cold or a misogynist. God no; the complete opposite. He loved and respected women. He just didn't want relationships. One of the things he loved about living in LA, was that women were strong and confident. Some were just looking to get laid. He was picky and careful, always. He never paid and he didn't get emotionally attached, ever. COVID had put a real damper on casual sex, however he managed to get through it. He didn't have to chase or convince, so why was he thinking about her?

He grabbed his phone and called Leslie. He had great respect and admiration for Leslie, and they had formed a good partnership for events and other business ventures.

Leslie Butler was an average-looking brown-haired, blue-eyed, hard-working woman. She was recently divorced. She had to give her asshole ex husband half of all the money she made as a caterer because his lazy arse never left the couch. However, she was happy to be rid of him. She managed to keep her catering business going through almost three years of COVID hell, in a city that always wanted to party. This will be her year, no lazy greedy husband, just party, party, party that she can cater and build up her clientele. Not to mention, big beautiful expensive weddings. Putting people back to work, made her smile. It also made her smile when she looked at her phone and saw Striker was calling her.

"Hey Carlos, how are you?" she answered.

"Leslie. Good, you?" Striker was a man of few words, especially when he wanted information.

"Great, thank you. Again, great job with the party last night. Everything went as planned."

"Glad to hear it. Thank you for the opportunity." Carlos paused. The events security was a huge piece of his business and partnering with people like Leslie was a great boost to his bottom line.

"I was wondering if you could give me the contact info of one of your waitstaff. She left a sweater in one of our cars. Blonde, petite, lives in an apartment building on Virgil?"

Leslie hesitated. She didn't like giving out personal info on her staff, especially those who were her friends, even to her security team. Even though she worked with Carlos on several events and trusted him, she tried another tactic.

"Why don't you just bring it to the next event we do together, which is Thursday evening, and I will give it to her."

Carlos smiled into the phone. She was protecting her staff. He liked that. In fact, his respect level for her just went up notches. "That sounds like a plan. If they call and need it earlier, just text me." Carlos conceded.

"Great, thanks for letting me know, and we will talk on Thursday. Should be a good time!"

Carlos hung up. He could have used his charm to get the info but didn't want to be pushy. He'd have to find another way. Surveillance was his only option, and he knew just the guy to put on it. He stood up and walked down to his control centre to speak with Ramone. He had a new job for him.

CHAPTER 5
Being An ER Nurse in LA Was a TRIP!

Ale decided to put Striker out of her mind and move on. Her shifts at Good Samaritan were three twelve-hour shifts, then three days off. Sometimes she did doubles. During COVID, they had zero time off and lived in hotel rooms. It was horrible and lonely. Her poor momma was devastated. Ale worried constantly about her family and her friends.

Before they could be together again, Ale had to self-isolate for 14 days, even after getting both vaccines. Only then could she visit her family. Momma just grabbed her and wouldn't let her go for the entire day. Ale sat on her knee the entire time and they cuddled. Couldn't buy love like that. Momma fed her over and over and told her to quit her job.

Today Ale was working the 7 a.m. to 7 p.m. shift. As usual, she rode the bus, 10 minutes door to door. She always dressed in nice clothes going to work, never her scrubs. Today she had on her worn in Levi's that hugged her butt. She tailored everything she bought off the rack. She had on high brown leather boots, a black ribbed crop turtleneck and a brown worn-leather motorcycle jacket. She carried a large black tote that held her wallet, hospital badge, change of clothes, makeup bag, and her lunch. Ale had a locker at work, so the lugging was minimal.

Ale loved her hospital; it always felt like home. She worked tirelessly to raise money, and she made it her mission to know and smile at everyone. They all knew her, especially the patients. She made an impact here. Out in the real world, not so much, but here at Good Samaritan, she ruled!

She greeted the security guard, Lou, handed him a nice fresh loaf of homemade bread, and he smiled like a child.

"Good morning, Ale! Thank you so much for the bread. You know you spoil me!"

"You deserve it, Lou," she replied. "Can't have our chief security guard getting hungry." She kept walking towards the staff quarters to find her locker and get ready for the day.

Mornings were always exciting in ER, shift change was confusing, people were cranky, and she loved it.

"'Morning, Nya!" Nya King was their big and beautiful African American goddess. She ruled the ER desk like nobody, and Ale adored her. She had a beautiful big toothy smile, long braids piled up high on her head, and a stubbornness that made her superb at her job.

"Morning, Ale! So glad to have you back girl. Hope you had a Happy New Year. Bahamas again?"

"Nope. I stayed here and helped cater a New Year's party."

Nya stared at her. "Girl, why?"

She laughed, "Leslie needed the help, and I don't know, travelling still feels surreal for me. Just wanted to stay close to home."

Nya shrugged. "Theo and I were asleep by 9 p.m. We are so *old*."

Nya's husband Theo worked for the fire department, and they too were considered frontline workers. Her household was a mess with kids doing school from home, along with her nursing schedule and Theo working long shifts. She prided herself on being organized and disciplined, but COVID demolished all of that. Nya was still trying to get things back to normal.

Ale reviewed the patient listing, looked at who she was working with, and started barking orders. She was lead ER nurse when she was on shift. She demanded the same type of care and attention from her fellow nurses as she gave. Anything less meant you were going to hear about it. They started calling patient numbers and getting ready for what would be another crazy day. Anyone with COVID-related symptoms still went through a different area. Those people who didn't get the vaccine and thought COVID was a hoax. You would think, after 10 repeat visits to the hospital with the same symptoms, they would get it, but nope. She had no time for people who wasted healthcare time and money because of their stupidity.

As always, the first half of her day went by quickly. Nothing too exciting. A broken ankle, STDs (yup, almost daily in LA), cracked ribs. Thus far, no accidents or emergency surgeries, however the day was still young. Ale went to her locker, grabbed her lunch, phone, and headed for the staff cafeteria. It was located on the top floor and on nice days (which was almost every day in LA) you could eat outside on the terrace. She loved that. She had received texts from Leslie, her momma, and Sophia. Ale filled up her water bottle and sat by the window. She loved sitting by a window and letting the sun warm her. She read Leslie's text and smiled. Leslie and Ale had been friends for years. They met at the coffee shop on their college campus and bonded immediately. Leslie was one of the strongest women Ale had ever met. Always moving forward, never feeling sorry for herself.

Leslie had texted: *Hey U, just chckg in to see how you're doing after the party?*

Ale texted back. *Great, tks. Tks again for the $$. Great night!*

Did you leave a sweater in one of the security team cars?

Nope.

Pause.

Leslie replied with the Hmmm emoji.

The owner Striker said a blonde who lived on Virgil left a sweater in his vehicle.

Ale stared at the text. She was the only one who lived on Virgil, she was blonde, and she did not have a sweater.

How to respond? Should she lie and say, *Oh wait a minute, yes,* or stick with the truth? Was he trying to find out info about her? Things just got interesting.

It wasn't me. I wore a coat and it arrived home with me in it, Ale replied.

OK, they must have it mixed up. No biggie. You working?

Yup, just having lunch.

OK enjoy! talk later—love you Ale Cat!

Love you too babe.

So, she wasn't imagining anything. Something was up with Striker/ Carlos. She decided to talk to the nurses, see what they knew about this dude.

CHAPTER 6
Surveillance

Ramone Ramirez loved his job with StrikeForce. His boss Striker was a badass. He was also fair to his employees and demanded loyalty. All staff had to endure vigorous background checks, constant fitness challenges, shooting certifications, self-defence and aggressive-driving training —you name it. Striker was committed to making them the best in the business.

Ramone was given his first surveillance task that didn't involve a criminal. At least that's what he thought since Striker didn't give him much to go on, except a description and address.

Ramone sat in his StrikeForce SUV that was fully loaded and parked where nobody would see or ask questions. The tinted windows helped. His target left home early, and Ramone took many photos. She was a looker all right. She jumped on the 16-16 bus, and he followed behind. She stepped off at Sixth and St. Paul and walked toward Good Samaritan Hospital. A nurse? Doctor? Patient? Visiting?

Ramone drove into the hospital driveway and circled to see which doors she entered and get a sense for things. He found a 30-minute parking spot as it was early enough. He parked and watched to see if she was visiting or working. Striker would want explicit details. He documented everything in his tablet, which was automatically loaded to the cloud every five minutes so Striker could read it. It saved a lot of back and forth.

He waited an hour and decided she must work there, and then drove back to head quarters. Not very eventful, but they knew a bit more than when they started. He uploaded the photos he had taken as well, especially the ones of her fine ass. Hey, he was only human.

CHAPTER 7
Nurses Know EVERYTHING!

Ale learned so much from just mentioning the name "Striker" to a group of nurses. The moans and groans and *Oh my Gods* that came out of their mouths was shocking. Ale just stared at them. *Seriously?* How is it that she knew nothing about this guy? Turns out, not only was he the owner of Strikeforce; he was also part owner of Miguel's! She thanked them for the info as they continued to gossip long after she was gone.

Why is it so hot in here???

She went back to work and walked into complete chaos. An ambulance had delivered a gun-shot victim, and there was screaming and blood everywhere. Cops were all over and *DAMN* did she hate it when her ER had chaos. She barged into the room and threw all the cops out. She was little, but mighty. She pulled the curtain around and stared at two nurses, Holly and Lisa, who knew she was pissed. The patient was trying to escape. Lesson 101: tie them down. She grabbed the cuffs that were beside the bedrails for just these moments and secured him. She did the same for his legs as he was kicking. The bullet was in his abdomen, which was bleeding profusely.

"Put pressure on the wound, Holly. Lisa, page Dr. Walker!"

The patient was still screaming, so Ale walked over calmly and stared at him. He stopped.

"What's your name, handsome?" she asked sweetly.

"JJJJohn," he replied, obviously in pain. She was getting the pain meds and antibiotics going while Holly was keeping the bleeding at bay.

She found the needle spot—he had tons of tracks. Obvious junkie. *This will be fun,* she thought. He was having withdrawal symptoms.

"Ok, John, I need you to stay calm for me. Can you do that?"

"Need a fix, bad. Need a fix bad," was all John could muster.

Ale cut open his shirt so she could get a good look at the wound. The bullet wasn't in that far, but she had to wait for Dr. Walker.

"Holly, please get him hooked up to the monitors. What was his blood pressure when he arrived?"

Holly checked the EMT form that the paramedics gave them and told Ale. His was low, not surprising. He's going to go into shock.

Ale heard ruckus outside with all the police and Dr. Walker trying to get in. Dr. Andrew Walker was one of her favourite doctors in the hospital. He was kind, polite, and cared about the patients. It helped that he was also young, good-looking, and didn't have an ego.

He entered with a smile, pulling on his gloves.

"Ale Cat, so good to see you!"

"Dr. Walker, Happy New Year!"

"OK, what have we got?"

She gave him the rundown. They worked together regularly, and they had a rhythm. It helped. She knew what he needed and how he needed it. It saved time and made things run smoothly.

Dr. Walker asked Holly to get ER Surgical Room 1 prepped. He spoke smoothly to the patient, explaining what had to happen. Then he looked at Ale and said, "Let's go remove a bullet!"

She loved it when the doctors asked her to join them in surgery. It wasn't often, but some gave her the opportunity and she jumped at it. They called an orderly and John was moved to Surgical Room 1. She followed Dr. Walker, ignoring the cops' demands for information and off they went to surgery. Her blood was pumping, and so was the patient's!! Doing any surgery on a junkie was always risky, but so was having a bullet in your belly. Dr. Walker found the perfect mix of sedative and John was out before you could say heroin. Typically, they would staple the wound after the bullet was removed but Dr. Walker and Ale were both old-fashioned and he knew how much she loved to stitch, so he let her do the honours.

Ale was thrilled. She took the bullet, now in a plastic baggie, out to the waiting detective. When he turned around, she almost passed out.

"Ale?" the guy with the beautiful blue eyes and gorgeous smile asked. He was grinning from ear to ear with his hands on his hips. "Alessandra Ferretti? Is that really you?"

Ale just stared. She hadn't seen or heard from Jason O'Malley in more than ten years. High school, to be exact.

Just then the surgery room door opened. Dr. Walker came out and asked, "Everything OK? It looks like a 9 mm to me," not realizing everyone was more interested in how Detective O'Malley knew Ale.

"Yes, Dr. Walker, all good here," Ale replied, trying to make a quick exit.

O'Malley gently grabbed her arm, which Dr. Walker noticed. "Not so fast, Ale. Aren't you happy to see me?"

Umm not really, she thought, however everyone was staring, and she had patients.

"Yeah, sure, O'Malley. Great to see you again. I would love to catch up but as you can see, its very busy here and I have patients waiting."

God, it's hot in here!

He smiled that beautiful smile and stared right into her soul. She thought for sure he could see to her uterus, or as her zia called it, her *purpose*.

"I had no idea you worked here. This will be great. I just transferred in from San Diego. Maybe we can catch up?" Ale prayed he had three wives and 20 kids.

"Sure, let's do that. Good to see you." Ale turned back to the desk to get her shit together and pretend she was busy. All cop eyes were on her ass. *Seriously?* She grabbed the tablet and headed to the next ER room to meet her next patient.

The cops cleared out and Ale took care of her patients, reminding herself to speak to Holly and Lisa before shift was over. That chaos moment was unacceptable. Dr. Walker caught Ale in the hallway and asked if she was OK. She said she was, just shocked to see an old friend. He smiled and told her she was great in surgery today. Ale spent 20 minutes with Holly and Lisa. They weren't happy with her, but they would get over it.

By the time 7 p.m. came, Ale had all her patient updates documented and her turnover to the new shift done. She was exhausted and rattled to her bones. *Jason friggin' O'Malley. Are you kidding me???* She headed for the bus stop.

Ale's short time on the bus ride home from work wasn't long enough to absorb seeing O'Malley again. Jason O'Malley was a year older than her and attended all the same schools as her. He was a *DOG*. He screwed anything that could walk, including her. Yup, he took her virginity in Grade 12 and never looked back. Needless, to say, not her finest moment. All the girls just loved him. He was an Irish troublemaker with a dick that never quit. Ale was shy, not exactly interested, but was definitely curious. The whole experience just came flooding back the minute he looked into her eyes. God why was she still ashamed?? It was 12 years ago, and they were kids. *You have, to lose it to someone, right?? It had to be him.* Catholic guilt.

Why did he have to come back here? Honestly, she thought he was run out of town or dead. She was sure he had illegitimate kids all over LA county. She wondered if he was married or divorced. Unfortunately, she had no time to dwell as she needed sleep, and 5 a.m. came early.

CHAPTER 8
Jason Friggin' O'Malley

Meanwhile back at LAPD headquarters, Detective Jason O'Malley sat at his desk contemplating what just happened at the hospital. The bullet was being analyzed by forensics and he had updated his report. The junkie wasn't as important as the gun and bullet. If it was from the same gun used in three other junkie shootings, they had a vigilante. That was never a good thing.

Alessandra Ferretti—or maybe she was married. Didn't notice a wedding ring.

O'Malley had left LA and gone into the navy right out of school. Primarily to escape angry fathers, brothers, husbands, and boyfriends. He was Irish and always horny. Still is. The girls in LA made it very easy for him. The navy was exactly what he needed. He had to put his hormones in check and get serious or be a porn star. The navy was a more practical option, however the thought of being a porn star still haunted him. After the navy, he went to the police academy and worked his way up to detective. He loved it. It was exactly what he didn't know he needed. He spent a few years in San Diego, but when an opening in LA came up, he jumped on it. He wanted to be closer to his aging mom and his siblings. He had some making up to do, lots of bridges burned, but he was not the same guy. Still horny, mind you, but more selective. Actually, if truth be told, he wanted a family.

The pandemic had a real effect on him. He wanted to be closer to his family. He was 31 and the things he thought he left behind or didn't need are exactly what he wanted. Maturity sucked.

He couldn't just do a search on Ale without probable cause as that was illegal, so he decided to check Google and social media. Always the good stuff on social media; women loved it.

Well, apparently not Ale. Maybe she was married. He decided to ask around the division. Some of the guys knew her from dealing with the hospital. First stop would be Detective Kevin Scott. He seemed a bit annoyed when O'Malley was staring at Ale, like he sensed some sort of relationship there.

"Hey, Scotty," he yelled.

Detective Kevin Scott looked up from his desk, annoyed. He wasn't pleased when O'Malley joined their division, and he wasn't pleased he was in LA. Everyone knew about O'Malley. His reputation was well documented, both as a cop and as an asshole. He really didn't like the looks O'Malley gave to Ale, either. Kevin had a soft spot for her. They dated once, but nothing had happened since. He still thought about her, though. Most of the cops did. There weren't many women like Ale in LA.

"Yo," he replied

"What's the deal with Ale? She married?"

"Nope, not that I know of."

"Something wrong with her?" O'Malley asked. Fuck, she was HOT. He didn't remember her being that hot in high school.

Scotty shrugged like he didn't know anything. O'Malley didn't buy it. He'd probe more later.

"Her parents still own that Italian place on Wilshire?"

"Yup," Scotty replied and continued updating his files.

"I feel like Italian tonight; want to join me?" O'Malley was grabbing his jacket and walking towards Scotty.

"No thanks, man. Got plans," Scotty muttered.

"OK, have a good night." O'Malley almost skipped out to his Dodge Charger. He couldn't wait to have some good Italian food and find out what Miss Ale had been up to these past 10 years. He'd had a hard on since she handed him the bullet.

CHAPTER 9
Strike Force

Carlos woke up horny and miserable. Normally he would just take care of matters, but nothing about this week was normal. He thought about the last three years with COVID: riots, protests, elections, and social unrest. A horrible time for everyone, but they plowed through it. He was hoping 2023 would be a great year. So far, though, it was just frustrating him.

The thoughts going through his head the past few days were disturbing. He was in unchartered territory. His mother told him it would happen one day. He always laughed and kissed the top of her head. Mothers always say those things to their sons. "One of these days, Carlos, you are going to meet your match," in her beautiful Cuban accent. His mother, Rosa Montoya was the most important woman in his life. Along with his two sisters, Justina and Mariella. Family was important to him. He worked hard to build his business so he could take care of them. His mother was a schoolteacher who really should be retired, but she loved her work. His sisters were also schoolteachers and he had one niece, Vanessa. He doted on her. She was 12 and growing up way too fast.

His father? That was a whole other story.

His mind went back to the discomfort between his legs and its cause. He was hoping to figure out her name, with the information Ramone had given him. He had his researcher/hacker, Stefan Rominiski, exe-cuting commands into the Good Samaritan employee database.

Legal? Absolutely not. Necessary? Yes.

CHAPTER 10
Pizza, Anyone?

O'Malley settled into the booth at Vito's Pizzeria and perused the menu. Everything had changed since he'd last been there. It once was a small Italian eatery, but now it was more upscale, large roomy booths with leather seating, neutral colours, nice tablecloths, and a party room. Updated fixtures, nice hardwood tables and very attractive waitresses. Things were looking up.

He asked the waitress if she knew Ale. Turned out she was a cousin, Anita. Bingo!

O'Malley ordered a large spaghetti with meatballs, plus a large pizza with the works and extra cheese to take home. Might as well get his dinner for tomorrow, too. To top it off, a giant pint of Guinness. Nectar of the Gods.

Anita scurried off to put in his order and disappeared behind the bar to pour his beer.

He watched her closely. She was very Italian-looking. Pretty, long blonde hair pulled back, lots of makeup, nice full lips. Probably early twenties. Cute little body. Looked nothing like Ale.

FUCK.

He just remembered something. Ale was adopted; she wasn't even Italian. He'd forgotten all about that. Unfortunately, there were other things he couldn't seem to forget. He scanned the restaurant. Plenty of patrons, lots of noise, great smells, and it reminded him how hungry he was.

Anita returned with the perfectly poured Guinness. "Ale in some kind of trouble?" she asked, staring at his badge. *Shit.* He'd forgotten to take that off or hide it.

"Nope." He paused and looked into her eyes. "Ale get into trouble often?"

Anita laughed. "You don't know her very well, do you?"

O'Malley had to stop himself from smiling. He knew her *intimately,* actually.

She continued. "Ale is a good girl and always has been. Super smart, educated, even has her doctorate in nursing. She works up at Good Samaritan as an ER nurse. During COVID we barely saw her."

O'Malley stared into his beer, then looked up and said, "That must have been hard on her husband or boyfriend."

She smiled. "Ale doesn't have either, and she's not interested. Don't get me wrong; she's not lesbian or anything. She just doesn't want the drama. She likes her life as it is."

O'Malley took that as a challenge. "Are her parents and her brother still around?"

Anita scanned the restaurant to make sure nobody was looking for her.

"Oh yeah, they're around, all doing well. Everyone survived COVID and the family is as strong as ever."

O'Malley laughed "How about zia Connie?" He knew Connie well. She had paid him a visit when he was 18, and he never forgot it.

"She's great, still in real estate, and spends lots of time at the bakery now. Her and Ale, are still very close."

He thanked her for the updates, and she went to get his meals.

Jesus, the food was incredible. He had forgotten how much. He ate like a savage. Anita brought him another beer and the bill. "You want me to tell Ale you were asking about her?" she asked.

"You got her number?" he asked.

She smiled "Yup, but I am not giving it to you. Ale is very private. I will tell her a cop with sexy blue eyes was in. My guess is she will know who I'm talking about. Have a good night, detective, and thank you for eating with us."

O'Malley dropped a few bills with a large tip. His stomach felt better but his dick was still in agony.

CHAPTER 11
Jesus, She's a Ferretti!

Carlos stared at the data on the screen, and he couldn't believe what he was reading.

Alessandra Ray Farrell Ferretti. He stared at one of the photos Ramone had taken of her. She was beautiful, not LA beautiful. Naturally beautiful. Authentic. Sexy. Smart. Fit. The complete *fuckin'* package. And she was a Ferretti to boot. That made things extra complicated.

Carlos had great respect for the Ferretti family and had worked with them on a few business ventures. He was very aware of what the Ferretti family was capable of, and he wanted to stay away from it.

Vito made the best suits in California, probably, the USA. Gio, his son, was a friend of sorts, business partner, someone who gave him work and vice versa. They co-existed and both profited. Carlos had to really think about this.

He continued reading. Adopted, Canadian, well-educated, speaks five languages. *WTF?* Why was she waitressing? She had an important job at a good hospital, made fairly good money. She had two trust funds that she's never touched. No boyfriends to speak of. An ex who owned an Irish pub in West LA. Nothing serious. Two years in Dubai. Likes to stay under the radar. God knows that would change if he decided to pursue her. He really didn't want to mess up her nice quiet life, but he might not have a choice.

CHAPTER 12
Gangs, Gangs, and Gangs.

Ale had a miserable sleep, but somehow that didn't matter once she arrived at her hospital. Second shift was always a bit harder on the system. She was going through the patient list and noticed a familiar name and called him into one of the exam rooms. Enter Diego Torres, leader of the notorious Cinco Reyes Gang.

A muscled, average-height Mexican who ruled LA and, as it turns out, a friend of hers. They had bonded over the numerous stitches she'd sewn into his multiple knife wounds. His body was covered in tattoos, and he had a beautiful smile, when he smiled. He wasn't particularly good-looking but hung like a horse. She knew this to be true. As a nurse, she had seen it, as had most of the Latinas in LA County. He had, like, four wives and God knows how many kids, but he looked after them as he looked after his beautiful, delicate momma, Ana. Diego had long black hair, parted in the middle, and a soft spot for Ale. He was always packing, usually knives, and was a generous donator to the hospital charities. Ale was always happy to help Diego and even more happy to take his cash donations.

He smiled brightly when she pulled the curtain over. All the nurses and doctors knew that Diego only wanted to see her, and nobody bothered with it. Ale was neither scared nor uncomfortable with him. He was always respectful and kind to her and she, sometimes, looked forward to his visits.

Today was another knife wound very, close to his kidney. Freezing was never an option. She cleaned and disinfected while he updated her on his latest child. She was sure they are all named Diego. Ale slowly and perfectly stitched him up and tried very hard not to alter any of his tattoos. Good as new. She put a large bandage on him and recited the normal instructions that she's sure he knew by heart.

"How are things, Ale Cat?" he asked in Spanish, smiling at her. He could be charming.

"Good, Diego. Always good."

"When are you going to go out on a date with me, *bonito*?" He asked this at every visit and the answer was always the same.

"As soon as you are single. I'm not a fan of sharing, Diego." They flirted like this. It was harmless. He laughed and grabbed his side.

"How's Pepe?" she asked. "He's usually with you." Pepe was Diego's driver/bodyguard, a large Mexican, with a sweet face, beautiful dark eyes, crazy hair and long sideburns. He was extremely protective and loyal to Diego, and therefore was the same with Ale. He too asked her every visit for a date. Apparently, gang members found her hot. Who would have thought?

"Pepe is in the car. Things are a bit heated, so we are being careful."

Normally they don't provide any details. She doesn't call the cops; that is a waste of time, even though for wounds like this or gun shot wounds, they were supposed to call them. That would not be a good idea, so they looked the other way.

Legal? No. Necessary? Yes.

He pulled a large manilla envelope out of his jacket pocket and handed it to her. "This should take care of it," he said.

He kissed her lightly on the cheek and whispered. "*Gracias mi amor.*"

She smiled. "*De nada*, Diego. *Te acompanare. Quiero ver a Pepe?*"

He frowned, "*Hoy no, hermosa. Es muy peligroso.*"

She accepted his answer and asked him to give Pepe her best. "*Ten cuidado.*"

He smiled and left.

She opened the envelope. It probably had close to $10k in it. Ale grabbed a plastic bag, put the cash in it, no prints. She covered it up and walked down to the business office and dropped it into the anonymous donation bin.

She thought about Diego and Pepe and always worried for the day they would bring one of them in on a stretcher and they wouldn't be able to put Humpty back together again. She would cry like a baby. These tough, crazy Mexicans had touched her heart. She plowed through the rest of the day and couldn't wait to get home and maybe have a nice hot bath.

CHAPTER 13
Legal? No. Necessary? Yes.

Carlos was taking his time walking through Alessandra Ferretti's apartment. He told himself he didn't have a choice. He was good at this. He had a *"special set of skills"* and she would never know he was here. The first thing he noticed was how incredibly neat she was. That in itself was a rarity. Most women he knew were messy and disorganized. Everything was in its place. She didn't have a housekeeper, which meant she did it herself. She knew how to cook and bake. Homemade chocolate chip cookies in the glass cake stand on the counter and homemade bread in bags on the counter. Interesting.

Her bed was made. She had two sewing machines in her bedroom. Two sewing mannequins with half-made dresses on each. Loads of material on the shelves of her closet. Peg boards with all the sewing necessities on the wall. All very neatly arranged. She was a seamstress. This was why he needed to look around. You could only find stuff like this on social media and she wasn't on it. Her furniture and décor were nice, not over the top. Quality versus quantity. Soft, neutral tones. Her closet and drawers were very organized. He found the safe, used his tools and skills to open it. *Jeezus!* What is with all the cash? This troubled him. Dangerous for a young, beautiful woman to have so much cash in her apartment.

He continued to open drawers, taking note of the very pretty panties and matching bras. Good quality bags and shoes/boots and, of course, her perfume. Loads of books.

He checked the medicine cabinet. You could find out a lot from looking in a medicine cabinet. Birth control, skin care, ibuprofen, Excedrin. No prescriptions, thank God. Of course, they might be in her bag she takes to work. He'd have to check that. He was on high alert for Prozac or anything similar.

Her education degrees were framed and hung on her walls. Photos of her with family and friends. He took particular notice of a black-and-white wedding photo: not Vito and Maria. Most likely her real parents. Her mom was stunning. It kind of made him sad. To lose your parents at age six and have nobody to look after you. He read that she was in foster care for a bit before the Ferrettis were able to adopt her. She had a story. *Private*, he thought, *something you never see in LA*. People post everything now; nothing is private. The more he saw, the more attached he became. He needed to get out of there. Ramone texted that she had just left work. He quickly exited as quietly as he entered and walked out the back to his Porsche Boxster. On his return to the office, he received an alert on one of his security properties. He changed gears and headed towards the building in trouble, hoping he could at least chase someone down or beat someone up. This might help with the problem between his legs.

CHAPTER 14
Giovanni Ferretti

Gio was at his desk in his office, located on the 20th floor of the Ferretti building. He had a "board meeting" in an hour and wasn't looking forward to it. All the uncles bitching and moaning. The last three years with the pandemic were hell, however, the Ferretti business was doing very well. Nothing to worry about. He had a business degree from USC, and yet they still gave him grief. He was always ready for them; he just dreaded the meeting in general. He'd been successful running the business for years, but what he didn't like was having to prove himself every damn month to his family.

Legal? Sometimes.

His mind was on his sister, Ale. Somehow, she had herself on some serious radar. People were asking about her, and he didn't like it. He had also heard Jason O'Malley was back in town. That was never a good thing.

O'Malley was a fuckin' dog in heat, and he had taken advantage of Ale when she was working late at zia Connie's bakery during her senior year in high school. Gio remembers going to his house and getting into a fist fight with him. O'Malley was Irish and a scrapper. His old man was a mean drunk, so he had learned to defend himself. Gio was sure O'Malley had got himself killed as it wasn't long after that he seemed to disappear.

Ale was never the same again. They never spoke about it, but he knew, and she knew he knew. It almost killed him. He was supposed to protect her, and he failed. Now, he had to pay O'Malley a visit and find out what his plans are. If O'Malley went near Ale, he'll have him fuckin' killed.

The other thing on Gio's mind was his wife and their lack of children. She was half-crazy with all the hormone shots and stress. Ale kept asking him to get his sperm checked. *What the fuck?* Nobody was checking his sperm. If Sophia would just chill, it would happen. It's constantly on her fuckin' mind and it was starting to really impact his ability to perform. *Jeeezus*, why was everything so fuckin complicated?

Gio stood up and headed to the boardroom.

CHAPTER 15
No Pain, No Gain

Ale woke up on her first day off and headed for the shower. She had a session with Mac, her personal trainer and an hour-long yoga session. She couldn't wait. She dressed in black-and-white striped wide-leg trousers and a black crop top. She jammed her workout gear, wallet, and water bottle into her bag, put her ear buds in, and caught the bus to the community college. Unbeknownst to her, a black SUV was following behind.

Her trainer, Mac, was a former Navy SEAL. He had strawberry blonde-hair, shaved military-style, and freckles everywhere. Beautiful blue eyes, a sexy deep voice, a body like a brick shithouse, plus he was the best fitness and self-defense trainer she knew. He taught Ale how to defend herself, where to apply the necessary pressure and how to handle herself in any situation. Being an ER nurse at a downtown LA hospital, you encounter a whole lot of crazy. She wanted to be able to handle herself should things get out of control before the police could get there. Mac's teachings helped guide her strength and always tested and challenged her. She finished each session soaked in sweat and in agony. It was awesome.

Mac was waiting for her in the work out studio after she changed in the locker room. He oozed masculinity. On occasion, Ale's lady parts would act up. They always worked closely and some days it felt like there was no air in the room. Mac was a serious guy, all business, but sometimes she caught him looking at her as if she was a snack. She was never uncomfortable in his care, but she was definitely aware. During COVID, they did some virtual sessions when she had time off and, of course, she could do her own yoga, but she really missed his hands-on sessions. Pardon the pun.

"She's here!" He smiled and hugged her.

"Happy New Year, Mac. It's so great to see you."

He clapped his hands together and looked her over. He did this every session. He looked for areas that might need improving. Most people would be uncomfortable as he looked like he was checking you out for other reasons, but Mac was all business. Today, she was wearing her black Nike tights and matching bra top. Definitely, all business!

They started with some warm-up stretching and then went right into combat. Next was kick boxing and beating the crap out of a rubber man. Then she had to crawl up the rubber man and wrap her legs around his neck and lower and raise her upper body 50 times. They were the most intense sit-ups ever, and she almost threw up.

Mac continued through each session, providing guidance and reassuring her. She wanted to kick him.

Next was moving the giant tractor tire across the floor. *Are you fucking kidding me?* Lastly, they did skipping; fast at first and then gradually slower and slower to get her heartrate down. She ended doing a slow walk on the treadmill for 10 minutes. She was sweating like a whore in church.

"Thanks, Mac. Really. I mean it," she said as she rolled her eyes and wiped her sweat with a towel.

He laughed and said, "Great workout, Ale Cat! Make sure you hydrate and maybe a nice Epson salt bath as your muscles will be sore. Go easy in yoga, please." Mac knew how much she loved yoga. She had a nice strong core and she used it.

She thanked him again and headed to yoga, not realizing a set of dark-brown eyes were watching her the entire time. Yoga was both intense and beautiful. Her heart, body, mind, and soul felt balanced again. She couldn't wait to get into the shower and head to her momma's for lunch! She quickly showered, dressed, piled her wet, curly hair in a messy bun. She put her sweaty clothes in a plastic bag and walked out the door. It was a bit cool today, so she pulled on her white short jean jacket. She put on her sunglasses and made sure she had her bus pass in her pocket. Turns out, she didn't need it.

CHAPTER 16
How or Never

Ale walked down the stairs of the community college building towards the parking lot. The bus stop was on the east side. Her spidey senses were tingling as she noticed a handsome Latino leaning against a Porsche with his arms crossed and wearing mirrored sunglasses.

She smiled and he asked, "Need a ride?"

"No thanks," she replied quickly and immediately picked up her pace. He didn't chase her; he just watched. Ale decided to stop and slowly turn around.

He took off his glasses and she asked, "Are you following me?" It was Striker.

"Maybe."

"Why?" He smiled like a lion looking at its prey.

"Good question, Ale. Maybe I want to get to know you."

"Hmm, so you know my name, but I don't know yours," she lied.

He put his hand out. "Carlos Montoya."

She took his hand, his very soft hand. "Nice to meet you."

He smiled and she just stood there, not sure what to do. She noticed Mac was watching through the windows. Surely this guy wouldn't take her somewhere and rape her, would he? In broad daylight?

"I don't usually get into strange cars with strange men."

He shrugged his shoulders, "I'm not a stranger. You've already driven in a car with me. I drove you home on New Year's and your family knows who I am. So does Mac. I'm not the boogeyman, Alessandra."

Gawd, the way he said her name almost made her knees buckle. She composed herself, took off her sunglasses so he could see her eyes, and she could see his.

"OK, but I'm not going home. I'm going to my parents for lunch. Since you were wearing one of Vito's suits on New Year's Eve, I am sure you know where his office is."

He smiled knowing she checked out his suit on New Year's Eve. He opened the car door, and she sank into the luxurious seats of his Porsche. Little did she know that this would be the start of a wild ride in more ways than one.

They drove in silence. He wore a black T-shirt with black fitted cargo pants and was packing. His arms were very muscular, and she found it very difficult to concentrate. Ale felt like he was reading all her thoughts and she started to sweat again.

Why was it so hot in here?

"Nice car." He looked over and smiled. They both had their sunglasses on again. It was much safer that way. She remembered all the photos of him not smiling and yet it was all he'd done since she met him.

They arrived at momma's, she thanked him for the ride, and ran into the house. She knew she was being rude as she didn't ask him in, but she was terrified he would say yes. Momma would have been ALL over that!!

She opened the back door, and the light was on in her papa's studio, so she knew he had a client. She took the stairs two at a time and crashed through the apartment door.

"Alessandra!" Her momma greeted her with the usual groping, hugging, and kissing, looking beautiful as always.

Hopefully, Carlos was long gone, and they could just have a nice lunch.

CHAPTER 17
Go In or Not Go In?

Carlos sat in his Porsche contemplating. He really wanted to invite himself in for lunch. He had never done that. He'd never needed to.

The memory of what he had seen today distracted him. He sat there thinking about watching Ale earlier while she worked out and did her yoga.

He knew Mac would be non too happy to see him. He and Mac went way back. Both with military backgrounds, both involved in black ops, both good at what they did, and they still remained with their toes in some dangerous business.

"Striker!" Mac had said earlier, coming over to give him the bro hold.

"How's it going, Mac?" Striker asked.

"Not bad. You looking to sign up for some lessons?"

"No, just admiring the view."

Mac's eyes went to slits. He didn't like that reply and his whole body tensed. "You referring to Ale?"

Striker nodded.

"She's one of the good ones. You don't want to mess with that." Mac turned and walked away.

Carlos then made his way over to yoga and what he saw took his breath away. He was never a yoga fan; he preferred weights and hitting stuff or people. Watching Ale's strength as she fluidly transferred from pose to pose was intoxicating. It was as if she was floating, with her strong body showing every muscle. She finished with a handstand where she raised her lower body up and down halfway, then raised her legs all the way up and spread them to do the splits. Fuck, he had leave. Seeing this did not help the problem between his legs.

He decided right then he was going to make his move.

He brought himself back to the present, sitting in the car at her parents' house; and decided what he needed was to get her to trust him. He drove off and would start putting his plan into place.

CHAPTER 18
Lunch with Momma and Zia Connie
(Pranzo con Mamma e Zia Connie)

Momma was in an Italian mood, so they were speaking Italian the entire afternoon. Zia Connie showed up in her red Mercedes convertible and once again she hugged and kissed Ale until she couldn't breathe.

Zia Connie was a breath of fresh air. She cursed, she drank, she talked openly about everything, and Ale could confide in her like she couldn't confide in her momma. Most girls probably felt that way. They were more comfortable talking with an aunt or a friend about personal stuff. Her momma was great, but she was staunch Roman-Catholic Italian and lived and breathed it. She wasn't the normal hypocrite who sinned all week long and asked for forgiveness on Sunday. Ale loved her dearly but some of the things she told zia Connie, she'd never say to her momma!

Zia Connie was beautiful in a very Italian way. Although zia and momma were sisters, they didn't look anything alike. Zia had dark curly hair, beautiful skin, dark eyes, and a nice wide mouth. She was a successful real estate broker, and owned Il Panificio, a popular bakery in downtown LA. Her baking talents were renowned, her pastry studies in France shown through in every bite. Zia and zio Tony didn't have any children of their own and they never spoke about it. Ale often wondered why. At any rate, it worked out fine because they doted on Ale from day one.

They ate lunch, drank wine, laughed, and gossiped. All in Italian, of course.

Ale only called Maria, momma. When they brought Ale to California, she was a shy, broken little girl and they all struggled. Ale really had no understanding of death or why her birth parents weren't with her anymore. Her whole world was upside down. Momma was so patient and loving and Ale eventually clung to her. She still did. She landed in the safest of arms.

One day, momma brought her the one photo Ale had of her parents. Ale said, "That's my mom and dad. They are dead." A seven-year-old doesn't know what that means. It's what they are told. She only knew that they were gone. Momma knew her real mom as they went to boarding school together, kept in touch and had a connection. Momma pointed at the photo and said to Ale, "Your mom." She pointed at herself and said, "Your momma." She didn't want Ale to forget her parents or replace them. That was the kind of person her momma was. So, the names stuck. She is momma and Vito is papa. Sweet, right?

They were nibbling on some grapes when Ale announced, "Jason O'Malley is back in town."

Zia just stared at her with concern in her eyes. She knew the history; Momma did not.

"Ale," momma said, "that is interesting news. If I remember, he was a looker. Is he married?" Momma was always on the hunt for either a wedding to plan or a grandbaby to spoil. Right now, she had neither and she was getting frustrated. Gio and Ale were not meeting her timelines.

Ale shrugged. "I have no idea. He's a detective with the LAPD, and I ran into him at the hospital."

Momma got excited. Zia got annoyed.

"A police detective? Oh Ale, I bet he's done well for himself. Did he have a wedding ring on?"

Ale's beautiful momma believed in the good of everyone.

"Not that I saw."

She smiled and grabbed Ale's hand. "Maybe this will be the year Alessandra finds love!" she said, gushing. Momma was also a hopeless romantic.

Jeezus, she needed tequila. That reminded Ale that she had to text Sophia and make a date so they could catch up on Striker. She quickly texted Sophia to see if she was free for lunch tomorrow, and she was. *Miguel's?* Sophia replied with *LOL* and *thumbs up emoji*.

Ale had no idea what this year was going to bring her, except that she was turning 30 and momma was in party-planning mode. Italians celebrated everything and they celebrated big. Ale just let her go. No sense in even trying to reign momma in. She had learned that from papa.

They discussed the party plans and Ale eye-rolled most of it, until they got to the *cake*. Ale was very particular about her cake. Only zia could make her birthday cake. She is the only one who makes the best Italian Lemon and Coconut cream cake that tastes like heaven. The first time Ale ate it, she was probably eight, and they were at a party for a family member. Momma had her all dressed up and she was starting to get comfortable with all the members of her new very, large family. Zia had her on her knee per usual and spoon-fed her a small piece of *the cake*. Ale was a difficult eater. Trauma of losing your parents, your life and moving in with strangers will do that to you. They managed to get her to eat pasta, sitting on papa's lap, of course, maybe grapes, cheese, milk, and that was about it. Ale had opened her mouth and zia let the cake sit on her tongue. Ale sucked it back like nobody's business. Everyone stopped what they were doing and watched in shock. Zia had started shovelling the cake into her and Ale couldn't eat it fast enough. They thought for sure that Ale would throw up later, but she didn't.

Zia made that cake for her every week and Ale thought she was the luckiest kid alive. She still does; she just doesn't tell them.

Ale informed her momma that she would be making her own dress. Momma stopped and stared at her. She knew Ale was a good seamstress, however momma had other ideas on Ale's dress. Probably some sick idea of an 18th-century ball gown! Nope. She was turning 30 and everybody was going to know it!

Momma hadn't seen Ale's idea for a dress, therefore thought about challenging her, however, zia kicked momma under the table.

"Great idea, bella. You should make your own dress. Nobody knows your body like you do," said zia, winking at Ale, hoping to cut off any argument that was going to start.

They cleaned up and she thanked her momma. Her momma always washed her workout gear while they had lunch. She does that. She just roots through her bag and finds it. *One day*, Ale thought, *I am going to put a big giant dildo in there and scare the crap out of her.*

Zia drove Ale home after having had four glasses of wine. Ale wasn't worried; this happened a lot.

"How was it seeing Jason again?" she asked.

"Weird. I honestly never thought that day would come. Everything came back to me."

"Alessandra, you were kids, and you have nothing to be ashamed of."

In her heart, Ale knew that. But she could tell by the way he looked at her, he remembered as much as she did and that made her very uncomfortable. She kissed zia goodbye and walked into her apartment building. She grabbed her mail and took the elevator to her floor. Her body was starting to scream from her workout, so a hot bath with Epsom salts was definitely going to be on the menu.

Ale started the tub, put in some nice bath salts and foam, scanned her phone for anything urgent, undressed, and carefully lowered herself into the steaming hot water. She could boil her bones it was so hot. It was *perfetto!*

CHAPTER 19
Sew What!

After her long, hot bath, Ale decided to get some sewing done for her papa. It was still early evening, and she hadn't sewn all day. Sewing allowed her to daydream and put all the days troubles out of her mind. She loved creating, loved the different materials, the different patterns. It was all beautiful to her.

She finished up the bins of garments that papa had sent and texted Danny to let him know so he could bring her a new load to sew. Ale moved over to her sewing mannequin and proceeded to work on her birthday dress. Her dress was a beautiful gold sheen wrap style, which could be belted with a short skirt. She loved it. It wasn't a typical Ale dress, but after going through the past three years and the significance of turning 30, she wanted to show off. She had nice legs and a cute, fit body. It was her time. She smiled and danced around with her ear buds on, listening to her playlist and sewing the hem on her birthday dress.

She had already purchased the shoes. Ale removed them from the box and smiled. They were also gold and beaded with a strap and buckle that fastened around her slim ankles. They had a single strap across the toes and a chunky four-inch heel. She adored them.

Three years in scrubs will make you want to be in pretty things the rest of your life!!

She finished hemming her dress and decided to try it on. It needed a bit more stitching, but it was finished enough to pull over her head and see how it looked with her shoes. She twirled around in the mirror and thought, *WOW, this is going to be a party!*

CHAPTER 20
O'Malley Needed to Get Laid

O'Malley decided after a day of chasing criminals, dealing with arseholes and druggies, he needed a night out. Thankfully, he didn't have to worry about the fuckin' pandemic. It could really put a damper on your sex life. He was hoping he could find a pretty young thing to bang and help take the edge off. He seldom had trouble in that area, especially in LA. He was happy to be back in his old stomping grounds, especially after seeing Ale Ferretti again.

He knew which hangouts to visit, and he wasn't interested in dance clubs or hooking up with teenagers. He knew how to look good and attract attention, too. He dressed in a well-fitted black T-shirt and dark-wash jeans. He was handsome, well built, and experienced. Ladies liked that.

He didn't need or want a girlfriend, just a good time.

He decided on Claytons, an upscale bar, which also served appetizers. As he walked in, he could already feel the eyes on him. He opted to sit on the patio and found a table where he could watch the door. The cute waitress in what could only be described as a short dress came over and he asked for a whiskey neat. Within ten minutes he had four whiskey neats on his table. He smiled. He perused the menu as he was a bit hungry when someone pulled up a chair across from him. At first, he thought it was one of the ladies or men who had bought him a drink, then he lifted his eyes from the menu and stared into Giovanni Ferretti's. *Shit.*

"O'Malley."

"Gio, long time." O'Malley greeted him awkwardly. He would need the four drinks after this conversation.

"I heard you were back in town, but I had to see for myself. Why'd you come back?" Gio asked, never moving his eyes off the cop.

"Took a transfer and wanted to be closer to family," O'Malley lied, sucking back the whiskey.

"Last I heard, your family didn't want you around; nor did mine," Gio pointed out.

Fuck. O'Malley really didn't want to get into this tonight; he just wanted to get laid and go home.

"Look, Gio. What happened years ago, happened. I'm not the same guy and I have no intention of causing any trouble for Ale or anyone else, for that matter." O'Malley tried to sound convincing. Just saying her name made him uncomfortable.

"You don't deserve to speak her name, O'Malley!" Gio's voice was getting louder.

"Agreed." Honestly, he just wanted Gio to leave. He didn't need to be reminded of his past. Fuck, people just don't let go of shit. This is what's wrong with the world.

The waitress came over to see if Gio needed a drink. "No thanks," he said. "I'm just leaving."

"Stay away from my sister and my family. I won't say it again." Gio got up and walked out.

O'Malley had to hand it to him, Gio had just threatened a cop. In Gio's mind, O'Malley was still the horny teenager who took his sister's virginity. O'Malley decided tonight was not his night. He laid down some cash and walked out. The past was making it very difficult to move forward.

CHAPTER 21
Striker and Karma

Carlos was feeling like a caged animal in his own control room. He was irritable, barking orders, and on edge. His latest potential client was a fuckin' nightmare. He'd already turned this chick down several times, used his lawyer to intervene, and she just won't take *NO* for an answer.

Lady Karma was a professional wrestler. Somewhat attractive, if you take in account all the makeup and surgeries. She had a wrestler body with fake boobs, fake tan, tall and muscled with long black hair, and green eyes. Men loved her, little girls wanted to be her, and Carlos wanted her to *fuck off.*

She contacted his company initially for a security system, which they installed and now monitor. Then she wanted personal security, 24/7. Carlos offered that to her, obviously for a large fee, but she wanted him to be her bodyguard. Absolutely *NOT*. First, of all, he didn't have time and, secondly, he already knew how she operated. Every time Carlos was in a room with her to go over the specs for her system, she would take her clothes off. She was extremely confident and aggressive, and Carlos wasn't interested.

Lady Karma kept calling and texting, so he knew he had to deal with it. And because he was in the security business, he had access to all the cool gadgets. He had one of his techs put a very tiny camera on the front of his jacket that would transfer the feed to his cloud server.

Carlos drove to her house in Hollyweird and parked in her drive after coming through the gates. He walked up to the giant doors and rang the bell. No surprise, she answered naked. He did not go in.

"About time, Striker. What the fuck? I am a paying customer and all you do is ignore me. Get in here now. We have business to discuss."

She walked away and headed towards the bedroom. Carlos didn't move. Obviously, this bitch didn't know what he did for a living or how he did it. She thought she could order him around like her servants, he was about to enlighten her.

Lady Karma finally realized he wasn't coming in. She returned, stomping on the floor with her high heels. She at least had a robe on, though it wasn't tied, of course. She stood facing him, hands on hips.

"I am not telling you again," she screamed. "Get the hell in here and fuck me. Then we will discuss you being my private security guard. This is non-negotiable." She stared at him, challenging.

"No," Carlos calmly replied.

She charged at him, and he stepped aside, lunging herself out the door and onto the concrete pavement. Lady Karma was screaming and kicking. He never moved. She rolled over, a bit scraped and bloody, cursing him up and down. He just stared at her, making sure the camera recorded the entire event.

She stood up on her feet and attempted to charge him again she was a wrestler and no amateur. He moved again, he was faster and had less alcohol in him.

"Fuckin' coward. You're not a real man. Any man would be all over me. I think you're gay. You're a fuckin faggot!" She was making a total scene now, screaming outside so her neighbours could hear.

Carlos spoke very clearly. "StrikeForce will not be providing private security OR any other service for you. Do not call, do not text, and please stop bad-mouthing my company and me. This ends now." Still remaining calm.

"Go fuck yourself. I'm going to post this on social media and show people how you really treat women," she threatened. "I will ruin you, asshole. You have no idea who you are messing with."

Carlos turned, got into his car, and drove off, leaving her standing on her front step with her mouth and robe open.

As soon as Carlos was through the gates, he pulled over and texted his technician to send him the feed. Carlos quickly forwarded the video link to Lady Karma. He was certain there wouldn't be any social media posting about him any time soon. Sometimes when people went into the gutter, you had to get in there with them. He never felt good about it, but that's business.

CHAPTER 22
Sleeping Beauty

After the incident with the wrestler, Carlos headed directly to the apartments on Virgil and sat in the parking lot. He had no idea why he was there or what he was going to do, but it was where he wanted to be. It was the middle of the night, and he was sure Ale was sleeping. What if she wasn't alone? He had to find out. It was risky, but he was an expert in B&E. All the years in black ops, he could hold his breath and control is heart rate for a very long time. Nobody would know he was there. He did a bit of recon to ensure she wasn't still awake. No lights on, no sounds. He took the chance and delicately broke through the security and slipped into her apartment. All was quiet.

He walked carefully into the bedroom and there she was. His heart stopped. She was sound asleep and beautiful. Her sexy curly hair piled on top of her head. He walked over and sat in the chair by the window. He just wanted to look at her. Jesus, he was turning into a stalker. *WTF?* He had infiltrated people's homes all the time as part of his business, mostly criminals. Doing this for personal reasons was not his style, yet here he was. He didn't care.

Meanwhile, Ale slept peacefully.

CHAPTER 23
Miguel's Por Favor

It was Ale's, day off and she could afford to be lazy, so she slept in. She had worked late sewing, and the only thing on her agenda was a lunch date with Sophia at noon. She stretched her legs out and just laid in the bed. She had weird dreams, like someone was watching or following her, so she double checked the locks. They were fine. OK, time for a shower.

Danny arrived with the new bins of sewing and an envelope of cash. She thanked him and told him she would be baking bread today and would call him when it was ready. He loved her bread. She quickly got the dough ready and put it in the pans and wrapped the bread pans with saran wrap to rise. She put the money in her safe and sighed. She really needed to do something with all this cash.

Dressing for lunch at Miguel's, Ale opted for a fitted pair of white capri Levi's and a cropped off-the-shoulder denim top with puffy short sleeves. She finished it with a nice pair of high-heeled wedge sandals.

She sighed when she looked at her hair in the mirror. Everyone always says they want curls and the ones with curls want straight hair. She usually wore her hair up as it was heavy and annoyed her when the weather was hot. She decided to leave it down and just use a finishing cream to touch up some of the curls. She put on some mascara and a bit of eye liner. Her skin had a nice tone, and she hated foundation, so she shrugged in the mirror and left it as is. A little bit of shiny body cream on her neck and shoulders and she was ready.

Ale pulled open her jewellery drawer. She had a shit-ton of beautiful jewellery. Italians gave jewellery or money for any occasion. She had more diamonds than the queen. She always wore her real mother's wedding ring on her right hand. Her momma had kept it for her and gave it to her when she turned 16. They had both cried. Ale selected a pair of diamond hoops that could be seen with her hair down. Her phone beeped. Sophia was outside the building waiting. She grabbed her wristlet and headed out the door.

Gio loved fancy, fast cars, and today Sophia was driving his Maserati. Ale's eyes rolled. Good grief.

They did the valet at Miguel's and walked in to one of Ale's favourite restaurants in LA. Except, of course, for Vito's Pizzeria.

Miguel's was not just a fantastic place to eat or drink; it was a beautiful space. It was designed perfectly. The left side was more the noisy pick-up area with long, winding bars and stools, which snaked and curved to allow for privacy. The ceiling was all tinted glass, which allowed for beautiful natural light and the strategic placed planter boxes of greenery throughout gave it an almost jungle like feel.

Directly behind the hostess booth was the kitchen. It had a wrap-around bar with the open kitchen behind it. The small hallway to the bathrooms was beside it and the elegant yet funky seating area was to the right. It too was designed to provide privacy. Lots of curved booths and tables in different placements with large plants broke up the space. There were various types of tables: high tables with stools, private tables in corners, large tables for groups. Miguel's had it all. The restaurant was always full and lively with Latino music piped throughout but not too loud. The colours on the walls were bright and bold.

Off the eating area was a set of patio doors that could be pushed back to present an outdoor patio. Sophia had made the reservation and requested a table outside under a big umbrella. It was a perfect day and they had plenty of shade and privacy.

Miguel, the chef, was of Mexican descent. He was round in the middle, had a bright welcoming smile, receding curly dark hair, and large bulging eyes. Not real attractive, but his personality shined. Ale adored him. He always greeted his guests. He loved people and it showed in his cooking. She caught his eye and smiled. He motioned he would bring her a margarita in a few minutes. Is it any wonder she loved this guy?

The food and drinks at Miguel's were off the charts. Yes, the ambiance was stunning, the staff friendly, and the location perfect. But it really was *ALL* about the food. They sat down and glanced at the menu. Ale already knew what she was having. Miguel soon appeared with her frozen prickly pear margarita. He set it down and kissed her on both cheeks.

"How are you, Alessandra?" he asked in Spanish.

"Great, Miguel, thank you!" She took a sip of her marg and smiled. "This is my sister-in-law, Sophia."

Miguel shook Sophia's hand and in perfect English asked her for her drink order. What he lacked in looks, he made up for in charm. Sexy as hell. Miguel quickly started Sophia's drink order and the waiter arrived with water for the table and a basket of homemade tortilla chips and salsa that would curl your toes.

Sophia's drink arrived and they placed their meal order.

"Ale, please tell me you aren't thinking of getting involved with Striker," Sophia said quietly.

Ale was about to answer her when in her peripheral vision she saw a very handsome Latino making the rounds to the tables asking people how their meals were. She looked back at Sophia and mouthed "*Striker is here.*" They both clammed up. Ale knew he would come to their table. This wasn't a coincidence. They had eaten here a million times and never once saw him do this. The ladies were giddy. He was flirting and sweet-talking everyone and then focussed those dark eyes on Ale and headed their way. He was dressed in a deep grey dress shirt and black dress pants. Tailored, but not too tight, like men want to wear them these days. What the hell is that? They look like they are wearing their little brother's clothes. Neither papa nor Ale like that style. When a client comes in and asks for it, they do it, but classic tailoring is exactly that. The look was ridiculous. Carlos looked perfect.

He smiled and arrived at the table. Women were watching him like hawks.

"Alessandra, good to see you again," he said, never taking his eyes off her.

"Do I call you Striker or Carlos?" she asked.

"Please, Carlos."

He looked to Sophia. "Sophia. How are you?" he asked, looking around the patio as women were waving and calling to him.

"I am well, thanks Carlos. I haven't seen you in a while. I hope you've been well." Sophia was always appropriate. Just like momma. Ale was more like zia.

"Yes, thank you." He turned and looked at Ale.

Their meals arrived, thankfully. Carlos moved to Ale's side and put his arm around the back of her chair while the waiter set their meals down and asked if he could get them anything else. They both replied, "No, thank you."

Carlos could have moved back to the centre of the table. But he didn't. He stood there close to Ale, with his crotch right at eye level. She just stared straight a head and was fairly sure Sophia wanted to crawl under the table as everyone was looking at them.

"Well, enjoy your meal, ladies," he said and lightly touched the back of her neck as he walked back towards the bar.

Jeezus… Why was it so hot here?

CHAPTER 24
Lauren Mitchell

Carlos made it back to the safety of his little office he had behind the kitchen. It was small but bright with windows and provided the necessities. A desk, chair, filing cabinets, supply closet, and some award certificates on the walls, photos with celebrities, and so forth. Most restaurants put those outside so the customers can view them, but Carlos wasn't like most people.

He sat in the chair and closed his eyes. Why was it that he could walk into his own restaurant and 100-plus women are all over him, except the one he wants? How did that happen?

He read the Miguel's reservation listing every morning to identify any VIPS, possible enemies or people of concern. Carlos always had his eyes and ears on every part of his businesses at all times. It's what made him successful. When he perused the reservation listing and saw Ferretti, party of two, he took a chance and showed up at Miguel's. Apparently, Ale frequented Miguel's a lot. Miguel knew her personally. Carlos had never noticed. Now he did.

She looked so pretty with her hair down. Her skin was soft-looking and glowing. She barely wore any makeup. She didn't need it. She was a natural with a smile that lit up a room. He saw how happy Miguel's visit made her and wished she responded to him like that.

A knock on his office door brought him back to reality.

"Striker? You in there?" said the female voice.

Fuck. Carlos knew the voice.

It was a mistake that haunted him daily. Lauren Mitchell *was* a cute actress who had a popular TV show about seven years ago but nothing since. Seven years ago, Carlos thought she was cute enough and had spent a few intimate hours with her. Since then, she'd been begging for more of him. She'd also been struggling as an actor. Lauren spent any money she had made—peddling ridiculous products or hooking up with rich assholes. She had ruined her appearance. However, Lauren thought she looked better than ever. Implants were in all parts of her body; she was over-tanned and dressed like a hooker. A lot of men liked the trashy look. Carlos did not. It was sad and pathetic. The more Lauren did to alter her appearance, the worse she looked. She hung out at Miguel's constantly with hopes of seeing him. She tried to send nude photos of herself to his phone, and although he had blocked her, she keeps trying. Lauren showed up at events to surprise him, usually wearing something inappropriate. God. He really needed to get a restraining order.

"Striker? It's Lauren. I know you're in there," she said sweetly.

Carlos took the cowardly route. He texted one of his larger security staff to come handle it. He didn't need a scene in front of customers or Ale. Within minutes there was a bit of a scuffle, swearing, and a text back that it was all clear. For now.

CHAPTER 25
Burritos, Baby!

Sophia and Ale ate their lunch quietly and per usual it was *delicioso!* Every. Single. Time. She looked at her sister-in-law. Sophia has been part of their family for years. She was Gio's first girlfriend and his last. The family adored her. Her long blonde hair was tied back in an elegant pony. Her eyes were big and brown. She was extremely thin and pale. Ale knew she was stressed about getting pregnant and decided to shift the conversation from her to Sophia. Carlos could wait.

"Talk to me; you look really sad today," Ale said, staring at her and sipping on her yummy drink.

"Honestly, Ale. I am so tired of feeling hopeless." She had barely touched her food and tears started to appear in those beautiful eyes.

Ale reached across the table and held her hand, and Sophia let her.

"Sophia, as a nurse, I can tell you there are many options regarding fertility. You are not alone in this. I am really concerned about your well-being. Fertility issues can wreak havoc on your mind, your relationships, your own health."

Ale paused. "Have you guys even considered surrogate or adoption?"

Sophia shook her head. "I know you care, and I appreciate you trying to help but, honestly, I feel like such a failure. The wife of Giovanni Ferretti can't provide him with his own baby. Do you know how that weighs on me?"

She was getting upset and Ale realized this wasn't going the way she wanted so she shut it down. To be continued later, after she wrung her brother's fat neck. Ale squeezed Sophia's hand. "OK, let's talk about something else. I didn't ask you to lunch to upset you. Talk to me about Striker." Ale's mad skill was changing subjects. She did it often.

Sophia let out a chuckle and wiped her eyes. "Well, as you can see, he's the full meal deal and extremely popular with the ladies. He's known for providing incredible sex and walking away, Ale. The women know the rules, and they beg for it. He seems to be nice and kind, just not relationship material, and he makes it clear. That is what I know about Striker."

"Why do you think he's sniffing around me?"

Sophia thought about it for a bit and said, "Well, you are beautiful and successful."

"Do you really think that is what someone like Striker cares about? I wonder if its because I am a Ferretti? I'm not his type, Sophia. We both know this."

"Tell me how all this started." She took a drink from her Miguel's specially made lemonade.

"I was working New Year's for Leslie and his company was doing the security. I saw him in passing, we both smiled at each other. The security company was driving home the wait staff and he drove me home."

Before Ale could continue, Sophia interrupted her and grabbed her arm, "Wait! Striker drove YOU home?"

"Yup."

"OK, that is bizarre. He has fleets of cars and drivers to do that."

Ale continued. "He asked if he could check out my apartment before I went in and I said no. I even tried to tip him."

Sophia burst out laughing.

"Yesterday he was outside when I finished my workout and offered me a drive home."

Sophia's eyebrows raised. "Did you say yes?"

"I was nervous at first, then I said OK, and had him drive me to momma's. When we got there, I quickly said thank you and ran into the building."

Sophia was laughing. Ale was glad she changed the subject. Sophia's colour was back in her face, and she started eating what was left of her lunch.

"That is hilarious, did momma or papa see who drove you?" she asked.

"Don't think so. It wasn't mentioned."

"And today he just shows up out of the blue? That's not a coincidence. You are right; something is going on here. You think its because of the family?" she asked, concerned.

"It's all I can think of. I don't look like any of these *'ladies'* he normally hooks up with, and I am not interested in being the next Striker conquest. I have enough drama in my life with momma." Ale sipped the last of her margarita and thought about ordering another, then thought better of it.

The waiter appeared and cleared their plates and asked about dessert. Both declined and he held out the bill. Ale grabbed it quickly so she could treat Sophia and Sophia glared at her.

"What kind of drama is momma creating?' Sophia asked, checking her makeup with her compact.

Ale pulled out some bills from her wallet and handed them to the waiter.

"My birthday party," she replied with an eye roll.

Sophia smiled. "It will be the best party ever, Ale. You know momma will not stop until every single piece of it is perfection."

"That's what I'm afraid of."

They stood up and moved towards the exit. The restaurant was still busy as Sophia handed the tag to the valet and waited for the car.

On the way home, Sophia asked about O'Malley.

"Oh yeah," Ale replied. "Like my week wasn't already strange."

Sophia knew the O'Malley story. "Gio knows he's back in town," she said quietly, almost like she didn't want to tell her.

"Dammit. Just what I need. Please tell him to relax. I can handle O'Malley, I'm not 17 anymore."

"Ale, you are Gio's baby sister. You will always be 17 and he will always be overly protective. You know this." She smiled. Sophia loved that about Gio, but that's because *SHE* wasn't his baby sister.

"Yeah, yeah."

There Ale was, trying to understand how for years there were no men in her life and this week there were now two. Almost made her miss the pandemic and isolation. Almost.

CHAPTER 26
Dr. Louise Norris

All the staff of Good Samaritan Hospital were offered, requested, and sometimes brow beaten into taking some sort of therapy after the pandemic. It wasn't mandatory to take, but it was mandatory for the hospital to offer it. Ale decided it couldn't hurt.

The suffering, the deaths, the families affected... it all weighed heavily on her. She knew what she signed up for to be an ER nurse, but the last three years were the absolute exception. They had little to no external support due to their isolation and some days were darker than others.

It was Ale's third day off and she had a 9 a.m. session with Dr. Louise Norris, a psychologist who worked out of the hospital. She was someone Ale knew and respected.

Dr. Louise was a tall woman, immaculate in her grooming. She had a soft, soothing voice and a reputation for getting to the root of the issue. Today she was perfectly dressed in a beige two-piece suit with a dark brown satin blouse. The skirt was pencil in style; the jacket was short and fitted. She wore a thick gold chain and matching earrings. Her beige pumps completed the look.

Ale enjoyed their sessions.

They started with the regular stuff and apparently something must have been off as Dr. Louise asked Ale the million-dollar question.

"You seem agitated today, Ale. What's on your mind?"

Hmmm... where to start? Ale did not want to get into the O'Malley thing; it seemed like a large rabbit hole. And the other topic wasn't going to be fun either.

So, she just spit it out: "Men," and let out a big sigh.

Dr. Louise smiled. Ale had ever seen her smile like that since they started talking.

"Tell me more. This interests me. For a while, I thought maybe you might be an alien," she said, still smiling.

"Alien?" Ale was confused.

"You have never mentioned any sort of relationship to me, other than your family or friends. You are a beautiful woman, successful in your field, friendly and confident. It was a mystery to me how you didn't have a relationship, a partner, someone to share life with."

Ale stared at her. Up until this week, she thought she was normal. Apparently, she wasn't. She was like this before the pandemic. What was wrong with her? She frowned.

Dr. Louise must have sensed her beating herself up. "Ale, there is nothing wrong with wanting a partner, whether just for sexual reasons, relationship, friendship. It's very healthy. Tell me about the MEN," she said. Ale blushed.

Where to begin?

"Well, I met someone, kind of. On New Year's Eve. I was working. My friend has a catering business and I help her on my days off. With the pandemic, I was isolated and couldn't help her or even see her. So, I wanted to do both. It gets me out and it's some extra cash."

"Is money a concern for you?" she asked, innocently.

"No. I like making it. I like saving it. But I would probably help her for free."

"You also sew for your father in your spare time. He also pays you," she pointed out.

"Yeah, I can see where you're going with this." Ale smiled.

"Not going anywhere, just doing my job to make you aware of behaviours. Let's table that and go back to New Year's," she suggested.

"Its really nothing. He was part of the security company that was working the party. He drove me home. He was nice and polite. Just something about him. I don't know how to describe it. He stirred something in me. Since then, he's showed up in a few places that I've been and it's making me uneasy."

"Uneasy?" she asked.

"Yes. Very. But not in I'm afraid of him. OK. Maybe. Gosh. Dr. Louise, I'm not communicating well here. I don't know how to explain this. He's not threatening. It's that he has a reputation, apparently, and I'm unsure why he's looking in my direction," Ale finished with a sigh.

Dr. Louise looked at Ale, being careful with her words.

"Are you attracted to him?" she asked.

Ale burst out laughing. "Everyone in LA County is attracted to him. He is beautiful. Successful. The 'full meal deal' as my sister-in-law says."

"And the problem is?" Her eyebrows raised.

Ale looked at her, stalling.

"I'm scared." Tears filled up in Ale's eyes. Gawd, where did that come from? *Jeeezus.* This is why everyone likes Dr. Louise. Ale wanted to bolt out of the chair and run home.

"Ahhhh. And there we have it," she stated and handed Ale a tissue.

"Is this what we call a breakthrough?" Ale asked timidly, wiping her nose.

Dr. Louise smiled. "Indeed. Ale, you just went through three years of hell with a pandemic, professionally and personally. You were on the front lines. You risked your life to save others. Not once did you mention fear to me."

Ale thought about that. She thought hard about that.

"We have some work to do here. If you want to do it. I want to help you be the best version of yourself. I want to help you work through your fears, whatever they may be. I believe, if anything, the pandemic has made you more aware of human emotions. Emotions you may have tucked away, for whatever reason. This man who has made it on your radar is stirring up those emotions and it has you scared. Perfectly normal. Would you like to continue talking with me about this?" she asked, not pushing.

Ale nodded. "Yeah, I think I need to. I can't keep pushing people away. Oh, and for the record, there is more than one man," she said, reluctantly.

Dr. Louise closed her book and looked at her. "Even better! I look forward to our next talk."

"Thank you, Dr. Louise." She got up, went to leave and Dr. Louise said, "Ale."

She turned around.

"Do me a favour. Do something fun this afternoon. Something you haven't done in say three years? Something that maybe doesn't involve you making money," she smiled again, widely.

Ale left her office, feeling a bit numb. She took the bus home, changed into one of her many bikinis, and put on a pair of jean shorts with a white V-neck T-shirt. She filled her beach bag with a book, phone, wallet, towel, sunscreen, and a few other necessities and ran out to catch the next bus. Ale was headed to the beach! *Thank you, Dr. Louise!*

CHAPTER 27
The Beach!

Ramone had been watching every move Alessandra Ferretti made. He followed her this morning to the hospital, even though it was supposed to be her day off. She only stayed an hour and came directly back home.

Now he was following her in the bus to God knows where. All the details were being fed back to the control centre and to Striker. Ramone had a strange feeling this job was more personal than professional.

Ale got off one bus and quickly got on another. Ramone almost wondered if she knew she was being followed. He continued driving and suddenly realized she was heading to the beach. *Jesus.* He was not dressed to do surveillance on a beach. He would look extremely obvious, especially in his StrikeForce uniform and boots.

He clicked on the display to call Striker.

"Yo," Striker answered.

"Jefe. We have a problem."

"Speak."

"She's headed to the beach."

"Shit. OK. Continue to follow and park somewhere close by."

"Want me to buy some beachwear, change, and pretend I'm a tourist?" Ramone suggested.

Carlos thought about it. Not a bad idea. Ramone was really coming into his own. "Great idea. Yeah. I will reimburse you when you get back. Keep the receipts and please try to stay under the radar."

"Got it. I'll keep my ear-piece in and continue to transfer the data."

Ramone hung up and eventually found a parking space. He quickly got out of the SUV and walked briskly to see where she was going and if she was meeting anyone, without looking suspicious. He noticed her immediately. The beach wasn't packed with people, thankfully. *Jesus.* Oh man. She was taking off her shorts and T-shirt off, revealing a bright yellow bikini. *Damn!* He quickly grabbed some photos without her noticing. She laid out her towel. Ramone felt confident she was staying put, so he jogged back to where the little shops were and got himself all surfed up. He returned quickly, dressed in a T-shirt, swim shorts, hat, and water shoes. He threw his stuff in the truck and headed towards the beach again.

CHAPTER 28
She Wore An Itzy Bitzy...

Ahhhhhhhh! Ale thought. This was the best idea. Why didn't she think of this before? The beach is always here. We take it for granted. New year, new behaviours, as Dr. Louise would call them. She was going to start including the beach in her days off!

She proceeded to put on her sunscreen. The beach wasn't crazy packed with people, thank God. She wasn't all that comfortable traipsing around in a bikini in front of strangers, but today she couldn't care less. It was LA. She didn't have the big, fake hooters, but she didn't look half bad.

She sat on her towel with her knees bent just relaxing for a bit, staring at the beautiful water.

It reminded her of the first time her momma brought her here. Ale loved the beach and water. She had a small memory of the beach where she was born in Canada, but the water was cold. When momma took her hand to walk towards the water, Ale pulled back. Momma let go of her hand and walked closer to the water to show her it was warm. It was confusing to Ale, but eventually she moved toward it and quite frankly, never looked back. It was so pretty today. Actually, it was pretty every day.

Ale turned over and removed her book from her bag to do some reading. Another one of her favourite things to do: READ. She would read anything and loved podcasts and TED talks.

She remembered to text her BFF Amalia to see if she wanted to meet her at the Crowe's Nest for wings after she finished work. They had a nice patio on the boardwalk and since Ale was already there, she could just walk over and meet her. Amalia replied with a big *thumbs up emoji.*

CHAPTER 29
Sweet Jesus

Carlos was having a hell of a day. He apprehended two criminals who missed their bail hearings, he had two long and boring meetings with his investors, and he was driving back to head quarters when he received the call from Ramone.

He pulled into the underground garage, walked into the elevator up to his condo. A quick shower and change of clothes and he was back in his office. Carlos took a few punches getting the criminals into the SUV and his jaw was a bit bruised and sore, but he would tough it out.

He walked to the staff kitchen and grabbed a sandwich from the fridge and a water. He hadn't eaten all day. Leslie's catering company delivered fresh food daily to his office. He had strict rules on diet for his security team, especially the ones in the field. He loved the set up. She provided good nutritious food for his staff, and he loved giving back to the local economy.

One thing for sure, the little blonde on his mind, was wreaking havoc with his appetite and his sleep.

Carlos made his way to the control room to check the status board again. He spoke to a few of the techs and felt comfortable that all was quiet. His cell beeped with updates as he walked back to his office. He had a meeting with his lawyer in ten minutes. Claire Matthews was his lawyer and friend. Because he dealt in such an "interesting" business, he needed a good lawyer who knew how to manoeuvre outside the lines. Claire was a good fit. She was also attractive and available. They kept the relationship strictly business, however Carlos knew she wanted it to be otherwise. Story of his life.

He brought up the feeds coming in from the field and almost choked on his roast beef sandwich when he saw the photos of Ale being sent from Ramone. *Are you fucking kidding me?* He just stared as he had no words. His dick started to act up, and his heart started beating fast. *What was happening?* It was a woman in a bikini. He saw photos of women like this daily, most without any clothes.

But. It wasn't just any woman, was it? He sighed.

His cell beeped, letting him know Claire was downstairs. He hit the code on his phone to unlock the door of the building and she strode in towards the elevator. He needed to stay seated for a bit and close the photos on his tablet.

CHAPTER 30
Wings, Anyone?

Ale closed her book and stood up to stretch and look around. She took a drink and headed towards the ocean, just to test the water. It was January, so probably a bit cool. She dipped her toes in and just walked along the edge. It was refreshing. She held on to her hat as she walked along, keeping an eye on her towel in case any thieves were around. She edged in to just above her knees. The waves were small, so she just splashed some water up on her upper body. It felt amazing. God, she needed this. She walked along the edge again and then turned back and walked up to her towel. She was meeting Amalia soon, so she put her shorts and T-shirt back on and packed up her stuff. She took off her hat and put her hair up in a wet, messy bun.

The Crowe's Nest was just starting to get busy, Ale walked up the staircase to the patio, grabbed a table with an umbrella, and plunked her arse in the chair. A sexy muscle-bound waiter approached asking if she wanted a drink. She ordered a Corona, which seemed ironic considering she spent three years cursing that word. She couldn't help it; she liked the beer. He left two menus and two glasses of ice water.

Amalia appeared, still dressed in workwear. Ale was super excited to see her. She stood up and gave her a huge hug.

"Oh my God, I am so glad you texted me. I really needed this!" Amalia said, sitting down and gulping down her water.

"You can thank my therapist," Ale told her.

She almost spit out her water. "Please explain," she smiled.

Amalia Carriera had been her best friend since elementary school, and she adored her. She was a stunningly beautiful Brazilian with cocoa skin, exotic eyes, and the most beautiful smile. She arrived in the US as a small child to live with her aunt. Their stories were so similar; it's no wonder they found each other as kids. They went through college together, they were roommates, and she lived in Ale's apartment when Ale went to Dubai. She was the sister Ale always wanted.

Mal just returned from Bahamas with their other friends. Ale was dying to hear all about it. Plus, she had a few updates to give Mal, herself.

Muscle boy returned. Amalia also ordered a Corona and they ordered a platter of wings with mozza sticks.

"My therapist suggested I do something fun today, so I went to the beach, and it was fabulous. I really need to do this more often; we all do." Ale looked at her. Mal was a workaholic accountant in a big firm In LA and worked like a dog. She was stellar with numbers and loved it, but she had no life. Pushing her on the damn plane to go to Bahamas was a chore.

Ale raised her beer. "Here's to Dr. Louise." They clinked and laughed.

"How was Bahamas?" Ale wanted to hear everything. It must have been so nice to be somewhere different after being stuck here for over two years. She almost regretted not going. Almost.

"It was amazing. There were so many people. The men! Oh my God, Ale. They were everywhere. I am fairly certain Katee got laid a few times." Ale burst out laughing. She was sure of it, too. In fact, she knew she did because Katee had texted her.

Katee was their actress friend. Again, they went to school together. She'd been the star of a TV series called *Lonestar*, where she played a deputy for almost eight years. She lived in Montana and flew back and forth for visits. She was now playing the captain of a spaceship in a sci-fi series that was blowing up on Netflix. She excelled at acting and loved it. She wasn't what you would call extremely attractive. She was pretty and had strong bone structure, probably Nordic or northern

European. Katee was blonde with a wide mouth and a very muscled body. She had to stay in shape for her job, and she took it very seriously. She also loved men. Apparently, they loved her too!

Ale listened intently to all the stories. She loved when Amalia told stories. She was so animated. They both laughed so hard; this was exactly what they both needed. Their food arrived, they dove in, and ordered more beer.

"Sooo…" Ale started. "Ever heard of a guy named Striker?" she asked, confident Mal hadn't.

Mal choked a bit and smiled. "Who hasn't?" *Jeeezus! Are you kidding me?*

"Me! I haven't! How is it that I don't know anything about this guy?" Ale pleaded, loudly.

Mal shrugged. "I guess I just assumed you did. We go to Miguel's all the time. Everyone in LA knows. Well, at least all the females do. Apparently, he's stellar in the sack. Very easy on the eyes."

Ale looked at her. "Have you seen him in person?"

She nodded. She wiggled her eyebrows and laughed. Gawd.

"Why are you asking about Striker?" She opened the wet wipe and wiped her hands.

"He seems to be interested in me." There she said it. Out loud.

Mal stared at her. "Ale! Holy hell. We just ate our entire meal, and you drop this now?"

"I wanted to hear about Bahamas first." Mal didn't buy it. "OK, I am out of my element here. Mal, guys like Striker don't notice me. This is really freaking me out. Oh, and while I have verbal diarrhea, O'Malley is back in town."

Mal's expression changed. She looked as shocked as Ale was and Ale could tell she was reliving that moment, just as she did.

"Ale." She reached across the table and grabbed her hand. "You should have started with that. This is huge. What is he doing here? I thought he was dead."

"He's a detective with LAPD. He showed up at the hospital and recognized me immediately. It was so uncomfortable, Mal, I almost threw up." That's the thing about your BFF. You can tell her anything.

She gets you.

"OK. I don't even know where to start with all of this. In the same week you have O'Malley return and Striker making eyes at you? Girl, you get a new perfume or something?"

Ale smiled. Exactly what she needed to hear. Ale continued to update her, they paid their bill and took the bus home. The other wonderful thing about her BFF, they both lived in the same building. It was an awesome day!

Once Ale arrived home, she baked the bread she had rising and bagged it. She texted Danny to tell him he could pick up his bread in the morning as she would be leaving at 11 a.m. for her shift. She took a shower and went to bed. Back at it tomorrow.

CHAPTER 31
Who's Watching Who?

Neither Ale nor Amalia realized they were being watched. Not just by Ramone, but also O'Malley. While O'Malley was watching Ale closely, Ramone was watching all of them and it was getting interesting. Ramone walked towards Striker's office. Not a bad gig to hang out at the beach all day and take photos of babes. He knocked on the door.

"Enter."

Ramone opened the door and sat down in the chair opposite Striker. He did a full recap every night before heading home. Striker looked annoyed. He also had a huge bruise and a small cut on his face. No doubt he got into a mix with someone. He was reading the information on the tablet and looking at the photos. Ramone handed Striker his receipts and Striker opened his wallet and threw some bills at him.

Ramone spoke in Spanish. "I noticed the cop following. He didn't notice me. He was very interested in Ale. He never took his eyes off her."

Striker looked angry. Ramone had no idea if he was helping or making things worse.

"Who's the girl?" Striker asked.

"Amalia Carreira. Long time friend. Accountant for Jones, Jones and Lang. Lives in the same apartment building."

Striker nodded. "OK, good work today. Go home, get some sleep. She's supposed to work noon to midnight, starting tomorrow. In the morning, I want you to introduce yourself and tell her I sent you to take her to work and pick her up because I don't want her taking the bus in the middle of the night. Let me know if she pushes back."

Ramone agreed, said good night, and headed home.

Carlos sat staring at the photos. Jason O'Malley. He knew him. What he didn't know was why he was interested in Ale, and it made him uncomfortable. No, not uncomfortable, it made him angry and a bit jealous. He scrolled down to the photos of Ale walking on the beach with the sexy beach hat and bikini. He closed the files and thought about his next move.

CHAPTER 32
Beach Bum O'Malley

It was O'Malley's day off, so he decided to find out how Ale spent her days. He checked the hospital, and she wasn't on shift, so he did more investigating and followed her to the beach.

Legal? No. Necessary? Yes.

O'Malley scanned the beach. There wasn't a large number of women to check out, not that he wasn't up for the challenge, but when he did finally spot Ale, he thought he would stroke out. There she was holding on to her hat and walking along the edge in a tiny yellow bikini. He was instantly turned on. *Jesus Christ* she was a beautiful woman. He knew her when he was a horny kid and she was a shy teenager, but this is different. How is she not married or engaged or knocked up? O'Malley needed answers. His body was responding in a way it hadn't in a very long time. Yeah, he got horny. This was something different. He wanted to mate. O'Malley had feelings going through him that he had turned off for years.

He watched for a while mesmerized and followed her as she headed to the patio bar. He recognized Amalia immediately as she hadn't changed much. She was still a looker, but she had a big sign on her that said, "Don't mess with me!" It was nice to know they were both still close friends. O'Malley followed their bus home and discovered where Ale lived. He was feeling good. He also had some beautiful photos to stare at to keep him company tonight. He was going to have to take care of business on his own. It wouldn't be the first time.

CHAPTER 33
Introducing Ramone Ramirez

Daylight was peeking in through the blinds as Ale awoke. Her shift started at noon so she could take her time getting ready. She headed for the shower, dressed in a pair of shorts and a tank, and put her wet hair up in a bun. She never drank coffee. Her morning pick-me-up was orange juice. She poured a glass, put two pieces of homemade bread in the toaster, and proceeded to make her lunch.

She sat eating her toast while scanning her phone for news. Prior to the pandemic, she hardly paid attention, but now she checked it daily. Her new normal. A small knock on her door startled her and she went to the peep hole and saw Danny's sweet face. She opened it, hugged him, and ushered him inside.

"You're around early" Ale said, handing him two loaves and a small container of peanut butter cookies.

"Yeah, Vito has me all over the place. Business has really picked up. Thanks for this, Ale. I love your baking." He stared at the items adoringly.

"You want some homemade soup? I have some frozen—you can take with you. It will be thawed by lunch time, and you can nuke it and have it with your bread." She moved to the fridge and opened the freezer.

"Thanks. You're going to make me fat."

She smiled and grabbed a paper bag with handles out of her pantry to put everything in along with some napkins. "There ya go; all set." She handed the bag to him.

"Sorry I can't drive you to work today. I'm heading the other way with deliveries and traffic will be a bitch."

"No worries. The bus always runs, and the weather is good." Ale tried to make him feel better as Danny was a soft soul. The family treated him with kid gloves.

"Enjoy your day, Ale and thanks again," he said as he closed the door. Ale locked it behind him and headed to the bedroom to get ready for work.

Today she felt like black fitted cargo pants that had a fancy buckle on the front. She made them herself and loved them. She chose a black ribbed sleeveless bodysuit and topped it with a yellow faux leather biker jacket and clunky black patent leather military boots.

She always made her bed and straightened up the apartment before leaving. She was filling up her tote bag with her lunch, water bottle. And other necessities when another knock on her door startled her. *It must be Danny*, she thought, as nobody else had a key to the building. Amalia was long gone for work. She peeped into the hole and saw a Latino male with a StrikeForce jacket standing there and it wasn't Carlos. She kept the chain connected and opened the door a few inches.

"Can I help you?" Ale asked.

"Miss Ferretti? My name is Ramone Ramirez. I work for StrikeForce Security. Striker asked me to come over today and drive you to and from work. He is concerned and does not want you taking the bus home in the middle of the night." Ale laughed. He sounded like he was reading from a script. He was a nice-looking guy, young, and seemed terrified. Her guess was he was told not to return unless he got her to say yes.

She smiled, unlinked the chain, and opened the door. He just stood there, waiting for an answer.

"Would you like to come in?" she asked.

"No, Miss Ferretti. If you agree, I will wait for you outside the lobby." She agreed and told him she would be right down.

Striker must have it bad. *OK, let's have some fun with this,* she thought.

She grabbed her bag and keys, locked up, and headed towards the elevator. Ramone was waiting outside the very, clean SUV. He moved to open the back door as she walked up.

"OK if I ride shotgun?" she asked. He nodded, gently took her bag, and opened the passenger door. Ale got in and he put her bag into the back. They buckled up and off they went, like any normal couple!

They both had their sunglasses on. Ale was checking out the vehicle as it was fully loaded. The screen had so many apps and gadgets, she was sure there were hidden places for weapons and that the glass was bullet proof.

She decided to converse in Spanish, to help make him feel comfortable. "I am guessing everything in this car is on video?"

He nodded.

"Soo, people are watching us right now?"

He smiled and nodded. Ale decided to flirt a little. She asked him if he was married, if he had a girlfriend, where he was from, about his family. She was trying to put him at ease as she was sure he dealt with arseholes most of the time. Especially in LA. She wanted to make sure she wasn't one of them. She grilled him the whole way into the hospital, knowing full well Carlos was listening to every word. They arrived at the hospital and Ramone quickly got out, opened her door, handed her the bag, and wished her a great day.

"If you are picking me up, I probably won't be ready until 12:30 or 12:45; should I text you?" she asked.

"My contact info is already in your phone." He smiled and got back into the SUV and drove off.

She stared at him and walked into the hospital. Apparently, they've hacked into her phone. Lovely. Nothing sacred here. Thank God she didn't take nude selfies. *Jeeezus.*

CHAPTER 34
Pepe y Jorge

The 12 p.m. to 12 a.m. shift was not fun. You had the leftovers from morning, and most people in LA don't get up until noon, so it tended to be very busy. Then you have a short break in the middle and all the crazies appear at night. She quickly changed and headed to the ER staff centre to get debriefed and start turn over. She was early, but usually was. She checked the staff charter and smiled as she would be working with one of her favourite humans, Lacey Livingston. Sounds like a porn name. They teased her all the time; however, she was one of the best ER nurses they had. Ale adored working with her and spending twelve hours with someone you trust and care about makes a huge difference.

They greeted each other like long-lost friends, gabbed about the holidays, and got down to business.

Lacey and Ale were always on the same page: get them in, get them help, and get them out. Not all medical staff were the same. They grabbed Dr. Lewis, who was the on-call ER doctor today and had him make the rounds with them on the existing patients, so they could hopefully empty some beds and start draining the over-crowded waiting room.

They managed to release eight patients with prescriptions and/or advice and started calling new names into the now sanitized and clean rooms. Ale took four patients and Lacey took the others. Appendicitis, broken nose, scraped knee that required stitches... so far so good. Her last room was a familiar visitor named little Jorge Rodriguez. He was four years old, in agony with chronic ear infections, and he badly needed his tonsils out. Everyone knew this, but his family didn't have insurance. Ale opened the curtains and smiled at the little guy. Jorge smiled back and Ale greeted his parents while holding his hand. They were all speaking entirely in Spanish, both parents were smiling as they knew Ale would always help Jorge with the pain, until it happened again. He would need a prescription. For now, she gave him some drops to take the edge off. She sat down with his parents and explained the situation again, and they just hung their heads. Jorge was settled for a bit and Ale needed to consult with Dr. Lewis. She gave Jorge a sucker and was rewarded with a huge smile in return.

She paged Dr. Lewis and they discussed Jorge and options. Of course, nothing had changed on the insurance side. The hospital had a slush fund for some charity cases, but it could take months to get approved. She decided to take advantage of her contacts and reached for her cell when she remembered it might be being monitored. Instead, she found a private office, called a number and left a message for her to be paged at the hospital.

Ale returned to the main ER station and called three more patients into the newly sanitized rooms. The waiting room was looking much better. Lacey was busy with her patients, so Ale started with the new ones. She went back to Jorge and his parents asking for just a few more minutes.

Ale was paged and went to take the call.

"*Presciosco!*" said a deep voice with a strong accent. It was Pepe. Ale smiled. She adored this man. She didn't care if he killed people. OK, wait, she did care. She just didn't want to know about it. She ignored it. He was in a gang, and she knew and understood what all that meant, she really did. She could only speak to what she knew. He had a big heart, and he was good to her, so she blocked the other shit out.

"Pepe, thank you for calling me back," she said in Spanish.

"What do you need, *nena*?" he asked.

Ale explained the Jorge situation. Diego and Pepe were extremely protective of their communities, and she knew they were aware of the family and would want to help. She asked if they would be interested in getting Jorge the surgery and of course the answer was yes. She thanked him a million times and hung up. *Yay!*

She informed Dr. Lewis He nodded and told her to get Jorge booked so they could do the surgery that afternoon.

The Rodriguez family were shocked and thrilled. They thanked Ale and hugged her like her own momma. They got Jorge ready and had the orderly take them to the Peds floor. She had them fill out the paperwork. They didn't need to know where the money came from—just an anonymous donor. She would go up later to check on them.

Ale's name came over the PA again to report to the main desk. She walked down to see what was going on and the admin clerk had a large manilla envelope for her. *Jeezus.* It was the money for the surgery. Hey, sometimes people like to pay in cash. She grabbed the envelope and took it to the cashier's office and attempted an explanation, as these types of transactions were delicate.

Legal? No. Necessary? Yes.

Once she had that sorted, she grabbed Lacey and they headed to dinner break.

CHAPTER 35
Striker and O'Malley

Carlos could not believe what he was hearing while listening to Ramone and Ale drive into work. *She was flirting with him.* He didn't know if he should laugh or be jealous. Obviously, Ramone was enjoying it. She knew he would be listening, and yet she just went for it. Unbelievable. Apparently, Alessandra Ferretti liked to play games. She wasn't all business, after all, and she didn't flinch when Ramone told her about her phone being hacked. Carlos expected fireworks. Instead, she just shrugged and went to work. Who does that? Carlos discovered something new with her every day. Time to turn on the heat.

He knew where to find O'Malley in the mornings. He seemed to like the lattes at Honeybeans, a popular hangout for cops and women in yoga pants.

Striker sat at one of the small outdoor tables waiting and slowly drinking his water. He wasn't a coffee drinker. He took very good care of his body and what he put into it. As a matter of fact, he was very picky about what he put his body into as well, especially these days.

O'Malley drove up, parked, and Striker watched him go in and order. When O'Malley came out, Striker was leaning against the Dodge Charger with his arms and legs crossed. O'Malley stopped short. He knew who Striker was. They had a crossed paths before and he wasn't all together sure why Striker was waiting for him.

"Striker. You lookin for a ride?" O'Malley joked, drinking his coffee.

"Nope. Looking for information." He had O"Malley's attention.

"About?"

"Why are you following Alessandra Ferretti?"

O'Malley tensed. "Police business," he said, hoping to shut this conversation down.

"Try again." Striker uncrossed his arms and put his hands in his front pockets.

"Let's take a walk." O'Malley didn't want to have this conversation here.

They walked towards the park and found a place with less traffic.

O'Malley looked at him. "Why do you care about Ale?" he asked. Striker took notice of him using the name Ale. He obviously had a personal connection with her.

"I run a security business and some people need to be protected." Striker kept it vague, and he knew O'Malley wouldn't push because he knew Gio would hire someone to watch Ale. Gio was that kind of brother.

"She's not in any police trouble. I guess you could say I was curious. She's a beautiful woman." O'Malley decided to end the stand-off as he didn't want trouble from Striker. He knew what he was capable of, and he knew Striker coloured outside of the lines.

"You might want to find a new hobby," Striker suggested and walked back to his car.

The conversation annoyed Striker. O'Malley had a reputation with the ladies, and not in a good way. He was going to start doing some research on where he'd been and what he'd been up to. Ale was off limits; Striker would make sure of that.

CHAPTER 36
Ale and Lacey

Lacey and Ale sat and ate dinner together in the cafeteria, mainly discussing the upcoming fundraiser gala for the hospital. They loved fund-raising and had helped the hospital reach some very aggressive financial goals.

Ale started getting involved in fund-raising while doing her Doctor of Nursing Practice. She wrote a thesis on Neonatal Abstinence Syndrome (NAS), specifically on how to care for the infants once born. There had been several papers, directives and procedures on this. While spending time with Neonatal, and helping during her off time, she discovered something very, simple, cost effective and easy to implement. It did require updating the neonatal floor with some soundproof rooms. This would cost money. They raised funds to do the construction and built four little soundproof rooms. Each room was decorated and made comfortable for the nurses, babies, and volunteers. The nurses worked with each baby individually as much as possible, however these babies were high needs. It was difficult to spend the amount of time with each baby that was necessary. Enter the volunteers. Women like Ale's momma and zia who loved babies and wanted to help. They could each take a screaming upset baby into one of the rooms, rock them and soothe them while the baby went through their withdrawals and not impact any other babies who might already be sleeping. They learned that some wanted the skin-to-skin touch, some wanted to be walked, some wanted to be wrapped and warm, and others wanted to be naked. It allowed the nursing staff to identify an individual approach to each baby and help them through what is truly the most difficult time. These babies deserved at least that. Ale was super proud of the program, which had been replicated throughout many hospitals who have high levels of NAS.

Today they were coming up with fundraising ideas. One idea that they've been throwing around for a while was a nurses' calendar. They both thought it was a perfect idea—the nurses needed some recognition, especially after COVID and the hospital needed a big financial boost. COVID diminished any funds they had in a reserve and really prevented any type of fundraising other than online.

Every year the LA firefighters produced a calendar, and it generated a lot of money. The calendars didn't have to be sexy, just a personal glimpse of the hard-working ladies and men who represent the nurses of Good Samaritan. Ale knew a good photographer that would be willing to do the work for free.

They documented their ideas, each with a tiny paragraph on their estimates to produce, and projections on possible donations. They had to get it finalized and sent to the hospital board quickly for approvals.

After their dinner and fundraising session, Ale and Lacey headed back to the ER and continued where they left off. The remainder of the night went fairly, smooth and Ale texted Ramone to let him know she would be ready by 12:30. She was showered and signed out, saying her goodbyes and heading towards the exit. As she exited, she stopped in her tracks. Ramone wasn't waiting for her; Striker was. Thank God the nurses used the staff parking exit and didn't see him. It would have caused a riot. *Jeeeezzus.*

Ale took a deep breath and walked towards the man who was wreaking havoc in her life. Gawd, he looked sexy. He didn't shave today; even more yummy. She played it cool and walked up to him, so they were toe to toe. He didn't move. He just smiled.

"Hi Carlos!" she said smiling.

"Alessandra." He pulled open the passenger door to his Porsche

Cayenne, and she sat in the front as he put her bag into the back.

"Is Ramone ill?" she asked while buckling her seatbelt.

"No." He was looking at her with those laser eyes as he pulled out of the parking lot and headed towards her apartment.

"Oh, I was looking forward to finishing my conversation with him."

"You can flirt with me if you want. I won't mind," he teased.

She looked at him and smiled, he was on to her!

"Are we on camera?" she asked. He grinned showing his beautiful white teeth.

"No."

"So, is someone paying you to babysit me?" she asked.

"No."

Gawd, man of few words. She decided to stay quiet. He asked for her key-fob to park underground. Holy shit, was he staying the night? *Wtf?* She handed it to him with a look of fear and his eyes smiled. Ale told him her parking spot number and he pulled in and opened her door before she could blink. The man moved like a panther.

They moved into the elevator and rode to her floor in silence. He took her keys, opened the apartment door, and asked her to wait while he did a walkthrough. *Why would he do that?* He returned to the foyer and put the keys into her hand, making sure he held it there for a length of time. Ale just stood there looking at him, not really understanding what was happening.

Carlos moved toward her, and she backed up until she hit the wall. He pressed against her, and she felt his firm body. *All of it.* She put her hands on his waist to keep her balance, and looked into his dark, dark eyes. She could feel her heart pounding against her chest. She was nervous, and he sensed it. He moved in with his mouth and skimmed it along her jaw to her ear. *Sweet Christ.* He smelled like sandalwood and oh how she really, really wanted to kiss him. He skimmed his mouth down her neck slowly to that sweet spot, all the while rubbing his front against her. She could only hang on. *It had been a while!*

He slowly moved his mouth back up to her lips as he brought his hand up and tucked a curl behind her ear. He looked into her eyes with his beautiful mouth right there for the grabbing and whispered, "Sweet dreams, Alessandra." He opened the door and left. She slumped and slid down the wall as her legs were like jelly. She sat on the floor for what seemed like hours before crawling into the bedroom and crashing on the bed, boots and all.

CHAPTER 37
Someone's Watching You...

When Striker drove out from the underground parking of Ale's building, he didn't take notice of the Dodge Charger parked in the dark, with O'Malley watching his every move. O'Malley was still annoyed by the Striker conversation and wanted to know what was going on. He had watched Ale happily get into his vehicle after work. In fact, they almost looked like a couple. Could this be the reason Striker wanted him away from Ale? Did he want her for himself? Striker didn't have girlfriends. He slayed and left. Everybody knew that. Did Gio hire him to watch Ale and keep him away from O'Malley? Or was there someone else after Ale, who O'Malley didn't know about? Why was everyone watching Ale?

CHAPTER 38
Sleepless in LA

By the time Striker got into his bed, he was wired. He had a hard-on that wouldn't quit, and he'd just made it worse. He was seconds away from kissing Ale's sweet mouth and man did he want to. He wanted to get her out of her clothes and see her naked. He wanted to kiss and taste every inch of her. He hadn't been this turned on by a woman in ages. She's all he thought about. He had women sending him naked photos and leaving messages and yet he just stared at the photo on his phone of Ale lying on the beach.

He would be very interested in her next move. He closed his eyes, hoping sleep would come.

CHAPTER 39
Gang and Bang

At around 5 a.m., Ale woke and realized she still had her clothes on. She stripped naked and crawled under the covers and slept another three hours. Her phone alarm went off and she clumsily turned it off. Her head ached and for some reason she was still aroused by that Striker encounter. No wonder all the ladies were after him. *Lordy*.

She headed for the shower and grabbed some Excedrin. After drying off, moisturizing with scent-free cream and putting her hair up, she headed to the kitchen. It was an oatmeal kinda day, so she made a package of instant, poured her beloved orange juice, grabbed some cut-up fruit, and perused the news. *SHIT*. Gang shootings. It was all over the news and the hospital would be crazy. She quickly scoffed down her breakfast, brushed her teeth and grabbed whatever was in her closest. A white bra shelf tank with thin straps, wide leg culotte jeans, and her furry plum sweater jacket. She put on burgundy leather ankle boots, some moisturizer, stud earrings, and she was ready. Ale remembered she had a chauffer and texted Ramone to let him know she would be going in early. Shocker: he was already downstairs waiting for her.

Ale's heart was racing. She worried about Diego and Pepe. She wanted them alive, while most people wanted them dead. She really needed to get to the hospital, *fast!* She quickly emptied her bag with yesterday's lunch containers and filled it with today's. Thank God she always made her lunches ahead of time. She filled her water bottle and grabbed some spare underwear and sweats, thinking it might be a long night. She headed down to meet Ramone.

When she exited her apartment building door, he was waiting with the door opened. *"Buenos dias, Alessandra."*

"Buenos dias, Ramone. Como estas?" she replied, getting into the SUV.

"Gran, gran!" He hopped into the driver side and off they went to the hospital. She was very quiet this morning as she was worried about what she would be walking into. Her silence did not go unnoticed.

He asked if she was OK, and she nodded. They drove in silence the rest of the way. She thanked him and walked into what would be hell for the next 24 hours. There were EMTs, doctors, security, cops, TV reporters and gang members everywhere. Usually, Good Samaritan took the overflow from other LA hospitals as they weren't located in areas where turf wars occurred. Today was the exception. She barged her way through. *Excuse me, excuse me,* all the way to the staff locker room. Some of the nurses were there, looking exhausted with their scrubs stained with blood. Some were crying. It always took a toll, no matter how many times you saw it, even gang members. A life was a life.

She quickly changed and ran into the ER to let Nya know she was there early. Nya looked sad. She never looked sad. Ale gave her a quick hug and grabbed the charts. She saw where she would be needed the most and headed there. The waiting room was overcrowded with gang associates and cops. It was extremely intimidating.

A blue pair of cop eyes were fixated on her, and she turned and went the opposite direction. She grabbed a pair of gloves and walked into ER Room 3. Ale had scanned the patient names and, thankfully, did not see the ones she was looking for. It didn't mean they weren't at another hospital, but they weren't at hers!

She took a deep breath, pulled the curtain back, and dove in. This poor dude had more holes in him than Swiss cheese. Dr. Lance Wright was in charge, and he was an absolute prick. Ale had chosen this one, because he usually made every ER nurse cry with his bullying; every nurse, but her. She could sense the tension and she gladly picked up the slack. They were attempting to get him stable prior to surgery, but it was like playing whack-a-mole as the blood was gushing out from everywhere. She pushed a very new young nurse out of the way and took over with the pressure and bandaging. The nurse looked relieved. Dr. Wright just glanced up and kept barking orders. Ale did everything he asked and just as they thought the patient was stable, he flatlined. Dr. Wright grabbed the paddles and went at him, blood now gushing everywhere, trying everything possible to keep this man alive. *Not today*. Time of death was recorded, Ale did the sign of the cross and she moved on to the next one, while Dr. Wright spoke to family, gang members, and the cops.

This continued for eight hours before the nurse supervisor demanded Ale take a break and get something to eat. She already knew she would be working a double so she texted Ramone to tell him she wouldn't be getting off work until noon the following day. She changed into her fourth pair of scrubs and ate her late dinner in silence.

She hooked back up with Lacey after she finished eating and they attempted to organize as much as possible. Most of the gang members were gone. The Good Samaritan public affairs rep, Susanna Cheng, was handling the press. They organized the gang-related injuries and patients to one area so they could work on other patients with an element of privacy and security. Lacey focussed on getting those patients treated and Ale made the rounds on the gang patients. They had all the surgery rooms going with six in waiting. This was as bad as it gets. She had just finished checking the vitals on a very young gang member, someone grabbed her arm and shoved her into a supply closet. *WTF?*

She caught her breath and stared into O'Malley's eyes.

"Jesus, O'Malley, what the hell?" she said, rubbing her arm.

He stood there, hands on his hips, looking at her. She had no idea what he was thinking or why they were in a closet.

"I needed to talk to you, and you are always avoiding me," he said calmly. Although his eyes looked the opposite.

"Is it related to a patient?"

"No. It's related to us. You and me."

Ale froze. "O'Malley, there is no us. We had a moment years ago. It's in the past. We've both moved on. It's all good," she tried to reassure him.

"Then why are your brother and Striker telling me to leave you alone?" He must have seen the surprise look on her face.

"I don't know." She looked at the floor. "Can we talk about this later? Please? I have so much work here and I am sure you do too."

"I want a date. I want you to give me your cell number so I can text you and we can go out and have a nice friendly dinner and a conversation. A conversation that we should have had ten years ago."

Fine. *Jesus.* She would have given him her ovaries to get rid of him.

She gave him her number and he put it in his phone. She quickly made her exit, praying nobody noticed. Of course, people noticed. It's a hospital for *Christ's* sake. It's not like *Grey's Anatomy* where everyone is boinking in closets. She wished.

Back to work, Alessandra, she said to herself.

By the time 6 a.m. came, Ale was feeling the pain. She took a break with Lacey; they both needed caffeine. She chose a Diet Pepsi and a muffin and Lacey grabbed a very large coffee and a bagel. They both sat quietly, deep in thought. So many young lives lost for no real reason. Senseless deaths after a pandemic just pissed them off.

Ale took a detour up to Peds as she wanted to check on Jorge. She checked with the desk and walked towards his room; she could use a pick me up today. She saw him immediately with his big bright smile. His mom sitting beside him, as he was sucking on a popsicle. "Ale!" he tried to say. His mom scolded him. He was supposed to take it easy. *Hard for child,* Ale thought. She went over and gave him a hug and a kiss. He showed her a picture he had drawn of a nurse and a little boy, and he had put her name over the nurse. It warmed her heart and he wanted her to have it. She thanked him in Spanish and took a few minutes to speak with his mom. The surgery went perfectly, and they are already seeing such a difference in their little boy. She thanked Ale over and over, they exchanged hugs, and Ale told her she probably wouldn't be back as she was off for the next few days. Ale also told her to watch for a fever and bring Jorge back if she felt things were moving in the wrong direction. She blew a kiss to Jorge and left. Her heart was a tiny bit lifted as she took her new picture and put it in her locker.

They somehow found their second wind and made it to the finish line. All the surgeries were complete. The doctors and nurses were all exhausted. They managed to save six out of 12 young men. The six were hanging on by threads in intensive care. It will be touch and go. The remaining gang members were asked politely to leave while the patients were in recovery. Contact information was exchanged as well as condolences for those that were lost. The hospital staff knew some of these people as they were part of their community. They were part of their family. Today hurt. It hurt bad.

When noon finally arrived, the ER was reasonably quiet. They did the turnover, showered, changed, and Ale couldn't wait to go home and sleep. She texted Ramone, signed out, and headed towards the door. She wasn't even thinking when she looked up and saw Carlos. He had a sad look on his face today and she guessed he may have known some of the victims. She walked out to where he was standing, and he just opened his arms. Ale fell into them and started crying while Carlos held her tight and whispered in Spanish. *"Estara bien, estara bien."*

Why was she so comfortable with him? It just felt good to surrender and let someone hold you up for a bit. Tell you it will be OK. Comfort you. *Gawd*, she had no idea how much she missed this from a man. She was in so much trouble and, honestly, she didn't care. At this point, she just really needed to take the edge off. She was ready to put herself in the Striker lineup and take the one-nighter and be grateful. One is better than none! She pulled herself back a bit, staying in his arms and looking up at him. She wanted to kiss him. She wanted to kiss him in the hospital parking lot with the world looking. She didn't care. He gently kissed her on the lips, and he ushered her in the car.

She was hoping he did that because he didn't like PDA, not because he wasn't attracted to her. She knew he was; she felt it. She was confused. First O'Malley; now this. What a *fucker* of a day. Good news: she was off for three days. Thank you, *Jesus*.

Carlos drove with one hand and the other holding hers. It was nice.

He had very soft hands. She looked at him and noticed he had a bruise on his face. It was turning yellow now. She hadn't even noticed that the other night; she had been a bit distracted.

"What happened to your face?" she asked. "It's bruised."

"Work," he said, obviously the Striker shell was back on. She was too tired to think about it, so she remained quiet all the way to her apartment door. She sure hoped he didn't want sex today because she would just be laying there while he did all the work. She was exhausted.

He did the normal check of the apartment. Ale dropped her bag, put her sweater on the chair, kicked off her boots, and headed to the bedroom. He stood there watching her as she was shedding clothes and walked. She kept her panties and tank top on, crawled under the covers, and said thank you in Spanish. He kissed her cheek, brought a bottle of water, and her phone in to charge. *Who does this?* When he left, she heard him lock the deadbolt. Apparently, he had made himself keys. *Jeeeezus.* Within minutes she was sound asleep.

CHAPTER 40
The Diner

Carlos reluctantly left Ale and headed to the LA Diner. He liked it there because he owned it, he always had a table, and the food and service was impeccable. It was a simple, old-fashioned diner with a long counter with stools and a row of booths along the windows. Jackie, the waitress, had been there for over 30 years. She was family. The cook and busboy were both from Cuba. Carlos took care of his own.

He pushed open the doors. Some of the booths were full and a few customers at the counter. He went to the end booth, which was reserved for him, and sat facing the door. Jackie brought him water and Carlos nodded in thanks. She was used to his moods and knew when to talk and when not to. Today was no talking. She put his usual order in: roasted chicken with vegetables.

Carlos sat in thought, and he pulled his phone out to check for alerts; nothing new appeared. He texted his mom to tell her he would stop by for dinner later as he needed to see and talk to her.

His heart was heavy as he knew some of the gang members that died today. He also knew that Ale probably fought like hell to save them. He wanted to take all that pain away from her. He had no idea how she did that daily. Such strength and yet she let him hold her while she wept. He could feel her relax against him. God, was he falling in love with her? *WTF?* His feelings for Ale were different than anything he'd ever experienced. He cared and wanted to protect her. He wanted her naked. He wanted to have conversations with her and learn about her life. He felt like he knew her forever and just met her all in the same week.

Images of her in her little white cotton panties were haunting him. Why is it that white cotton panties on Ale seemed sexy? *Focus, Carlos.*

Jackie appeared with his lunch, and he scoffed it down. He had an afternoon of meetings and then the most important meeting of all: his mama.

CHAPTER 41
Familia

Carlos finished with his business meetings and headed to his mom's. She lived on a quiet street in East LA. He parked in the drive and noticed his sisters were already there. He suspected an Intervention was on the menu.

He opened the side door into the small but efficient kitchen. His mom was at the stove and Justina and Mariella were cutting up veggies and setting the table. Vanessa was on her phone with her earbuds in. His mom dropped the spoon and ran over to hug him. He hugged her hard and spoke to her in Spanish, asking about her day. His sisters came over, hugging him. Carlos got the subtle hint that he needed to visit more often.

They gathered around the small dining table. Everyone talking at once. Carlos was asking Vanessa about school, trying to get a sense of what was going on in her life. He monitored her social media, so he had an idea, but he wanted her to feel comfortable talking to him. She was a shy girl. Her dad left years ago, and Carlos tried to fill that role. Carlos tried to fill most of the male roles. The exception was his brother Milo. Milo helped a lot, but he was the polar opposite of Carlos. He kept to himself, and he avoided violence. They got along, but they didn't mingle in the same circles.

Justina was closest to him in age, and she was fierce. Nobody messed with her. Carlos was terrified of her. She was all Latina, beautiful and bossy. Mariella was youngest and more like Milo. She was quiet and shy. She was very pretty but did nothing to bring attention to herself. Almost as if she wanted to hide. He understood why as they had an abusive bastard for a father. He left scars on all of them. They were all laughing and talking like they hadn't ever been apart. His mom was loving it. He was sure she was wishing Milo was there, but Milo marched to his own drum. They finished the delicious Cuban meal and sat drinking coffee. Carlos had a glass of red wine and sipped it. He rarely drank alcohol. They continued to sit at the table and talk, while his mom put out their favourite dessert, *torticos de moron*. He ate one, so he wouldn't have to hear about it.

When there was a lull in the conversation, he spoke. "I think I've met someone." Justina dropped her wine glass on the floor, his mom's eyes almost bugged out of her head, Mariella gasped, and Vanessa jumped up and started hugging him. OK, not what he was expecting. They cleaned up the wine glass and Justina hugged him so hard he had to push her away to breathe.

"Oh my God! Are you freaking kidding me?" she screamed. In Spanish, of course. They bombarded him with questions. Once they finally calmed down, he told them his story.

"A Ferretti? Oh Carlos, are you sure?" Justina asked. She always did all the talking.

"I am sure. I am very sure." After he said it out loud, he knew. He showed them a photo of Ale and they all *oohed* and *ahhed*. He knew his mom would prefer si Latina, but the heart wants what the heart wants. For years he didn't even think he had one.

They pounded him with questions, and he did his best to answer them. What does she do, how old, family? Been married? Kids? Speaks Spanish – *BOOM* – that got his mom. Ale could completely win these ladies over. He had no doubt. Now he just had to make her his. That shouldn't be a problem, right?

CHAPTER 42
Teaghlach ("family" in Irish)
Mommy, I'm Home...

O'Malley sat in his Dodge Charger on the street across from his mum's house. This was the house he grew up in. His neighborhood and he ruled it. He chased girls up and down these streets for most of his young life. It kept him from having to go home. He adored his mother, but his father was a complete arsehole. He was an abusive drunk. O'Malley felt his old man's fist more times than he could count. So did his mother. When his father finally drank himself to death, O'Malley left for the navy. He knew his mum and sisters would be safe then. He was fairly certain that they didn't see it like that.

He called a few times over the years; the conversation was cold. His mum resented him, and he knew it. His sisters didn't speak to him either. This would not be easy. Time to pay the piper as they say. He got out of the car and walked across the street and up the stairs to ring the bell.

An elderly lady with beautiful blue eyes opened the door and stared at him. He took off his sunglasses. Her gaze softened and tears started to fall. She pushed opened the screen door and hauled him into the house. She hugged him around the middle and cried uncontrollably. OK, he thought, *maybe it wouldn't be that bad.*

O'Malley unhooked her arms from around him and pulled himself back so he could look at her. She had aged and seemed shorter. He took her face in his hands and, for the first time ever, he kissed her face.

"Mum. I'm sorry," he said, looking into her eyes.

"My Jason. Is it really you?" she asked, tears still flowing.

"In the flesh. Let's go sit down and get you some tissues." He steered her to the kitchen, and she sat on a chair. *Christ*, he thought, *nothing has* fucking *changed in this house*. It was depressing.

He found some tissues in the tiny bathroom and wiped her eyes. He sat down and moved his chair directly in front of her. "You want some tea?" he asked. She nodded and he put the kettle on and realized that absolutely everything was exactly as he left it. He knew where the tea bags were, the cups, even the biscuits. He made the tea, put some biscuits on a plate, and brought everything over to the table.

He sat down and asked her about her health, and she shrugged. She probably wouldn't tell him. He'd have to get that out of his sisters. He was sure there wouldn't be any hugs or crying when they saw him.

She put her hand over his. "How are you?" she asked, still with a hint of Irish. "Are you married? Kids? Where have you been? All these years, worrying. You are so handsome. Just like your..." she stopped. He knew he looked like his old man, that was *fuckin'* irony for you.

O'Malley filled her in while she went into mum mode, hauling left-overs out of the fridge. He had to admit, he really missed her cooking. She heated up the leftover beef stew, cut him some fresh homemade bread, and sat down to watch him eat. This is what mums did. Christ he was a coward. Why did it take so long? He put this poor, sweet woman through hell worrying. Funny how you think you are doing what's best for someone and it turns out to be the worst thing ever.

He asked about his sisters. Emily was the oldest, married her high school sweetheart, and they had four kids. His mom showed him photos. Meghan was the middle child. She had gone through some rough patches growing up but turned her life around. She was living with a guy, and they had a kid. O'Malley knew his Irish-Catholic mother wasn't happy about that, but she was probably happy Meghan was doing well and lived close by. He asked for their numbers, and she wrote them down for him. No technology here.

He looked at his mum, realizing she was now in her sixties, but looked so much older. Having a husband like Patrick O'Malley would age you quick.

She brought out pie and they talked about the pandemic. He had so much guilt over not being there for her. O'Malley never felt guilt until he hit 30. Now, it was all-consuming.

The front door opened, and he heard, "Ma, you there? Why aren't you watching *Jeopardy*?" Emily stopped in her tracks. He knew he reminded her of their father. Then he knew she'd be upset it was her brother. Either way, it was a lose, lose. "Jace?" She teared up; his mom teared up. "Christ, Jesus, I thought you were fucking dead!"

He got up and she almost toppled him over. She just wept in his arms. O'Malley was crying too. "What the hell? Why didn't you call or write or Facebook or something? My God, Ma's been worried, we've all been worried. You just left and we had nobody." She was blowing her nose and he just let her get it all out.

Emily went to the cupboard to get the whiskey. Apparently, they could have it in the house now. She poured them all a drink and brought it to the small kitchen table. He had no idea how they had all fit into this damn house. It felt claustrophobic.

She texted Meghan. It would be a real family reunion as her husband was bringing their kids over. O'Malley would meet everyone. He knew Emily's husband; they'd been together since school. Emily looked good, she had put some weight on, but she kept herself neat and was extremely proud to be a mom. She showed him photos of the kids. O'Malley had stalked her on social media, but she didn't know that, and he wasn't going to tell her.

He updated her on his life.

"A fucking police detective? Are you kidding me?" Emily asked. Apparently, his mom was OK with swearing. O'Malley got his mouth washed out with a bar of Irish Spring soap any time he swore. *WTF?*

Minutes later the door burst open and Meghan, her brood and Daniel, plus Emily's husband with three of her kids, as one was playing soccer, all bounced in. The kitchen was getting extra crowded, so they all moved into the living room, which wasn't much larger. More whiskey was poured, more tears, more photos, and more stories. It was *fuckin'* fabulous. He didn't want to leave.

O'Malley was going to put down roots here, and he knew exactly who with.

CHAPTER 43
Ben and Jerry's

Ale woke up disoriented. She had no idea what day or time it was. She checked her Fitbit and it said 12:08 a.m. She was starving. She reluctantly got up, padded to the bathroom and grabbed her warm, comfy pink robe that her momma had made for her. She found her pink inside UGGs and went out to the kitchen to make a mortadella and provolone sandwich. Yum. She poured a Diet Pepsi with ice and sat and ate while checking her phone. Carlos had turned the volume down and put it on vibrate, so she didn't hear anything. *Shit*, hopefully the hospital wasn't looking for her. Or worse: momma. She unlocked it and was bombarded with texts. *WTF?*

Ale! OMG were you hugging Striker outside the hospital? (Lacey)

OMG Ale, wtf? I saw you kissing Striker, outside the hospital. Are you dating? (Amy)

Alessandra. I need to talk to you. Call me when you get this. (Gio)

Chiamami bambino. (momma.)

Ale Cat. Confirming lunch tomorrow. Text me. (Olivia.)

It's O'Malley. Checking to make sure this is your number. Text me back.

SHIT

DOUBLE SHIT

Ale forgot her phone was being monitored and chances were that Carlos had seen that last message. Oh boy. It was the middle of the night and she decided to wait and answer them in the morning. She was craving something chocolate, so she went to her freezer for her favourite Ben & Jerry's Chubby Hubby ice cream. She grabbed a spoon and headed over to the couch to turn on the TV. She rarely watched tv and wasn't sure why she even had one, but she found a cheesy movie, laid down with her faux-fur blanket and proceeded to feel much better with the help of B&J!

CHAPTER 44
The Aftermath

Diego Torres was a mean motherfucker, make no mistake. He ruled his gang and most of LA in weapons, women, and money. He also owned and managed several legit businesses, which assisted him in laundering the gang money. He stayed away from drugs. It's a fuckin' shit show, and he didn't want anyone in his communities strung out on it. OK, weapons were bad, so were the women, but drugs? He drew the line. When someone tried to introduce it into his territory, he got a bit annoyed.

The last few days were a result of someone trying to do just that. Diego preferred to operate without the violence. Yes, he sold the weapons, but he didn't advocate using them. He was more of a peaceful sort underneath. Not many people saw that side. He wouldn't be the leader of one of the largest gangs in California if they did. He had several special women that he called his wives, and they all got a long and gave him beautiful children. He took care of them all. He took care of his entire family, especially his mama, Ana. She was his heart.

The result of the gang violence was heavy as they lost four soldiers. There is always sacrifice. They know the rules and the consequences, but it still bothered everyone. They would mourn, they would celebrate, and they would never forget. A gang turf war was almost always the beginning of something and, as a result, Diego and his team were on high alert. He didn't want the people closest to him to pay the price, so he picked up his phone and started making calls.

CHAPTER 45
Lunch with Olivia...

Olivia Manikas sat at her usual table at the Beverly Hills Wilshire Hotel, scanning her phone when her best friend Ale entered, walking behind the hostess. Ale looked beautiful as ever. They hadn't seen each other in person for ages, due to the pandemic, so Olivia was looking forward to this lunch and reconnecting. Ale always looked good, but for some reason, today she looked different, Olivia thought. She always dressed appropriately, and today was no exception. She had on a nice snug white, one sleeved off-the-shoulder top with a pair of navy and thin white striped palazzo pants. Her beautiful curly hair was in a messy pony. Even when she didn't try, she was gorgeous. Every head in the restaurant turned, but Ale wouldn't notice. That's the best thing about her: she had no idea just how beautiful she was. None. They screamed when they saw each other and hugged until they almost fell over.

Ale and Olivia had met at a party. Ale was working and Olivia was attending. Olivia noticed Ale wasn't like the other servers, so she tried to strike up a conversation with her, but they were given strict orders not to speak to the guests. Olivia was persistent. Ale thought maybe Liv was hitting on her but no, she was just being nice. Liv was bored with the people at the party, and she really wanted to get to know Ale. That is the quality Ale loved about her. Liv didn't care who you were or how much money you had. If she liked you, she liked you.

Ale plunked down in the comfy big booth and turned to smile at her beautiful Greek friend.

"I'm so happy to see you!" they both said at the same time. The pandemic really made them realize just how important friendships were.

The waiter filled up their water glasses. Ale ordered a Diet Pepsi with ice and perused the menu. She wasn't in the mood for a salad; she was never in the mood for a salad, but Olivia would order the salad. Ale went for the turkey club and oh, yes, fries with lots of ketchup! Ale heard her phone beep in her small purse. She checked it and the number was blocked caller. *Hmm*... sometimes Diego did that. She excused herself. She really, really needed to hear his voice if it was him.

"Hello?"

"Amiga." It was him.

"Thank God. Are you OK?" she asked, in Spanish, of course.

"All good, baby girl. Keeping low, still not safe in the community. I wouldn't recommend the Medivan for the next little while."

The Medivan was like a mobile clinic that drove to challenging neighbourhoods. It provided care for those who could or would not go to hospitals. Flu shots, antibiotics, coughs/colds (non-COVID) COVID vaccines, infections, etc. Issues that didn't require surgery. It was a program implemented a few years back and was hugely successful. Everyone worked on a volunteer basis. Diego and his gang funded most of it.

"Goodbye, beautiful. Enjoy your lunch," he laughed and hung up.

She looked around. *Jeezus,* was he here?

Olivia looked at Ale like she lost her mind. "Sorry," Ale said. "It's been a rough couple of days with the gang war and all the bodies. I was waiting to hear from someone." She decided to lower the volume on her phone, tuck it into her purse, cover the purse with her jacket, and then she shoved it way over to the other side of the booth. She had no idea if Carlos was listening to her conversations, but she wasn't taking any chances.

"You alright?" Liv asked with concern.

"Oh yeah. This is nothing, I got through a pandemic, remember?"

The waiter arrived with Ale's Diet Pepsi. Liv just stuck with water.

"How are you? How is Joe?" Ale asked, smiling, rubbing her hands together. FBI Agent Joseph P. Chase was Liv's sexy boyfriend, and Ale had a huge crush on him. She didn't hide it either. It was a joke among all of them. He was dreamy.

"Joe is great, I'm great, but I want to talk about you. You look different, like you're glowing," she teased.

Christ, was it that obvious? Ale looked at her. "I think I'm just in heat." Olivia went into a gut-wrenching laugh and everyone in the restaurant looked at them. Ale started laughing too and shrugged. There was no other explanation for it.

"God, Ale. I needed that. Seriously, I love the stuff that comes out of your mouth. No filter. You are so damn refreshing."

"That's one way to put it. Guess who's back in town?" Ale asked.

Liv looked at her, serious this time. "Who? And is he the reason you're in heat?"

"Ha! No, I don't think so. Although he has stirred up some feelings. Jason O'Malley."

Liv raised her brows. She knew the story as Ale confided in her on one of their late evenings drinking too much wine. Liv wasn't around when it happened, but she understood the significance of the event.

"Wow, OK. Did you see or speak to him?" she asked.

"Yup, he's an LAPD detective, and he's even more handsome and charming than he was when he was 18."

"Hmmm…" she said, trying to get a read on Ale. "I can't tell if you're happy he's back or if you aren't."

"Great question. I don't know either. Its confusing, to say the least. But that's not all."

Liv smiled again.

"*Striker?*" she asked.

Oh fuck, Ale thought, *are you kidding me?*

"How did you know?" Just then the waiter brought their food, he did the pepper thing, and asked if they needed anything else. Ale ordered another Diet Pepsi; her caffeine levels were low! She dove into her food. She was almost always hungry, but today her body was really out of whack with the shifts she'd been working. Liv, per normal, picked at her food. Ale never understood that. She bet anything Liv really just wanted her sandwich.

"Want a fry?" Ale asked her and she took one.

"I want to know about Striker."

Ale updated her while Liv continued to play with her lettuce and drink her water.

Who lives like this??

"Wow, just, wow Ale!" Ale's food was gone, even though she did all the talking.

"Yeah, it's been an exciting, few weeks."

"Now I understand the "in heat" comment," Liv said, laughing.

"As your lawyer and your friend, it's my duty to tell you that hacking into your phone is illegal. But I'm sure you know that."

Ale nodded and thought to herself, *Why do you think I wrapped it up and threw it cross the room?*

"So." Liv started, pushing her half-empty plate away and clasping her hands on the table.

Jesus, Ale thought, *how long does it take to eat lettuce?*

"I do have some details on Striker. I know nothing of O'Malley, but I'm sure Joe could do some digging, if you wanted."

That's our Liv, always so helpful, Ale thought.

"Striker is all alpha. Very polite, considerate, and sexy," Liv started. "He has a rep, but I'm sure a lot of it's spun with social media and the bimbos who live in this freakish city. He has a very successful business. He's well respected and, of course, has a dark side, but seems to be trying to legitimize more. Obviously, not all his practices are above board, but he's always on the side of the good guy. He has a hate for criminals and enjoys taking them down."

"Do you think someone hired him to watch me?" Ale asked her.

"No," she said quickly. "Striker is man who sets boundaries. He is known for it. It's what makes him who he is. If someone hired him, he would be treating you like a job. You would be 'handled' if you will. He has guys to do that. He wouldn't be picking you up from work, holding you while you cry, and tucking you into bed. And if he wanted to just fuck your brains out, he would have done it already and moved on. Something else is going on here."

Liv had a law degree; thus, she was the best at presenting the facts. She made too much sense in that one last sentence.

"Do you think it has anything to do with my last name?"

She shook her head. "He's done business with Gio and your father. I can't see any situation where that would be a reason." Liv grabbed her hand. "Maybe it's just as simple as a handsome man meets a beautiful woman, and he falls for her?" she teased.

"Olivia, Striker isn't the '*fall in love*' type, remember?"

"People change, Ale. This pandemic has had a huge affect on people and how they want to live their lives. Maybe he realized he was missing out on something special by not having a partner."

It did make sense if the person wasn't Striker.

"Anyway, I have no idea where this is going or if it's even anything. I'm just going with the flow," Ale said drinking down her Diet Pepsi and scanning the room.

"Tell me about O'Malley," Liv asked as the waiter appeared and asked about dessert. Ale of course said yes to cheesecake. *Hormones?*

"I definitely get the sense he wants to get me naked again and do it right this time. He wants us to get together for 'a date' so we can talk about things. He sounds sincere, but Christ, it's O'Malley, and why is all this happening at once? I haven't dated since Matt. I wasn't looking or asking, and I'm so out of practice with this shit. Liv, I'm terrified."

"Just be careful with O'Malley. One date and you're knocked up and married by Saturday," Liv teased. *TRUTH!* She still had Ale's hand. "Honey, it's your time. Enjoy this. You have been so structured and organized. We all love that about you, but you deserve some man fun. Embrace it and have them both going at the same time. Liven it up! Life has thrown us all some curve balls lately. Yours just happen to be attached to two good-looking eligible men!"

Ale went into hysterics. *Seriously?* She was sure Liv had been waiting the entire lunch to say that. Ale finished up by eating the entire piece of peanut butter and chocolate cheesecake!

They said their goodbyes and set a date for another lunch. Ale texted Ramone and walked to the front doors of the hotel to wait for him. Everyone drove a black SUV in LA, so she waited until he got out, but the dark, haired Latino wasn't Ramone, it was Carlos. *SHIT. DAMN.* Doesn't he have a company to run?

He smiled. He could see her annoyance as he opened the door and she got in, buckled up, and exhaled loudly. He drove efficiently through LA as she sat in silence. She wasn't in the mood and was tired of his games.

CHAPTER 46
Car Talk...

Ale wasn't sure where they were driving to, but it wasn't back to her apartment. In fact, they were driving away from the city. She remembered what Diego had told her and pulled her phone out to text Dr. Walker about the MediVan. They were scheduled to take it out tomorrow. She put the phone back in her purse and noticed they were headed for the coast. Where was he taking her?

Carlos looked over at her. "You look beautiful today, Alessandra."

"Thank you," she said, uncomfortably.

"How was your lunch with Olivia?" Of, course he knew who she had lunch with. She was just hoping he hadn't been able to hear their conversation.

"It was great. Liv is one of my best friends. She always makes me laugh. Where are we going?"

"For a drive," he replied.

No shit.

"I want to talk to you and have some privacy."

Ale assumed the hospital parking lot kiss had been a hit on social media and probably scared the crap out of him.

After a tense drive up the coast, her stomach doing flip flops as he handled the curves in the road, the coastline so beautiful yet she couldn't help but be a bit scared. Nobody knew where she was or who she was with. She really needed to be more careful about her surroundings and her decisions.

Finally, he pulled off the road in a parking area that overlooked the ocean. There was nobody else parked there. They could get out and walk to the beach, but she had a feeling he wanted to stay in the vehicle. He lowered the windows down a bit and turned the engine off. Carlos unbuckled his seatbelt, turned to face her, and removed his sunglasses. She had to admit, he had a beautiful face. His eyes seemed to see through her and know everything she was thinking or feeling. It made her jumpy and uncomfortable. It also made her horny. She removed her sunglasses and took in his size. He was built! She was sure there was a six pack under his T-shirt and his arms were solid. He made the SUV look tiny.

"What did you want to talk about?" she asked, trying not to stare at his lower regions.

"For starters, who called you today on the blocked number?"

"I don't know, wrong number," she lied.

"Alessandra" he said in that sexy voice.

Gawd, she was so bad at this. Carlos was having a difficult time as well. Being so close to her, all he wanted was to reach over and pull her on top of him. She looked so damn adorable today and his eyes kept drifting to her breasts. Her nipples were obviously interested as it wasn't cold in the car.

She crossed her arms. "It's a friend, someone who wants to remain anonymous. And, by the way, you hacking and monitoring my phone is illegal. I want you to stop, please. I feel invaded."

"Do you want to know why I monitor your phone?" he asked.

She looked at him. Was this the moment of truth? "That would be nice."

"I like you. I like you a lot. I want to get to know you, but before I do that, I like to get a sense of who people are and how they behave. I would never do anything with the information. I have to say, you take the least amount of photos of anyone I know. No selfies or sexy photos of yourself," he smiled.

She raised her eyebrows quickly.

"You will never see a sexy photo of me!"

"Maybe I found other ways to get them?" he said, thinking of the ones from the beach.

"Well, I can't do anything about others taking my photos, but I don't do things like that."

Ale sounded like a prude but seriously, taking sexy photos on your phone was just asking for trouble. Especially considering how easy it was for him to hack it.

He reached for her hand, and she let him. She liked his hands.

"Ale, do I make you nervous?"

She nodded. Her nipples were dying to introduce themselves and she tried uncomfortably to cover them.

He smiled, "You cold?" She put her eyes down.

"I don't mean to make you nervous." He continued to hold her hand and rub her fingers. It was making her sleepy and she had difficulty looking him in the eyes.

"Why are we here? Why me? Why do you want to get to know ME? Does this have anything to do with my family?" She needed real answers, not this dance he seemed intent on doing.

He smiled. "We're here because I wanted to be alone with you. Your family has nothing to do with anything. I want to get to know you because I'm very attracted to you. You have this magic quality about you. I find it endearing and I can't seem to stop thinking about you."

Ale just stared at him. That was unexpected. This was the most he'd ever said to her.

"If that's true, am I allowed to ask *you* questions? Personal questions?" she asked.

"Of course; that is how this works. That is how we get to know each other. Ladies' first."

"How old are you?" she asked.

"Thirty-one. My turn. Are you attracted to me?" He already knew the answer. "Is this something you want to pursue?" he added.

"OK, well, technically, that is two questions. Carlos, the entire LA county is attracted to you. I would have to be dead not to be. I am, however, unsure about your lifestyle. Are you interested in just banging me? Because all of this is unnecessary, we can take care of business and you can move on."

He grinned, showing those beautiful teeth.

"Is that all it takes? I just ask?" he said. "I thought you would make me work for it."

"Nah. Honestly, I haven't had it in a while, and I could really use something to take the edge off."

He burst out laughing. She'd never seen him laugh.

"You've been busy saving lives in a pandemic. More important things on your mind."

"I wasn't getting any before that either," she said, rolling her eyes.

"That wouldn't have been the case if I knew about you." His eyes grew darker.

"I thought you were 'one and done' when it came to sex: no complications, no dating, no romance. Just BAM!" She didn't want that to be true, but she knew of his rules.

"Maybe I've changed and maybe I want something else."

"Like?" Ale thought about what Liv had said about the pandemic.

"I'm not sure yet; it's why we are here talking, I guess."

Ale laughed. "You are as awkward with talking as I am with sex!"

"Then we can learn from each other. There are lots of things I want to show you, Ale."

"Soo, I am a charity case?" she asked, smiling.

"No, we are utilizing the barter system. You work with me on my 'communication' skills, and I will help you in the areas you need improving. Win-win." It all sounded so logical. *Jeeezus.*

There was a bit of silence.

He spoke first. "Is there a reason for your lack of sexual activity? I'm curious as you are beautiful, smart, sexy, established woman. I don't understand why you're not in a relationship or even dating."

"I suck at it, pardon the pun. It's a long story. I have baggage, I guess. I don't really know. I just gave up on it and focused on other things. I have fun and enjoy my life. I just don't get laid," she shrugged. Best explanation she had.

"Then, let's change that. Can I ask about Jason O'Malley?" He must have noticed her tense up. He responded by holding on to her hand tighter. "Ale, he seems very, interested in you. I am asking because I want to know who my competition is."

"O'Malley is not competition. He was a mistake from years ago who just reappeared in my life and I'm dealing with it."

"Would you like me to handle it for you?"

He was very serious. *Jeeezus.* "Umm. No, O'Malley is harmless, really. I promised him we would go out for a drink to clear the air. I'm sure he will no longer be interested after that." She hoped.

"My turn. Have you ever been engaged or married? Or even thought about it?" Ale asked.

"Not until recently."

She shivered. "Any chance I'm getting laid tonight?" Ale blurted out.

He laughed again. "Nothing I would love more, truly. I want our first time to be special and I want it done right."

She rolled her eyes. "Why couldn't I have met you when you just banged and left?"

"I promise you, Ale. I never would have left. You are incredibly special, whether you realize it or not. You've changed me, just by being yourself." Carlos was an expert at staying calm and keeping his emotions in check. He made a living at it for *fuck* sake, right now he just wanted to throw caution to the wind and get them both naked. *What was happening?*

Ale sighed. She really, really just wanted the sex. *Why was it so hot in here?*

Ale decided she wasn't going home empty-handed, so to speak. "Will you at least kiss me?" She felt brave and was going for it.

Carlos knew this was a bad idea, but he went for it anyways. They slowly leaned toward each other, he let go of her hand so he could cup her face and gently set his lips on hers. Ale went all in and completely shocked him. *Jeezus,* the man could kiss, and apparently, she was pretty good at it as she heard him groan. Ale shoved him back and straddled him gracefully without getting caught on the steering wheel or gear shift. Carlos hit the button for the seat to go back and she was on top. Yum, her favourite position. His hands were moving south, and she were grabbing his sexy thick, dark hair. She couldn't help herself; it was like someone lit a fuse. She was writhing, rubbing herself all over him, their mouths never disengaging, tongues teasing, hearts beating faster. Gosh, it was almost too much.

Finally, he broke off the kiss. "Ale, babe, please." His voice was breathy.

She felt like she just ran a marathon, and *why was it so damn hot in here*? She rested her head on his shoulder while he rubbed her back and butt. Her nipples were dying for attention.

Ale sat up, took his hands and put them on her breasts. His eyes went pitch black and she could feel how hard he was. *I am almost there*, she thought. Carlos was out of his mind horny, he moved up her breasts and damned if those big, beautiful nipples didn't smile at him through her bra and top. He grabbed Ale by the neck and kissed her again, hard this time. He was slowly losing control. Ale was praying to God she could get him to change his mind and they could both take the edge off. She was close to begging. He was making her feel things she hadn't felt in so long—her body had been aching for this and now she craved it. *Please God, let it happen!* she thought.

He stopped again. Ale groaned. "I don't want our first time to be in a car," he said, kissing her face and her neck.

"My place?" she suggested.

He smiled. "Ale, as you can tell, I am beyond horny right now. The old Carlos would have had you naked and screaming. I want more than that with you. Please understand."

She didn't understand, and she really wanted the old Carlos!

She reluctantly climbed back over to her side as he put his seat up. His phone went off, and he dug it out and spoke in Spanish. Ale knew from his responses their evening of fun was over, so she buckled up.

"Sorry, babe, I need to get back." He looked at her like she was lunch. "Christ, Ale. You have the most amazing nipples." He started the SUV and they were headed home. Ale was still dizzy and under the Striker spell. She crossed her arms to hide her amazing nipples and felt more confused than ever.

The drive down the coast was quiet. He held her hand and kissed it. When he gazed at her, she looked like he had taken her favourite toy away. He hated that, but he really needed to be sure before he went all the way with her. Hurting Ale was not an option. He signalled and drove into the underground parking garage of StrikeForce and parked the vehicle. Ale had no idea where they were. She assumed it was his headquarters as there were a large number of black SUVs, as well as his Porsche and other sportscars. Ramone was standing by the entrance waiting for them.

Carlos unbuckled and leaned over and kissed her thoroughly. "To be continued." Carlos said as he got out of the car and spoke quietly in Spanish to Ramone.

Ramone nodded and got into the car, put his seatbelt on, and smiled at Ale. "Miss Ferretti, lovely evening," and they exited the parking garage.

Ale needed to channel her energy, so she asked Ramone to stop at Fortino's, their family grocery store, on the way home as she had placed an order for pick up.

Her zio Guido Ferretti owned and operated all the Fortino's grocery stores in LA. They were stocked full of fresh food and Italian groceries. She smiled when she walked in.

"Alessandra!" He and Ale spoke entirely in Italian. Zio Guido asked if Ramone was her new boyfriend, the usual banter. She thanked him and kissed him on both cheeks. Ramone helped carry out her order, which they put in the SUV and headed to her apartment.

By the time Ramone left, Ale was exhausted. *Making out was exhausting*. She put her groceries away, prepped the chicken, and put it in the oven. She started up a batch of dough, covered it, and let it sit. She took a long, cold shower, put on some comfy clothes, and decided to sew. Ale either sewed or baked when she was edgy—sometimes both. She sewed for almost two hours and texted Danny to let him know she had a pick-up. She removed chicken from the oven, cut up the dough, laid it into pans, and covered until morning. Lights out.

CHAPTER 47
Lunch with O'Malley

O'Malley woke up feeling very happy. As long as he woke up with a woody, he thought life was grand. All systems go. He had a date with Ale today and he couldn't wait. He checked his phone to make sure she hadn't chickened out. No updates since she had replied to his text yesterday.

He lived in a small two-bedroom house. Nothing fancy. It had been recently renovated but still had some of the original character. It also had a nice backyard with a grill. The decorating was lacking; he hoped his sisters would volunteer to fix that. He showered and dressed, keeping it casual. He ate some toast and watched the depressing news. The last thing he needed was to be called in to work on a Saturday in the middle of his date with Ale.

He had picked a pub called the 3-Mile for their date. It was quiet and casual, with good food and beer. A bit out of the way, as he didn't want to run into anybody they knew. He wanted Ale all to himself. Work had been nuts lately with the gang wars; he hadn't had any time to follow her. He was back in the good graces of his family so that also kept him busy, especially his mother.

He cleaned up, brushed his teeth. and walked out to his newly detailed car. It was an LAPD vehicle, and the only one he drove. He arrived at Ale's at 11:45 a.m. and texted her that he was outside. She came to the door a few minutes later and, as usual, she took his breath away. She had on a cute little red and white checked sun dress that was off the shoulder and above the knee, with little shiny flat sandals. Her hair was down and sexy. He barely had time to adjust himself before she opened the door.

Ale slid a bare sexy leg inside the car, she smiled, said hello and buckled up her seat belt. O'Malley just smiled the entire drive to the pub. It was quiet on the drive over, only polite conversation. They discussed the gang war at a high level, expressing concern over the unnecessary death, work, his family reunion. He would wait until they were in the pub to make it personal.

The 3-Mile was a casual pub that had survived the pandemic. It had been in business for more than 30 years. There were pool tables on one end in a separate room. The entire inside was rustic with wood beams and a wooden bar with stools, wooden booths, and benches. Very masculine but still inviting. It had large windows and was known to have great pub food. *Salads be damned!*

They took a booth in the corner for privacy and they each ordered beer. O'Malley was a bit surprised as he took her for a wine girl. The fact that she chose a Corona was ironic. As they both studied the menus, the waitress returned with their beer. They both ordered cheeseburgers with fries. Another healthy meal, Ale thought.

O'Malley thought she looked a bit nervous, so he decided to break the ice.

"Ale, I owe you an apology," he said. She lifted her eyes up and looked at him. He had the most beautiful blue eyes she'd ever seen. The Gods really blessed him with looks. Curly brown hair that he kept short. Tight, lean, and muscled body and a smile that made all the ladies say "yes"—including her.

"Jason, you don't owe me anything. It was 13 years ago and we were kids. It was bound to happen at some point, whether with you or some other teenager."

He watched her. She never called him Jason. Even as a kid, his gut flinched when she said his name.

"I hurt you and I left, and there is no excuse for that. You have to know, Ale, I didn't think things would go that far. I had no intention of doing that. I wanted to kiss you and maybe get to first base." He looked off towards the bar as if searching for words.

She put her hand on his. "I know. I do. Things got out of control and—"

Before she could finish, he interrupted her. "Out of control? Jesus, Ale. I felt like I raped you. I know it hurt, and I couldn't stop myself. I beat myself up every day for not being able to stop. And I left you there bleeding. You think I don't remember that?"

Ale started to cry. Maybe this wasn't a good idea. She grabbed the napkin and wiped her face. "I was OK; there is always blood the first time. I was just as into it as you were, believe me. I had never been kissed like that and I'd never seen a boy naked. I know you weren't expecting it to happen because you always have condoms. Everyone knew you carried them. I worried for a month that I was pregnant, and I was terrified. I didn't regret what you did. Honestly, it felt good for the most part."

He smiled. "My God, how can you say that? I prayed to God I didn't knock you up. Your family would have had me killed."

She nodded. "You're right, I actually thought when you left town that maybe they did have you killed; nobody knew where you went."

She looked at him with those pretty eyes. She still seemed innocent to him. He remembered everything about that night. She was so tiny and soft. He had been mesmerized by her small breasts and large nipples. She didn't tell him to stop. She was squirming and kissing him like she was interested. She touched him with her small hands, and he was frantic to get inside her. Still, he knew better. He couldn't justify his actions; he was a complete asshole.

"What happened after I left?" he asked, part of him not wanting to know.

"I cried, tidied myself up, and called my zia. She took me to her house and checked me out. I was OK, just not a virgin anymore, and scared to death I was going to have your baby."

"*Jesus Christ*," he exhaled.

"Jason, it's all in the past. Can we please let this go now?" she asked.

Just then the waitress appeared with their meals and two more beers.

They thanked her and dug in. Ale was wiping her face and moaning as the food was so good. He could only look at her and smile. "Oh my God, O'Malley, these burgers are incredible! How did I not know about this place?"

They ate their food, enjoying every minute of it. Ale was a slow eater on a good day. She ate each fry one at a time, dipping it in ketchup. O'Malley attacked his food and within minutes his plate was empty. She just stared at him.

"Sorry, old habits. Eat as fast as you can before your old man beats the shit out of you." He turned, embarrassed it came out like that.

Ale's heart softened. "How is your mom? She must be thrilled to have you back." Good ole Ale knew when to change the subject.

"She's good, actually. Seeing her and my sisters again has been great. We are finding our way back to each other. Lots of mending to do."

"I see Em and Meg all the time. Usually at the hospital with the kids—always something," She kept dipping and eating.

"They were kids when I left." Catholic guilt.

"Hey, how about we just focus on today and moving forward," Ale suggested. "We can be friends and hang out. There shouldn't be any awkwardness between us. I'm glad we did this. We both needed to put things right and remember that we were kids, and we don't always make the right choices. But look at us now? You are successful and I'm doing great. We survived a pandemic and life is good. Are you married, or were you married? Any kids? I know nothing about you, really." Ale had verbal diarrhea thanks to two beers.

O'Malley smiled. She never could hold her liquor.

"Thank you, Ale. I really needed to hear that you were OK. I left for the navy right after school. Soon as the old man kicked it. I knew my mom and sisters would be safe, so I took off. I needed to get out of town and if I am perfectly honest, I needed to get away from you."

Ale just stared at him, that kind of hurt. "Me? Because you thought I was pregnant?"

"No." He took a drink and signalled to the waitress for another. "I wanted to see you again. I had feelings for you. I still do. I knew your family would have killed me and I wasn't sure how you felt."

Well, *shit*. "Jason. WTF? I had no idea. I figured I was on a list or something. You got around and I didn't ever think I was special."

"Jesus, Ale, you were more than special. I wanted to kiss you for months. I still do." Silence.

"Wow. *Gawd*. This just got awkward. OK, can we just be friends for a bit and get to know each other? It's a lot to absorb in one lunch." She smiled, hoping he would understand. She did not want to bring up the whole Striker mess.

"Of course. I just wanted to be honest with my feelings. You were never a name on a list."

Ale finally finished half her burger and all her fries and excused herself to go to the washroom. She needed to give them space.

When she returned, the plates were cleared, and the waitress had brought ice water.

"That was delicious. Thank you for bringing me here." She slid into the booth.

Ale updated O'Malley on her life and her family's, and he did the same. They laughed, talking about people they knew, who was divorced, who had kids, keeping it light and friendly.

"Impressive, Ale. Seriously. You have really done well for yourself. I still can't believe you aren't married or in a relationship. Please tell me it had nothing to do with that night."

"Absolutely not! I had a brief relationship with another Irish guy, but it didn't work out. I kind of focused on me, furthering my education, going to Dubai, travelling. I haven't been avoiding it; it's just not a priority. The pandemic took three years of my life, and I am still adjusting to life outside a hotel without a mask."

"That must have been awful, especially for your mom," he said, knowing Maria.

"Oh, momma was nuts. Seriously, when I was finally able to spend time with her, she just held me on her knee for hours and tried to convince me to find another job."

O'Malley laughed out loud. "Your family is awesome, Ale. You lucked out there."

Ale knew his dad was horrible and their home life was hard. Everyone did. The fact that they all survived and thrived is a testament to their strength. "Did Gio corner you?" Ale asked, knowing full well he did.

"Yeah." O'Malley smiled. "I knew it was coming. He adores you. I can't blame him for hating me and wanting to protect you. I would be the same."

"It's no excuse. I will tell him to back off. He needs to move on and focus on his life," she said, thinking she should probably make time for Gio today and will text him later.

"He and Sophia doing OK?" he asked, innocently.

"Yeah, good. She wants babies and it's not happening." Ale didn't want to gossip about them but felt comfortable O'Malley wouldn't repeat their conversation.

"God, that has to suck, being Italian and all."

"Right? Jesus, momma is off the charts with wanting grandbabies. I also get the '*When are you getting married?*' spiel. It never stops. Right now, she is busy planning my thirtieth birthday party. She's completely out of control. Expect an invitation. She will invite everyone."

O'Malley was smiling. "Ahh, The big three-O. I celebrated mine in isolation. Probably a good thing."

"Imagine someone telling my momma that she can't have a big party due to COVID?" They both laughed.

"Your mom still as beautiful? "

All the boys remembered Ale's momma. "Yup," she replied and hauled out her phone to show him a photo.

"*Christ, s*he doesn't age."

"Nope. Sadly, I will get none of her genes."

He smiled, looking at her breasts. "You do all right, Ale. Plus, you have her grace."

Ale blushed. They talked for a bit more and decided it was time to leave. O'Malley drove her home and she could tell he desperately wanted to kiss her.

O'Malley drove home thinking he made good progress today. They could joke around and be comfortable. The seducing will come later. He was an expert at that.

CHAPTER 48
Sopa

Gio agreed to pick Ale up at 6 p.m. for dinner at Vito's. *Christ*, if she keeps eating like this, she will weigh 400 lbs. She texted Mac, her trainer, to see if she could get in a workout on Sunday after church and he replied with a big thumbs up. Yoga would have to wait and, hopefully, her workout gear would fit.

Her phone beeped. It was a text from Carlos who was now a contact on her phone. Amazing how that happened. He was asking if she was home. She was sure he already knew that, but she replied yes anyway. Not even ten minutes later, the locks on her door were being unlocked as she stirred her homemade chicken noodle soup in the crockpot. Her freshly baked bread was sitting bagged on the counter.

Carlos walked in and smiled. He grabbed Ale and pulled her in for a kiss that seemed to last for days. She just hung on.

Daaaaauuuum!

When they finally stopped to catch their breath, Ale pushed back and said, "This is a nice surprise."

"I had a few minutes before I have to head to the airport. I'm on my way to Miami for business." He didn't look happy about it. "I won't be around for a few days. Please use Ramone to drive you anywhere so I don't worry about you." Carlos hated the idea of leaving town. Normally he enjoyed a new city, new woman, but not since meeting

Ale. He just wanted to be near her.

Ale nodded. "OK." She wasn't going to challenge him. He looked like he had lots on his mind.

"How was your lunch with O'Malley?" he asked, grabbing a chocolate chip cookie from the glass cake stand. "These are really good."

"Thanks, lunch was good." She was avoiding his stare and stirring her soup.

"That smells delicious. What is it?" he asked coming up behind her, really close.

"Chicken noodle soup. Want to try some?" She spooned some out, blew on it, and he tasted it.

"Mmmm, that tastes amazing."

"Thanks, it's my speciality." He grabbed her by the waist and turned her around. "After last night, I beg to differ."

She blushed. "Don't you have a flight to catch?" *Why was it so hot in here?*

He grinned and kissed her again. "Yes, and when I get back, we are going to talk about your lunch." He headed to the door. *"Adiós amor."* And with that, he was gone.

Honestly, she welcomed the break while he was gone. Carlos could be stifling. She knew most women would be begging him not to go, but Ale would have driven him to the *fuckin'* airport.

CHAPTER 49
Gio "Fratello"

Going to dinner with Gio was like going to the principal's office.

When they arrived at Vito's, they greeted everyone, with kisses and hugs, speaking all in Italian, of course. Ale's zio Luigi was a lot like her papa: quiet and calm. His daughters? They were all slutty and crazy-assed Italian. Ale loved them dearly, but they were nothing alike. They posted pictures of themselves, half-naked, every minute on social media, and they chased everything that walked. When Anita texted her that O'Malley was in the restaurant, Ale half expected him to take Anita home and get lucky. He would have only to ask.

They used the private room as it was empty and soundproof—nobody needed to hear Gio. They both ordered, and he proceeded with, "What is going on with you? I think this pandemic has affected your brain." His hands were going, and his eyes were bulging out of his head.

"What are you talking about?" Ale pretended to be bored.

"O'Malley, Striker, Diego. *Jesus H. Christ*, Ale. You alone can start a gang war. What the fuck are you playing at?"

Ale just stared at him; she really wasn't putting any of this together in any context until he said it out loud.

"Gio," she said calmly as he took a drink of his wine. "O'Malley just appeared out of nowhere. I was as surprised as you were that he was here. And just so you know, he and I had lunch today." His eyes were as big as the pizza she ordered. She put up her hands. "We are good. We talked about everything that happened years ago and we agreed to move forward and let it go. I need you to do the same. If I can move on, Gio, you can. This didn't happen to you; it happened to me."

He looked around the room. "OK. I'm glad you worked it out, honestly. But I am still going to watch the fucker. I don't trust him. He's like his old man."

Ale shook her head. "He's nothing like his old man. Please don't say that. He feels horrible about how things happened. Just leave him be."

"Fine. Let's move on to Bachelor Number Two." Gio had a crazy sense of humour on a good day, but that made her laugh out loud. The funny expressions he made were even more hilarious.

"Striker. Fuck, Ale. I don't even know what to say about this. Are you crazy? You can't get mixed up with this motherfucker. He is dangerous and crazy. He probably has STDs and God knows what else. You have to pull yourself away from him. I mean it. I am scared for you. He has enemies. You don't belong in his world." He drank his wine and their food arrived. Pizza made by God himself didn't taste this good. *What's another couple of pounds?*

Ale thought about what Gio said while they ate. She had similar concerns. She knew nothing about Striker, really. Only what he wanted to tell you. He sucks you into his world and before you know it, you feel comfortable. All she knew was, she liked it when he kissed her, she liked it a lot.

"I don't have an answer for you on Striker, Gio. I don't even know what is happening. He says he likes me and wants a relationship."

Gio lost it. "A relationship? WTF, Ale." He was rubbing his fingers together like Italians do. She never understood that gesture. "His relationships last an hour. *TOPS.*"

Ale burst out laughing. All of this was becoming too comical. "He won't let anything happen to me. He watches me 24/7."

"Do you hear yourself?" he asked, wiping his chicken parm with the delicious garlic bread. "It's like he's got you under a spell. You are smarter than that. You don't want to be a notch on his belt. You are better than he ever deserves. You know this."

"Gio, OK. Please stop. This whole, '*You are better than them*' stuff is getting old. I have been hearing this my whole life. Look at me. I am about to turn 30 and I have had two lovers and one doesn't even count. I am…" she stopped and sighed. "OK… I am horny. I am off the charts fuckin' horny and I want to get laid."

Gio stared at her like she just told him she bought a new purse at Waldorf's.

"OK, Bachelor Number Three."

Ale drank some wine and almost choked. Apparently, the Striker conversation was over. "Diego is a patient and I sew him up when he comes into the ER. I help out with his communities in the Medivan and he donates to the hospital. He has a sweet spot for me, as does Pepe. Neither have been inappropriate. They would protect me, without question. Probably more than even you or Striker. They flirt and tease, but they are kind and sweet to me. That is all."

Gio sighed and grabbed his chest. "I swear you are going to give me a stroke."

"Good thing I am a nurse! I'm not the reason you are stroking out. Your turn."

He looked at her. He knew what she was talking about.

"Fuck, Ale. Soph is making me nuts. She is bat-shit crazy with the hormones and injections. I don't even want to fuck anymore. It's like a chore. It's like cleaning the fucking toilet."

She reached across and took his hand. Primarily to keep it from moving. Everyone thinks about the woman in these situations, but Gio had a huge ego and he loved Sophia to death. Not being able to get pregnant bothered him as much as her. She could see it in his eyes, and she just wanted to get up and hug him. Life was unfair sometimes and fertility issues were rampant these days.

"Gio, I know this is hard, but Sophia is unhealthy right now."

He looked at her. She was a nurse. He listened when she spoke about health; the entire family did.

"What do you mean?" he asked, concerned.

"She's not eating, she's not sleeping. She's not taking care of herself.

She's giving up. I am very concerned about her mental health. This so much bigger than getting pregnant. She is putting all of this on her shoulders, and you need to be more supportive. I'm sorry."

"I suck at being supportive," he said.

"Will you at least get your sperm checked? I can set it up at the hospital and nobody will know."

"I'm not jerking off in a fuckin' cup."

Sigh. Men are so fuckin' stupid. "Adoption or surrogate?" she asked.

"Ale, Soph would lose it if someone else carried our baby. She would go right off the deep end. She wants a baby in *HER* belly."

"Maybe you could ask Diego; his sperm count is good." Ale smiled and Gio broke out laughing.

"Just what I need; a little Diego running around calling me papa."

"If you won't think of other options, can you at least keep an eye on her and be a bit more understanding? She's a mess. All she wants is to have *YOUR* baby. It's all she's ever wanted."

Gio had tears in his eyes, Ale stood up and wrapped her arms around his big fat head and hugged him. "*Ti amo fratello.*"

They resolved nothing, but they both felt better talking about it.

CHAPTER 50
Shooting Practice

Sundays, when Ale is not working or sleeping from a shift, were meant for church. It was never said; it was implied. Momma expected you there, so you went, and everyone went to zia's after for a *light* brunch. *Another 10 pounds.* Plus, they got to gossip about the other Italian families.

This Sunday was no exception. Ale was up early, and since her Saturday had been full of drama and too much food, she swapped her workout appointment for an earlier time. Mac was able to meet her so she could go to church after and, of course, Ramone was her chauffeur. Besides almost throwing up, her workout was great. She showered and changed into an appropriate dress and joined Ramone in the parking lot. Off they went to church.

They were having their usual Spanish banter when, out of nowhere, a loud bang. Ale thought they blew a tire, then it was *tap, tap, tap* on her side of the SUV. Ramone hit the gas and made a sharp left. He pushed her head down between her legs and yelled, "Get down!" Ale ducked, as she now realized the sound was from bullets continuing to hit the back of the SUV. Thank God the SUV was bulletproof. Ramone found an alley and pulled in to get them coverage. *WTF?*

"Are you OK? Are you OK?" he screamed. Ale didn't know. Was she? Ramone had his gun drawn and was out the door and she stayed in the car, curled into the fetal position. He went around to her side. She heard him swearing in Spanish as he opened the door gently. She was sobbing and in shock. Normally she was great at holding it together, after all she *was* an ER nurse, but this was a whole other level of drama. *Sweet Jesus, was someone actually shooting at them?*

Ramone gently brought Ale's head up and looked her over, one eye watching out in case whoever had been shooting at them followed. He unhooked her seatbelt and helped her out of the car. Her legs were jelly, and she just leaned against the wall of the building. She saw the side of the SUV when he moved to call someone. It was covered with holes and dents. She bent over and threw up.

Ramone put his hand on Ale's back to steady her and kept saying, "Everything is OK" in Spanish. Within minutes, a parade of SUVs arrived with StrikeForce guys in full SWAT gear. Vests, large automatic weapons, knives—you name it. Ramone went over to talk to them and then took Ale by the arm to another SUV and put her in the back. Another guy brought her purse and workout bag.

Shit. Church. Momma will be pissed, and Ale's new headache was growing larger by the minute. She hauled out her phone and texted Gio: *Not feeling well; won't be at church. Tell momma.* He replied with the angry emoji. Probably annoyed that he had to sit through it, and she didn't. Little did he know about her day.

She drank from her water bottle, rinsed her mouth out, opened the door and spit. They all looked at her. She took some Excedrin and put a breath mint in her mouth. She leaned her head back and started doing deep breathing exercises to calm down. Ramone got into the driver seat, turned around, and told her to buckle up. Another much larger guy got into the front and yet another got into the back beside her. She felt very small.

Ramone was the first to speak. "We are taking you back to your apartment, Alessandra. I will stay with you. I know it's uncomfortable having a stranger in your home, but your safety is priority. Unless you want to go to Striker's apartment, which is in our secure building. Striker is on his way back from Miami."

"I will go to my place, Ramone. I have work tomorrow, and all my stuff is there. Thank you for everything." Ale started to cry. They all drove back in silence. She was certain police were not called as there were no sirens. She was also sure the SUV with bullet holes would not be found. She wasn't sure what she would be allowed to talk about; she didn't even know if the target was her or Striker. Well, it had to be Striker, because who would be shooting at her? They arrived at her apartment and Ale told Ramone to help himself to soup he could heat up, or make a sandwich, grab some cookies—whatever he wanted. She went into her bedroom, changed into sweats and laid down.

Hours later, Ale woke up to voices, very disoriented. She checked her Fitbit. It was 7 p.m. Guess she was tired. She walked out into the main area of her apartment where Carlos and Ramone were speaking. Carlos walked over and grabbed her and held her so tight. "Ale, are you OK?" he asked. She pulled back and nodded. She went to the kitchen for a Diet Pepsi and realized she was *hangry* and started putting out food on the table; it's what Italians do. They sat down, ate together, and nobody said anything.

Once her stomach was full, she spoke. "Quite a day." They both looked at her, their faces blank. She actually felt fine once the caffeine and food settled. She stood up and brought the cookies over. Apparently, they were both hungry too. She looked at Carlos. "How do you want me to handle this?" He just stared at her. How was she so calm? Was she in shock? She should be pissed and angry. He thought he was keeping her safe and look what happened? This is unacceptable.

"Are you OK with lying until we can find out who did this?" he asked, holding her hand, she nodded. She wasn't OK with it, but she'd never been through anything like this. They had the experience. Her gut was telling her they should call the police, she should call Gio, something besides sitting here and waiting.

"We'll tell your family you weren't feeling well and Ramone drove you home. We will handle the rest," Carlos said, checking her eyes to make sure she understood. Ramone took his dishes to the kitchen, thanked her for the food, and left.

"Ale, I am so very sorry. I provide private security for a living; this never should have happened." Ale noticed he was almost shaking. He was keeping himself calm for her sake, but his body was simmering with anger. His eyes were a colour of deep brown she had never seen before, it scared her.

"So, police are not an option?" she asked, he shook his head.

"Did anyone else get hurt, like an innocent bystander?"

"No, thank God. Otherwise, we would have a *fuckin'* mess on our hands. I just need to contain it and draw whoever it is out. I'm grateful for bulletproofing. I couldn't live with myself if something happened to you, especially in my care." His eyes lowered.

"Go if you have to," she said. "I will be OK here."

He shook his head. "Either Ramone bunks here or you come live with me." Her eyes widened and he smiled. "That would move my timeline ahead greatly."

"That would send my momma on a tangent; bullets have nothing on her!"

He laughed, he needed that. "Ramone it is then; and thank you for keeping it quiet." He stood up and drew her up into a long, warm soft kiss. He held her so tight. She just wrapped her arms around his waist to hold on. *Jeeezus.* He could distract anyone from a gun fight! When he finally stopped kissing her, he just held her, he knew she needed it because he needed it more. He really wanted her to stay with him, but she wasn't ready. He kissed the top of her head and thanked her for the food. Carlos left and Ramone reappeared like magic.

So, it looked like Ale had a roommate for a while. *Sweet!*

CHAPTER 51
It's My Birthday!

The next three weeks went by like a blur. Ale worked, sewed, baked, slept. She did her workouts on her days off and visited momma. She had Ramone with her 24x7 and Carlos was nowhere to be seen. The good news was nobody was shooting at her and gangland had settled down. Nobody heard or spoke of the shooting incident, and she didn't bring it up.

Ale took a few days off around her birthday so she could help out. Really, she needed the break. She took very little time off after COVID as she wanted the other nurses who had families to take their vacations. Now it was her turn AND she was turning 30!

Her party was on the Saturday at the Hoxton Hotel in downtown LA. Ale offered to help decorate or do anything to help but momma just said no. She managed a workout on Friday and yoga, as well she had a good session with Dr. Louise. She didn't bring up the shooting, but they talked a lot about her adoption and Carlos.

Saturday morning, her actual birthday, and the day of her party, Ale had an appointment at the Sunflower Spa. Her friend and hairdresser, Jessica Connell, was the owner and manager. Ale met Jess when Jess was in community college studying to be a hairdresser. Ale and Amalia would go and get cheap highlights, facials, pedis because the students wanted real people to work on. It was a win-win situation. After Jess graduated, Ale followed her as she was one of the few hair stylists that knew how to properly cut curly hair. Jess was also one of the sweetest humans she'd ever met. Most spas in LA were overpriced, staff were rude, and the people who went there were even worse. The Sunflower was a happy place and Jess didn't tolerate otherwise. Ale loved going there and so did her friends and family.

Ale arrived at the spa, probably looking like she'd been shot at. Oh, wait, she had!

Jess greeted her with a beautiful smile. "Ale! Oh honey, it's so good to see you. We're thrilled you're here getting pampered before the big party!" Jess was always up and spoke in such a calm voice. Ale was used to Italians and loud, so Jess seemed like she was always whispering. Ale felt better just seeing her and getting a hug. The Sunflower Spa always smelled like rosemary and mint as it was their signature scent in all its products. It was a small spa, but very elegant and calming. Ale knew all the staff and they were all invited to her birthday party; probably the entire city was invited to her birthday party!

"Thanks, Jess," Ale said, half smiling. She knew she looked tired and rundown. This was just the place to fix her up. Jess handed her a glass of OJ and ushered her into the change area to put on a robe.

"I want you to relax and let us spoil you today," she said, rubbing Ale's hand as she held it.

"Sounds great."

"Your mom and Connie were in yesterday. We are all excited about the event of the year. Why don't you look happy?" she asked, tucking Ale's curls behind her ear.

Why do you always feel comfortable talking to your hairdresser? They must teach them therapy 101 when they take their training. "Long story," Ale said. "Lets' gab when you do my hair."

She smiled. "Sounds good. Meantime, try to enjoy your day." Jess left her to undress and put on a robe and slippers.

There was something magical about having someone else's hands on you. Not a sexual feeling, but a healing feeling. Her first stop was waxing, not exactly healing. Then it was all the good stuff. Body wrap, facial, pedicure, manicure. Ale didn't care for manicures and nurses aren't supposed to wear nail polish for work, so this is a one-time thing, her nails are kept short for a reason, so she doesn't claw patients to death when she is working on them. Next was hair. Jess was just going to put in a few highlights, give her a trim, and try to calm down the curls a bit. Ale had only ever straightened her hair once and it took so damn long, not to mention that everyone hated it. It curled right back up after she washed it, and she kept it that way.

While Jess was working on her hair, she filled her in on things. Left out the men drama and the shooting. Mostly about family, work, friends. She was sure momma already filled her in.

"Your mom is so excited about this party," Jess said as she was brushing in some highlights.

"Yeah. I've just let her run with it. It's just easier," Ale said, rolling her eyes in the mirror as Jess laughed.

"You know it will be beautiful and she will leave no stone unturned. Tell me about your dress!" Normally Ale would just haul out a photo but because her phone was being monitored, she didn't have a picture to show. Ale described it as best she could. Besides, she really wanted people to be surprised when they saw her.

Ale felt so much better already. The body-wrap and massage helped her relax and gave her energy at the same time. Her face and skin were glowing. Jess was starting to wear off on her and it made Ale excited about her party. Ale didn't realize how much she needed this pampering. It was almost another two hours before she was done, and she looked like a new woman. She changed, tipped everyone with her wads of cash, and headed to the counter to pay her bill. Jess was waiting for her.

"How do you feel?" she asked.

"Fabulous," Ale said and meant it.

"Good, we will all be there tonight. Can't wait to see you with your dress on. You will look beautiful." She was getting teary. *Jesus*, you'd think Ale was getting married. Ale went to pay the bill and Jess put her hand on her arm and said, "It's been taken care of."

Ale looked at her. "Momma?" Jess shook her head, then she turned around and presented Ale with a round black box with gold lettering that said, "Beverly Hills Roses." A red and pink ribbon was tied around it. Ale just looked at it, then at Jess.

"Jess, please tell me this is not from you."

Jess laughed. "No, Mr. Tall, Dark and Handsome stopped by to pay your bill and asked me to give it to you."

Carlos. Ale sighed. She had to admit, not seeing him for weeks has had an affect on her. Now she knew how all the ladies in LA felt; her nipples were distraught.

She opened the box and removed the card. It read:

Feliz cumpleanos hermosa. Disfruta tu dia. Ahodame un baile.
Carlos

Ale smiled. She knew his company was working security for her party, but she wasn't sure he would be there. She really wanted him to see her in her dress and maybe they could even have a dance. Italians loved to dance!!

Jess was beaming and impatiently waiting, so she pulled the tissue back and the box was filled with the most beautiful red roses with pink roses forming a heart in the centre. The smell was intoxicating. These flowers were off the charts. *Wow!!* All the girls were gushing. Ale had to admit, the man knew how to put a smile on her face. They were perfect.

"Striker knows where to shop!" Jess said. Ale just smiled, thanked and hugged the staff, and walked out with her box of flowers to Ramone who was waiting in the car.

"Feel better?" he asked.

"Yeah, much. You hungry?" Ale asked him.

He shrugged. "Let's stop at In and Out Burger. I feel like grease," he smiled.

They bought take-out, took it home and pigged out.

Happy 30th birthday, Alessandra, she thought. She texted Carlos to thank him for the flowers and he sent her the *heart* emoji.

The rest of the day was a blur. Ale fussed with her makeup and her underwear or lack there of. She used some boob tape to bring the girls together as she needed cleavage but didn't want to wear a bra. Momma would not be pleased. She wore what can only be described as a piece of gold triangle for underwear. Once she pulled on the dress and put on her heels, she knew it was the right decision. *She looked good!*

Ale was happy she had changed the original design of her dress and removed the belt. The result was just a short wrap dress in a shiny gold sequin material, which stopped above her knee. The boob tape worked wonders for the cleavage and her legs were all glistened up and the gold-sequined strappy shoes made her legs look even longer. The shoes had a chunky heel, so they would be perfect for dancing. Ale chose a pair of gold drop earrings with the large square diamonds. Her momma and papa had given them to her when she earned her first master's degree. They were stunning but Ale always felt uncomfortable wearing them as the diamonds were huge. Wearing them tonight, though, might distract momma from her cleavage and the length of her dress. Ale put her earrings on and looked at the photo of her real parents and her heart felt squeezed in her chest. She didn't have many memories of them as she was so young when they died. She hoped they were watching her from heaven and were proud of the woman she became. It pained her that they weren't part of any of her milestones. She wiped her tears and fixed her makeup again.

She shook her head as if to bring her back to reality and smiled. The family she had now will soon be all gathering after three years of being apart. This would be more than a birthday party. She was really getting excited. Maybe a big party was just what they all needed. Or was it?

CHAPTER 52
It's My Party...

The Hoxton was an elegant boutique hotel in downtown LA, a perfect location for a large party and easy enough to secure and lockdown if necessary.

Striker was reviewing the blueprints with his men in one of the small meeting rooms. He really didn't want a party right now, especially since the shooting. They hadn't made any progress on finding out who had shot at his vehicle and the special cargo inside. He had been heads down focused on it. Visiting enemies, interrogating people his way, and yet nothing. It disturbed him. He still didn't know if it was aimed at him, his business or at Ale. That disturbed him more.

He had received a text from Ale, thanking him for the beautiful flowers and the spa treatments which made him smile. God, he missed her. He couldn't wait to see her tonight, even if it was from afar. His priority was security. The large ballroom was decorated beautifully. Striker could not believe what he was seeing as he made his final walk-through. The Ferretti's knew how to do it up right. As people started to fill in, it was time to make his team invisible.

Striker watched the security monitor from another room. He knew most of the people. He recognized family and friends of Ale's, nurses, doctors from her hospital. Striker made it his mission to investigate everyone in her life. He had to. He had to keep her safe. His jaw dropped when he saw her mom, Maria. My God, she was a beautiful woman. She was dressed in a beautiful navy sequined dress that showed off all her curves. Her breasts were out of this world—and real. Striker shook his head. This was Ale's mom! *Christ*, he needed to get laid.

The room was filling up fast and his team was doing their jobs. StrikeForce had people integrated with the staff: working valet and at the front desk, serving, cleaning up—you name it. It needed to be secure without being obvious or intrusive. He received a text from Ramone that he and Ale were on their way. Striker notified his team that the package would be arriving in approximately ten minutes. Ramone was just going to bring her into the main party room and disappear among the guests. They both probably needed a break from each other, and they wanted Ale to enjoy her night.

Ten minutes later, Striker wasn't prepared for when Ale arrived and took off her coat. Are you *fucking kidding me?* He couldn't take his eyes off her and apparently neither could his men. He could hear them saying: "*Holy fuck*"; "*Oh my god*"; "*I would bang her...*" Striker got on the comms. "*Hey!* Package has arrived. Keep the comments to yourself." He was angry and horny. Mostly horny. He couldn't blame them. She looked incredible and she knew it.

Ale braced herself for the reaction when she arrived at her party. This wasn't a normal Ale dress. Everyone gathered around her, wishing her a happy birthday, giving her compliments. Her friends and cousins were touching the beautiful fabric, asking where she had bought it, asking about the shoes. It felt nice to be the centre of attention. She normally avoided these kinds of things, but tonight she felt different. She'd grown in the last few years with all that was thrown at her. It was her time to show off, and she will enjoy every minute of it. Her momma looked stunning as always. She just wrapped herself around Ale and whispered, "*Sei la donna più bella della stanza. Buon compleanno, piccola.*" "You are the most beautiful woman in the room. Happy Birthday, baby." They hugged each other hard, and Ale thanked her for everything. Neither of them wanted to let go. They never did. They both wiped away happy tears and headed towards their table.

Ale looked around the room in awe. Momma knew her style and incorporated it everywhere in the elegant decor. Small bouquets of pale yellow and light pink orchids with lilies in crystal vases. Cream-coloured tablecloths on round tables, which surrounded the large dance floor. Ale's eyes caught what had to be the largest lemon and coconut cream birthday cake sitting on a huge table in the middle of the floor. It had to be three feet tall. She gasped and grabbed her zia Connie. They both cried and hugged. The cake was the most beautiful thing she'd ever seen, and she couldn't wait to eat it!

Ale was overwhelmed with the number of friends and family that had shown up for her party. She was being hugged and congratulated in Italian, Spanish, and English. Some family members she hadn't seen in years. One in particular caught her eye—Mossimo, her cousin from Italy. They were the same age and best friends. Ale adored him. She ran over and jumped in his arms. He hugged her so tight and whispered to her in Italian. Oh my God, she had missed him. What a gift! They talked and laughed, she promised him a dance. Seeing everyone here celebrating with her was everything. She felt all the love.

Meanwhile, in the surveillance room, Striker's body tensed, and he almost reached for his gun. Who the fuck was the guy hugging Ale? He'd never seen him before. He texted his hacker with a photo and asked him to run it.

CHAPTER 53
The Party Continues...

Ale was having the time of her life, catching up with family from Italy, Santa Barbara, New York, Boston. Family she hadn't seen in years or even heard from. She made the rounds, talking and dancing with friends, family and co-workers. She had given the DJ several playlists and he had everyone up dancing. But the best part of their family parties was watching her parents as they danced. Everyone stopped and stared at them as they floated across the dance floor, holding each other through each perfect step. Ale could watch them all night.

Their family's table included momma, papa, Gio, Sophia, zia Connie, and zio Tony. Ale really didn't need a chair; she usually sat on momma's or zia's knees. Sitting on knees was her thing.

Leslie's catering company and the hotel outdid themselves with the food. It was an enormous and succulent buffet with everything and anything people would want to eat. The presentation alone was making Ale hungry, with decadent ice sculptures and beautiful trays all arranged perfectly. The seafood and shellfish section was isolated for allergy reasons. People were lining up as the hot food started appearing. Italians loved to eat!!

It took a while for everyone to get their food and finish eating, and once the plates were cleared, it was time for speeches. Ale really hated this part, and she begged her momma: no speeches. Obviously, she listened.

Papa walked up to the microphone. Firstly, he thanked Leslie, the hotel staff, and StrikeForce. He thanked everyone for coming, he introduced the family members who had travelled from afar and told the story of how and when they adopted Ale. His eyes teared up when he spoke of how small she was and how she lit up the room whenever she walked in it. He told stories of how she followed Gio everywhere, clung to momma—and still does—and how she could melt his heart with just a look. Ale let the tears flow down her face. She was truly the luckiest daughter in the world to have this family. They were everything to her. He bragged about her accomplishments and how proud they were. He snuck in some funny comments, and everyone was quite shocked that papa was even speaking sentences, never mind being funny. People were crying and laughing, especially her. He finished with how much they loved her and wished her a Happy 30th birthday with a toast. *Salute!!*

Ale ran up to the microphone to hug and kiss her papa. She landed in the safest of arms with this family. She wasn't blood, but you would never know it from looking around. She was truly blessed.

Gio made his attempt to get up as a joke and Ale kicked him. *Sit your ass down* was the look she gave him, and he laughed. Sophia and he seemed to be enjoying themselves. Of course, there were babies and kids everywhere so Sophia could at least get her baby fix.

It was Ale's most favourite time of any party: the *CAKE*! Time to cut that big-ass cake. Yes, please! Everyone sang Happy Birthday, in Italian and English at the same time. She made a wish. *Bet you know what it is!* And blew out the giant 30 candle on the top. This cake was a work of art. Leslie handed her the beautifully engraved knife to use, but she looked at zia and thought, *It's my party!* Ale grabbed a hunk of the cake with her hand and shoved it into her own mouth. Everyone burst out laughing and zia's voice rang out the loudest. She ran over and grabbed some cake and did the same. They destroyed that cake. Good thing there were three layers. They had cake everywhere and they couldn't stop laughing. Best party ever!

Ale wiped up what she could and headed to the washroom to clean up. From out of nowhere, an arm grabbed her and hauled her into a small meeting room. He pushed her against the closed door and laid a kiss on her that had her *purpose* singing like a wild pirate! She recognized those lips and that smell of sandalwood. She wrapped her arms around Carlo's neck and dove in. When they finally came up for air, those almost-black eyes were staring at her like she was his everything. Carlos stepped back and took a long look up her legs, at her cleavage, and smiled.

"Mmmm, you taste like cake. Happy birthday, Ale." He kissed her again, softer and with a lot of tongue. Ale could only pray she would get her birthday wish! She put her hands on his sides. His suit jacket was open, and she ran her hands up and down his muscled abs. She really wanted to see him naked. She ignored the gun and the holster.

"Are you about to give me my present?" she asked, looking innocent but nothing was innocent about that request or her outfit.

He laughed. God, he wanted to fuck her right there, right now. "You look good enough to eat." He continued to stare at her nipples. They were staring back as no amount of boob tape was going to hide them. Carlos lowered his hands and slowly brought them up the sides of her legs. He stopped and looked at her with his eyebrows raised. "Do you have panties on, Ale?" he asked.

She smiled a dirty smile and replied, "Not sure—maybe you should check."

He checked. He double checked. Then he grabbed her butt and brought her forward to rub against him. *Oh, please God.* Her arms went around his neck, and they were at it like animals. Sadly, he pulled back. "Jesus, Ale, where did you learn to kiss like that?"

Hmm. Good question. She had no clue. She tried to compose herself, but she really needed to get back to her party, and she really wanted to stay in this room with him. She moaned.

"Thanks for the kiss, Carlos." She left him with a wink and a woody.

The party continued until long into the morning. She slow danced with O'Malley. She was sure his service revolver was in his front pocket. *Helllloo?* He held her very close. He was actually a good dancer. He kept whispering how incredible she looked and asked if she would like to go back to his place after to get her gift. HA! It was nice dancing with a man she wasn't related to. She was fairly, sure Carlos had his gun out and was aiming it at them the entire time.

Ale made the rounds to all the tables, trying to talk to everyone and thank them for coming. She made a date to have lunch with Mossimo, her cousin from Italy, who was staying at a hotel in LA for a few days. His family were all gathered at their big house while visiting, but not Moss. That would cramp his style.

Momma gave her a break from church since they probably wouldn't get home until almost 3 a.m. But only if Ale went to zia's later in the day to open her gifts. They will take the loot back there after the party. Ale agreed; at least she could sleep in a bit. Despite telling all the guests *"Best wishes only"* on the invites, there was still a pile of gifts and cards. *Jewellery or cash!*

As the party wound down, Ale thanked, kissed, and hugged everyone as they left. Momma and papa were gathering their things when Carlos appeared. Ale introduced him to momma and he and papa shook hands. They left and Ale had no idea what was going on. Carlos quietly removed her coat, took her hand and walked her to the dance floor. Apparently, he had made prior arrangements with the DJ to play one of her favourite slow songs once everyone left. The song was Little River Band's, Cool Change. Very few people knew this. Yes, it was from years ago, but her momma played it all the time when she was growing up and it stuck with Ale. *How did he know she loved this song? Oh, right. Her playlist on her phone.* Carlos was a beautiful slow dancer. He held her tightly and moved seductively. She could have stayed in his arms all night. He whispered sexy things in Spanish, and she cuddled right into him. The music stopped, and Carlos kissed her softly.

"You have guests," he said. His gaze went behind her and she turned around to find Pepe and Diego watching them. That made Ale very happy. She ran over to hug them, and Carlos just shook his head, put his hands on his hips, showing his weapon. O'Malley and Gio would have shot them.

"Feliz cumpleanos hermosa" and lots of hugs, maybe a little groping. Ale accepted it all. It was so sweet they showed up. They handed her a beautifully wrapped gift. Ale was touched; Carlos was glaring.

"Don't open in front of the big guy," Diego said winking. He always called Striker the big guy, even though Pepe was twice his size.

"OK, do you want some food or cake? There is plenty; they just started packing up. We can sit and talk."

They happily agreed and the three of them sat, ate, and talked for a bit. Carlos excused himself to deal with security and seemed content that Ale was in safe hands. Never mind: Pepe carried two giant revolvers crisscrossed on his belt behind him, legal or not. She was safe! They chatted while they ate, and Ale couldn't resist another piece of cake. Diego and Pepe both loved the cake as much as she did. Ale thought how nice it was to sit and talk to them like humans. She knew people called them monsters and she knew what they were capable of; right now, though, they were two of her friends who had come to her party. She really wanted to open her gift, but Diego asked her to wait until she was alone. *Hmmm. OK.* They thanked her for the food and hugged her again, whispering how sexy she looked, still asking for dates. It never got old! She walked out with them to find Ramone waiting for her. She was a bit disappointed it wasn't Carlos. *It was official*, she thought, she was 30!

CHAPTER 54
Are You Freaking Kidding Me?

Ale woke up, slightly aroused from a very nice dream to someone nudging her. Wait. What? She lived alone. Christ, was it Ramone? She slowly opened her eyes. It was Carlos, in full SWAT gear.

"Ale, honey, wake up." She pulled her covers up and stared at him with a snarl on her face.

"Carlos, what the heck?" She checked her fitbit and it was 10 a.m. on a Sunday and she could have sworn she just went to sleep after her awesome birthday party.

"Babe, listen to me. I need you to get up and get dressed. We need to get you to a safe house." Ale could hear men whispering in her living room. Was she dreaming this?

"What? Why? Carlos, what is happening?" He gently grabbed her arm to get her out of bed and quickly realized she only had a tank top and panties on.

"Christ." He swore and left the room, reappearing with her robe. *Jesus*, Carlos thought to himself. *Does she prance around the apartment wearing just her panties and tank top when Ramone's here?* He needed to talk to her.

Ale reluctantly pulled on her robe on, and Carlos ushered her to the bathroom to get ready and fast. He would explain later. *OK, well, 30 is not starting out so great*, Ale thought. She splashed water on her face, brushed her teeth, fixed her hair, left it up. She grabbed a pair of jeans and a T-shirt, and put some spare things in her leather tote, along with toiletries. She was off this week, so she didn't have to worry about work.

She walked out to her living room still half asleep and there were men with guns everywhere, including O'Malley and Detective Scott. They must have saw the look on her face because Carlos rushed over and rubbed her arms. "Everything is going to be OK, Ale."

She looked at him and started to cry. "My family? Are they OK?" It's all she could think of. Her family, because they had money, supposed ties to the mob and had been targeted before; she kind of knew the drill.

"They are safe. We're going to take you to them now. OK?"

She nodded and grabbed a can of Diet Pepsi and a bottle of water from her fridge. They all followed her out. Ale felt like a zombie. She just did what they told her to do. She stared out the window of the SUV while someone drove. She wasn't even paying attention to who was in the vehicle, she was just hoping it wouldn't get sprayed with bullets. They arrived at a house she'd never seen before; it was really a mansion. Enormous and beautiful with gates and a large fence surrounding it. The security guards and dogs were everywhere. She sighed, *What the heck was going on?*

They opened her door, took her bag, and walked her in where momma and the whole family were already waiting. They clung to each other, and momma was crying.

"It's OK, momma," Ale said. " I'm fine, just tired."

Momma looked at her. "Ale, have they told you anything?"

Ale shook her head. Momma turned and looked at Carlos and O'Malley. *OK, when did they become so chummy?* Ale thought. Seriously, what is happening? Momma grabbed both of Ale's hands and led her over to a what looked like a very comfy high-back chair. The ENTIRE family was there. *Jeeezus*, it was like her party all over again. Kids, babies, zios and zias, cousins. Everyone talking and, oh, her head hurt, and she needed caffeine. She searched for her bag, removed herself from momma's grip and walked towards the kitchen where she noticed a ton of food being prepared with zia Connie in charge. All of her zias were now in there. This is how they coped: they cooked or baked. Ale snuck in and hugged her zias from behind. They all turned and gave her a group hug.

Ale allowed herself to be smothered by them, all with their aprons on and so loving. She grabbed a glass and went to the ice dispenser, poured herself a Diet Pepsi, and sucked it down. *OK*, she thought, feeling a bit more normal. Gio came in and did the finger wave, telling her to follow him so she did. She brought her drink with her and stole a sandwich on the way. They went into an empty room that was being used as someone's office.

"You, OK?" he asked, sitting on the desk while Ale sat in the chair and ate her favourite sandwich, mortadella and provolone.

"Yeah, all good. You?" she said, almost moaning as the sandwich was incredible and she was super hungry. She remembered seeing meatballs in the kitchen. Her zia Francesca made the best sweet and sour meatballs; she'd have to go back.

"Alessandra!"

Ale snapped back to Gio.

"You seem out of it and oddly calm," he said, taking a bite of her sandwich.

"I don't know what's going on, so why panic?" She drank the last of her Pepsi.

He bent down in front of her. "Someone is trying to kidnap you," he said, looking her right in the eyes.

She laughed. *Seriously? What would they want with a nurse?* "What? Why?" For some reason, nothing was really registering. She wasn't freaking out over this. She must have just gone into some sort of self-protective state as she didn't freak out when the bullets were fired at her either. All she did was… *Oh shit*… She quickly got up, found the powder room, and woofed up her wonderful sandwich. She was fairly certain her lovely dinner from last night and the four pounds of cake had come out too.

Momma was frantic. "Ale, let me in. Let me in, honey," she kept saying. Jesus, momma, she thought, *I am a bit busy!* The nausea finally stopped, she splashed water on her face, and rinsed out her mouth, cleaned up. At least, none of it got on her clothes. She opened the door, and everyone was quiet and looking at her. She wanted to shut it again. Momma grabbed her again and was soothing her.

"It's OK baby. Its OK."

Ale asked her to get her bag so she could brush her teeth. Ale hid in the bathroom for a bit just trying to get her head around all of this and another knock came. She guessed she shouldn't hog the bathroom with all these people in the house, so she opened the door. Carlos was standing there.

"Come here," he said, and she fell into his arms.

NOW everyone was looking. Shit, she was going to have to explain this. She put that aside and just cuddled into him. *Gawd*, he loved it when she did that, he could hold her forever, but Jesus this was a fucking mess and he needed her to get her head right. All Ale could think of was food. She was really hungry now.

"Do you think you can keep some food down?" he asked. She nodded, and they went back to where the food was displayed. Seriously, there was enough for a small country. She grabbed a plate and headed for the meatballs, pasta, rice—you name it. She found a chair and sat down to eat. Carlos appeared with a plate of food and a fresh Diet Pepsi in a glass with ice.

She smiled. "Thank you." He must have been hungry too, as he dug into his meal. Food was always good at family gatherings. She really didn't know how she didn't weigh 400 pounds. Then again, she had thrown up a lot. That helped.

"Do you know who is trying to do this?" Ale quietly asked. He shook his head.

"So, the bullets were meant for me?" Ale asked, even more quietly. She had tears in her eyes, and he reached and pulled her into him and rocked her. *Jesus H. Christ. Why is this happening?*

After Ale realized the significance of the situation, she finished her meal and zia came over with a hug and a piece of leftover birthday cake. Hallelujah! She thanked her and dove in. Damn, this cake was the cure for everything.

CHAPTER 55
Isolation Again? No way!

Mossimo came through the front door after being grilled by security and Ale quickly ran over to hug him. They spoke in Italian, and she led him over to the table and introduced Moss to Carlos. They shook hands and Carlos excused himself. He looked back at her and said, "We need to talk to you. The team has some questions when you are done here." His tone and stare told her everything.

She sat with Moss while the zias prepared his plate. He could do it himself, but they always fawned all over him. Moss always attracted the ladies. He was charming, good-looking with light brown hair, and soft blue eyes. He was growing a beard and Ale thought it looked good on him. He had several "lovers" as he called them, never girlfriends. The family always teased him. He owned a high-end lingerie company called *Carino* and made some of the most beautiful ladies' underwear in the world. Ale and her American cousins were always sent free samples and her underwear drawer was packed full, all matching, of course. He was very successful, and he knew it. To Ale, he was just her cousin.

When Ale was in Dubai for two years of nursing, she had ten weeks of vacation time, and flights to Europe were dirt cheap. Ale would fly to Italy and stay with Moss's family the entire time. They would take trains everywhere, which allowed her to visit almost all of Europe. She loved being there and he always spent so much time with her, showing her Europe through his eyes. Moss lived posh and ate at the best restaurants, shopped at designer boutiques. She had wonderful memories of them being young and free, doing what they wanted, when they wanted.

Carlos came out of the "war" room and looked at Ale. She sighed, excused herself, and went down the hall towards him. He led her to a larger room, where all the men were gathering. O'Malley, Scott, Gio, Carlos's men, security, zios… You name it, even Mac was there. He came towards her, his muscled body moving so quickly, and lifted her up in a hug. "Ale. I am so sorry. I will help in whatever way you need me." His deep voice made her feel very safe. Meanwhile Carlos was glaring at them.

They asked all the normal questions, like "Do you know anyone who would want to harm you?" Anyone come to mind? What's your relationship with Diego and Pepe? Any patients who might want revenge?" Apparently, they all knew about the bullet incident now; she'd hear about that later. Ale honestly couldn't think of anybody who wanted to hurt her for any reason; and she knew Diego and Pepe would want to protect her as much as they would.

Ale decided to start taking things in her own hands. No more victim. "How did you find out someone wanted to kidnap me? Who told you? I mean, did someone call papa or Gio?" This was all confusing to her and she wanted some answers. They all looked at each other and she could tell they didn't want to tell her, but she was starting to feel like herself again and wasn't leaving the room until she had answers.

"We found the guy who opened up on you and Ramone," said Carlos. "We interrogated him, and he told us there was a post on an underground network stating a large payout if they brought you to them."

"It's like a fuckin' social media for terrorists," Gio added, pacing the room like a caged animal. Gio could never sit still.

"Sooo, they want to pay someone to kidnap me and then they want to ask for a ransom?" she asked, more confused than ever. "That makes no sense." They all looked down on the floor again, not wanting to answer. She thought for a moment. "They want me, but not for money.

They just want me so they can keep or kill me?" she asked, thinking she might throw up her lunch again.

O'Malley came over and took her arm. "Ale, we don't know that yet, but we have our best people working this, trying to get more information. The important thing is that you stay safe until we can figure it out and get the bastards." Ale looked at him and then she looked at all of them.

"Well, that's not happening." She said defiantly.

Gio threw his hands in the air. "Fuuuck...here we go!" he was still pacing.

"I am not hiding. I spent over two years in a hotel during the pandemic. I wasn't able to see anyone or do anything. I am NOT doing that again. I am leaving here and going to my apartment. I am not having anybody move in with me or drive me anywhere. I am DONE. They want me; they can have me. There is no amount of torture they can give me that will be worse than what I've been through."

Nobody said anything as none of them could relate to how she managed the past few years. She never once spoke about it or complained. Nobody even friggin' asked her; they just assumed she'd gotten through it. Fuckin' idiots. All of them. She was angry now and she was going home.

"Ramone, can I ask this one last time for you to please take me home. You can get your stuff and leave. Thank you again, for everything."

"The rest of you should let my family go. Nobody is looking for them. You've scared the crap out of everyone for no reason."

"No reason?" Gio screamed. "For Christ's sake Ale, get your head out of your ass."

"The kidnapper doesn't want them. They are being specific on who they want. Let them go."

She turned and walked out of the room, with Carlos, hot on her heels. "Ale, please."

She kept walking. "Momma, I am going home. Everything is OK. We can all leave," Ale announced, and everyone looked at her. She grabbed her bag and headed for the door.

Carlos grabbed her arm, and he was trying desperately to keep his voice down. "Ale, please, be reasonable." Ale looked at him. He was pleading. God he was handsome.

"I've been very reasonable, Carlos, but I need to live my life. Whoever wants me can have me. I'm not living in fear. I did that a few times."

She walked outside and Ramone was waiting for her. Carlos gave the nod and off they went. What a fuckin' day.

CHAPTER 56
Fun and Games

After Ramone left, Ale locked up and headed for a hot shower. She wanted to wash the day away. She was in there forever, scrubbing and trying to feel clean again. She wrapped a towel around her and opened the bathroom door. Carlos was standing there, leaning against the wall.

"So much for my locks," she said, grabbing her lotion and heading back into the bedroom.

He followed her, watching intensely. Carlos was pissed. Ale was being careless and irresponsible. Part of him wanted to drag her to the bed and fuck her brains out and the other part wanted to spank her like a child.

He spoke calmly, "If they want you, they will find a way in. Ale, is there anything I can say or do to get you to reconsider?" She laughed and thought about just letting the towel fall and trading her safety for sex, but that would have been too easy.

"What would you be willing to do, Carlos?" she asked, keeping her hand on the top of the towel watching his eyes go *horny* dark. She could tell the differences now as she'd seen his eyes change with moods. Neither of them spoke. Both wondering what would happen next. Ale caved.

"Just what I thought. Listen, Carlos. You're a sweet guy and for some reason you've taken a liking to me, but I think it needs to stop. All these kisses and little games are just distracting. Especially when you have no intention of following through with it. It's unfair to me and I want you to leave. My life was uncomplicated before you came into it. It's a mess now. You're a good man and I appreciate everything you've done and are doing. But this stuff between us. It ends. Please respect my wishes."

She let the towel drop, climbed under her covers, and turned out her light. She was beyond tired.

"Goodnight, Ale," he said and left. She heard him use the key to lock the deadbolt. She didn't even care if the door was wide open. She cried herself to sleep.

CHAPTER 57
Regrets Suck, Big Time

Carlos walked out to one of his SUVs, which was waiting and running. His driver Zeus was waiting for him. "You talk any sense into her?" he asked. Zeus was a huge man, his body riddled with tattoos, he had long blonde hair, like Fabio, and constantly bit his nails. Carlos relied on him greatly as he was heavily skilled and committed to Carlos.

"Nope; she talked some sense into me, though," Carlos said. He was pissed. *Jesus.* She was fuckin' stubborn, extremely intuitive, and she had hit too many of his buttons today. He needed some sleep and he needed to let it go. He couldn't keep someone safe who didn't want to be safe. But how the fuck was he supposed to turn that off? He adored her, respected her, and he continued to mess it up. He could have easily gone to bed with her and kept her with him 24/7 as his partner. What the hell was stopping him?

Zeus laughed. "She's a little spitfire. I kind of like her. She's nothing like the divas we usually get stuck with."

Carlos agreed. She wasn't like anyone he'd ever met. He needed a new plan. They headed back to StrikeForce to regroup. Thoughts of her naked and climbing into her bed were running through his mind. Meanwhile, a kidnapper was out there waiting for the right moment.

CHAPTER 58
Lunch with Moss

Ale woke up feeling more tired than ever. Her sleep was restless at best, topped with weird dreams and a bit of regret for what she had said to Carlos. Why had she jumped all over him? He was trying to help and keep her safe. She headed into the shower to wake up, ate some break-fast, and did some sewing. She was meeting Moss at the posh Beverly Hills hotel, and she was eager to start enjoying her week off.

Carlos had texted her in the middle of the night, telling her he left a vehicle in her parking slot to use as long as she wanted. He also told her to be careful and included a heart emoji in his message. She figured it was a nice compromise. Danny texted to tell her he was on his way over with more sewing and her birthday gifts. *Shit*, with everything going on, she totally forgot about them. It seemed weird to open them alone and momma would be pissed. She'll have to stop at momma's on her way home from lunch and apologize.

A knock on her door made her jump. She checked the peep hole, and it was Danny with a dolly stacked with bins. She opened the door and smiled at him. He came in and gave her a big hug. "You're causing all kinds of trouble, Ale," he said jokingly.

"So, what else is new?" she said, shrugging her shoulders. He handed Ale the boxes of gifts and cards while he went in to unload the bins in the bedroom and reload the finished ones. He left the envelope of money for the sewing on the counter.

He looked at it and smiled. "You might want to open that and those cards. You know there will be cash in those envelopes. It shouldn't be sitting out. Put it in your safe or go to the bank."

She smiled at him. "Yes, Dad."

He just shook his head. "Please be careful Ale. You matter to us." And off he went. She opened the envelope from papa; momma had put a note inside telling her she loved her. She took all the envelopes from her birthday and stuffed them in her safe. She really needed to do something with this cash. As she looked at the gifts, she remembered the little box that Diego and Pepe gave her. She found it and opened it carefully. It wasn't ticking. Inside was a new cellphone with a card that read in Spanish. *Happy Birthday beautiful. Use this to contact us. The big guy is monitoring your phone!* She smiled, removed it from the box, and turned it on. It had two contacts, Mickey and Minnie. *Hmm...* She wondered who was which one.

Ale decided to up her game for lunch. Mossimo was used to eating with beautiful Italian ladies who always dressed stylishly. She put on one of her favourite dresses. It was a bronze and white striped linen tank dress that had a low scoop neck. The dress ended just below her knees and zipped up the side. It had a matching bronze duster. She had made it, so it fit like a glove. She chose a nice bronze-coloured push up bra, which added a bit of cleavage. It might have fit too snugly after all the food she had eaten this weekend. Eek. Probably should have salad for lunch.

Her hair was in a messy pony, as she didn't have any hair skills. She let some curls hang loosely and put on some mascara and liner. She didn't look half bad for someone who was about to be kidnapped. She grabbed the cash her papa sent her and stuffed it into her clutch that matched her Italian pumps.

Carlos loaned her a beautiful Porsche Macan to drive. It was fully loaded and probably had a tracker. A little note on the dash said, "*Te amo.*" She rolled her eyes and drove out of the parking garage, headed to the Beverly Wilshire hotel for lunch. Nothing but the best for Moss!

When Ale arrived, Moss was at the table near a window. He stood up to greet her. "*Sei bellimissia.*" He kissed her on both cheeks and held the chair out when she sat down. Moss had impeccable manners. The waiter filled up their water glasses and didn't ask if she wanted anything. Ale must have had a strange look on her face. "I took the liberty of ordering for both of us. I hope you don't mind," Moss said.

She smiled. "Of course, not." She minded. She really, really minded. *WTF?*. Just yesterday she told a room full of men she was making her own decisions and now this? What year was this again? They conversed in Italian, and everything felt awkward. The waiter appeared with their overpriced salads; Ale played with her food while Moss constantly checked his phone. He seemed nervous and edgy. She wasn't sure if it was because they were older now, or that they no longer had anything in common. Usually, they just picked up where they left off, but it was different this visit. He suggested several times that she return to Italy with him. He even suggested she relocate and look at working at hospitals in Italy, near family. Moss was family on her momma's side. They lived in a beautiful area near Positano. Moss's factory was located there, and he also had an office and an apartment in Milan. Ale had never thought about moving and living in Italy, however she told him she would think about it.

Moss had another appointment, so they finished up their salads, hugged, and went their separate ways. She headed to momma's; she needed real food. Momma almost knocked her over when she walked through the door. "Oh Alessandra." She'd been crying.

"Momma, it's ok. Please stop crying." Ale hugged her tight. She never wanted to upset her momma.

They separated and her momma looked approvingly at her attire. "Oh baby, you look lovely. I love that dress on you. Sit and I will make you something to eat."

Thank GOD. She removed her duster and heard papa coming upstairs. He smiled and hugged her. "Hi baby," he, said. It felt nice, just the three of them.

"Momma, I'm going to wait to open my birthday gifts so you can watch. I was just going to wait for things to calm down a bit," Ale said, grabbing a Diet Pepsi out of the fridge. Momma only had Pepsi in there for her. Momma piled fresh buns and cold cuts, cheese, tomatoes, cucumber, olives. and mustard on the table and papa started building his sandwich. *God, I loved my parents*, Ale thought. Papa looked at her and winked. Man of few words.

She put her sandwich together and moaned when she took the first bite while saying, "I had lunch with Moss today." Her papa looked at her stuffing the sandwich in her mouth and seemed confused. Ale smiled, wiping her mouth. "He ordered me a salad without asking. Who does that?" She kept stuffing the sandwich in, her papa smiling. *He gets me*, she thought.

Momma spoke up, "Oh, good. I think they are heading back to Italy tomorrow. We are having a dinner for them tonight at the restaurant. Why don't you come?"

Ale nodded. "OK, then maybe after dinner, you can come back to my place, and we can open the gifts. Maybe zia and Gio will come." Momma got excited. See? *Wasn't this better than a freaking safe house?* "Moss was acting weird today," she added. "Usually, we talk non-stop, but I found him awkward this visit. I don't know how to describe it."

Her parents looked at each other. "Well, maybe he has a lot on his mind. Everyone is a bit on edge with what's going on." Ale didn't believe her momma. In fact, Moss didn't even mention the kidnapping, which was very odd.

"He even suggested I move to Italy and work in a hospital there," Ale said, drinking the last of her Pepsi.

"That's just *crazy*! Why would you leave your family to move there?" Momma scowled.

"Anyways, are you busy papa? I see you sent more sewing to me." Ale knew when to change the subject.

"It's, crazy, everyone is looking for new suits and everyone gained weight during COVID. Will you be OK to do sewing while you're off this week?" he asked. Obviously, he wasn't bothered by the so-called kidnapper.

"Yup, no problem. I might go up to zia and zio's in Santa Barbara for a few days, just for a break. I'd like to ride the horses and visit with them. Unless you think I'd be putting them in danger?" Ale asked.

Her zia Carmen and zio Nick owned a beautiful ranch in Santa Barbara and Ale spent a lot of time there as a kid. They'd taught her how to ride and take care of the horses.

"I wouldn't worry," Papa said nonchalantly. "Nick will shoot them if they step foot on his ranch." OK then, guess she would be safe there too!

"Whose car are you driving?" Momma asked.

"Carlos lent it to me, minus the chauffeur.

Papa chuckled.

"That was nice of him. He seems like such a nice man, and he sure likes you, Ale. My gosh." Momma was grinning.

Oh, here we go, Ale thought.

"All those big hunky men fawning over you yesterday. And all of them single!"

Ale groaned and papa smiled. "Momma, right now I just want to be left alone."

"OK, I just wanted to point out that you have quite the following," she winked. *Jeeezus.*

"Has Gio had a stroke yet?" Ale asked, changing the subject.

"Nope. Not yet, but we do have some possible good news."

"Maria," Papa said.

OK, wow, Ale's never seen him do that.

"Oh, Vito, I can't keep this from Ale. She deserves to know."

OK...

"Is Soph pregnant?" Ale asked, excitedly. Momma shook her head.

"No, but we have a cousin in Italy whose wife died during childbirth and he's not handling her death very well. The baby girl is fine, but the only close relative is the grandmother, and she is too old to take care of her. We are discussing Gio and Sophia adopting the baby. The dad is in some sort of depression and the baby is a reminder of the dead mother. It's a horrible situation. Gio and Sophia are flying over to talk to him and meet the baby."

Ale just stared at momma, as tears rolled down her cheeks. Momma stood up, walked over and hugged her. "I am sorry; I know this probably hits home with you. I didn't tell you to upset you, honestly honey."

She kept rubbing her arms. Papa was shaking his head. That's why he didn't want momma to tell her. Nobody in Ale's birth parent's family could take care of her either. She knew what that was like. Her heart ached for this baby. But, if it worked out, this baby girl would land in the safest of arms. Ale was living proof.

"It's OK, momma," she said. "It's always hard when I hear stories like mine. I really hope this works out. Gio and Sophia need some good news for a change." She might be a zia soon! Oh, that made her happy.

"Can I mention it or were you supposed to keep it a secret?" she asked momma, who looked the other way.

"You might want to wait until he brings it up," she said, covering herself.

Papa was finished with lunch. He excused himself from the table, kissed Ale on the top of her head and kissed momma on the mouth. "I need to get back to work. You two, stay out of trouble." He glared at momma. That's as much trouble as she would ever get into with him. He adored her so much, he couldn't even get mad. Ale wanted that. She wanted what they had. It was the most beautiful love story.

Ale stood up, helped momma clear the table and put stuff away. She said her goodbyes and headed home. It was hot out. Maybe she would sit by the pool today.

CHAPTER 59
Pool Day!

Ale arrived home safely and decided to do some cleaning, just in case her family descended on her apartment after dinner. She scanned both her phones, and updated Amalia. Ale knew her phone was being tracked, so she was careful with her words. She also told Mal she would be by the apartment pool in case she got off early today. She texted Mickey (aka Diego) with an update on the kidnapper thing, again, being careful. She was sure they already knew, but she wanted them in the loop and wanted to let them know she was OK. The pool belonging to their apartment building was quiet, no kids or teenagers.

She put on her cute, fuchsia-coloured bikini, this one was bandeau-style with frills on top and bottom. The top also had a peek hole in the middle. She covered the swimsuit with a tank and a pair of tiny jean shorts. She threw a bunch of necessities, including her hat, into a beach bag and headed downstairs for some quiet time.

Ale always jumped into the pool to cool off first, then applied sunscreen and laid down to relax and read. She loved flipping through fashion magazines as they gave her a look into upcoming styles and ideas for sewing. Her hair was up, hat on, and the sun felt warm on her skin, making her freedom seem even better. She put in her earbuds and let out a big sigh.

CHAPTER 60
Everybody Was Watching Ale...

For the first time ever, Carlos thought he was going to have a stroke. Even though Ale had demanded everyone back off, everybody was still watching her. She had to know they wouldn't stop. Her phone, the SUV she was driving. He had men everywhere. So did O'Malley and probably Diego and Pepe, too. Christ, most of LA.

It didn't help that she just paraded around her apartment pool area in a tiny pink bikini. What in God's name was she thinking? Carlos just stared at the feed. She was the prettiest little thing he'd ever seen. He had given up trying to keep his guys from saying stuff. They were all in love with her. He just shook his head. He'd give her an hour, tops, and he would have to intervene as she was too exposed out in the open and she barely had any clothes on.

O'Malley and Scotty were in a van looking at the surveillance video and trying to stay professional. They had other cases they were working, and this wasn't exactly O'Malley's area of expertise, so they could only assist as needed. Some of the LAPD teams were very territorial. Needless to say, most of the LAPD Abduction and Kidnapping Division were now in love with Ale, too.

CHAPTER 61
Family Dinner...

Ale was laying on her stomach in the shade feeling so very relaxed. Her vacation time was awesome. She jumped when she felt someone touch her shoulder and reached for her mace as she turned over quickly. *Jeezus!*

"Carlos! What the hell, you need to stop doing this!" she said loudly.

"I'm sorry; I thought you heard me walking up." He sat on the chaise beside her. He had his mirrored sunglasses on so she could only see herself. *She looked pretty good.*

She took out her ear buds. "What time is it?" Ale asked. She didn't want to be late for family dinner.

"It's almost 4 p.m." Carlos sounded angry. "Ale, can you please come inside, you are so exposed out here." He lowered his head, expecting her refusal.

Ale surprised him. "OK. I was going to go in soon anyways."

He looked up at her with relief. She stood up and put on her shorts and tank back on and gathered up her things. He took the bag from her and led her into the building. He unlocked and checked the apartment while she headed to the shower. She needed to get the chlorine and sunscreen off.

Ale finished showering, put on her robe, and grabbed her lotion. Carlos was sitting in the chair in her bedroom. He looked tired and serious. It made her sad. She put on her lotion, slipped on a pair of panties, and walked over to him. She turned around, sat on his knee, leaning back as he wrapped his arms around her.

"I thought you wanted this to stop?" he asked moving his mouth close to her ear.

She shuddered. "I'm just sitting on your knee," she lied.

"You like sitting on people's knees, I noticed. Mmm, you smell good, Ale." He was whispering, kissing her neck, and holding her tighter.

"I have to get ready for dinner with my family at Vito's. Did you want to be my date?" Ale asked.

"I'd love to," he said, still rubbing his lips up and down her neck.

God why was it so hot in here?

Carlos texted someone and Ale texted momma to let her know that she would be bringing a plus-one to dinner. She'd let her stew as to who it is. Momma is still learning emojis, and she sent Ale a thumbs up, thank God. Ale decided on a black jumpsuit with a tank style top, added diamond string earrings, a diamond tennis bracelet, and a diamond anklet. She kept her hair up in a messy bun and finished with a pair of strappy high heels. Someone knocked on her door and handed Carlos a garment bag. Ale smiled. It was a Vito's leather garment bag. He quickly changed into a black suit with navy shirt. Carlos looked her up and down and smiled. Most women took years to get ready, not Ale. And she would still be the most beautiful woman in the room. Her new tan had her glowing, as did the diamonds wrapped around her limbs. *Sweet Jesus!* They headed out. Ale assumed they would take the SUV he had loaned her, however they went out the front doors instead, where a very large man named Zeus was waiting for them.

Momma was in the door waiting when they pulled up. Carlos opened the vehicle door for Ale and momma came running out squealing, "Oh Ale! Hi, Carlos!" She grabbed his hand and almost dragged them into the restaurant. The family was eating in the private dining room, which was normal as there were so many of them. There was also additional security. Everyone was excited and of course speaking Italian. Ale tried to remind them to speak English for Carlos, but it was mostly ignored. He didn't seem to mind. He kept his hand on her back the entire time. She didn't think he ever stopped working or knew what it was like to relax. Except, maybe in bed.

Their meals, as always, were delicious. Ale always had pizza. Carlos had pasta primavera. Ale had white wine and he had red. She realized this was the first time they'd eaten together in a restaurant. She kept giving him looks and smiling. She really did like having him around. So did her nipples!

Moss was across the table and seemed uncomfortable with Carlos being there. Ale tried to start up conversation, but the responses were short. He preferred to keep speaking in Italian, which she found rude, so she stopped talking to him. She had no idea what was going on with Moss, but it was starting to annoy her.

After dinner and goodbyes, zia and momma agreed to come back to Ale's place. Papa seemed quite happy to be rid of them. Gio and Sophia were already on their way to Italy to see the baby.

They all squeezed into the SUV with Zeus driving and zia wanted the front seat so she could flirt with him. Carlos was able to really experience zia's personality. Zia Connie had him and Zeus laughing the entire time. Carlos checked the apartment and kissed Ale good-night, with both momma and zia watching closely. They all sighed.

Ale dug out all the cards and put all the gifts on the coffee table, while zia poured the wine. Carlos said Ramone would come back and take them home when they were ready. He already knew zia had kicked back two bottles of wine at dinner.

Opening her birthday gifts was always uncomfortable for Ale. She always received so many beautiful pieces of jewellery and had lots of it already. Her zio Tony had made a killing on this event. Ale's zia gave her a beautiful rose gold (her favourite) rectangle bar with a diamond on a necklace, which had her named engraved in it. Ale loved it. Her momma and papa gave her small rose gold and diamond hoops to go with the necklace and $10,000 in cash. *WTF??* She thanked them with tears and hugs. They were always so generous. In total, Ale had received over $15,000 in cash. *Seriously?* And loads of gift cards for the Sunflower Spa. Gio and Soph paid for a year's training session with

Mac, and her nurses gave her a yearly yoga membership. Ale felt very spoiled. Momma wrote down who gave her what, of course. Ale *HAD* to send thank you cards, naturally.

Ale felt brave after a few glasses of wine and brought out the beautiful roses Carlos gave her. She had them in her bedroom next to her bed. They both went crazy.

"Oh Ale, a man doesn't send you Beverly Hills roses if he's just a friend," said momma.

"And he paid for your spa treatments? My gosh, that's so thoughtful," zia piped in, winking at her. She had *a lot* of wine tonight. "He is hot, Ale, you need to get him between the sheets, NOW. You are at the best time of your life, nice and ripe."

Umm, RIPE? What the heck did that mean? "Ripe? Seriously, zia." Ale said, exasperated.

She nodded. "Obviously, you are ripe. Suddenly, you have all this testosterone surrounding you. It's the only explanation." She shrugged and momma looked as confused as Ale was.

"What exactly does ripe mean?" Ale asked her, taking a long swig of her wine as she really didn't know if she wanted the answer.

"Your body is sending out pheromones. You are at that perfect age for mating and it's sending out the signals."

OK. Wow. Why was it so hot in here?

They continued to discuss Ale's ripeness while she texted Ramone that the two drunk Italian ladies were ready for him. God help him, he may never make it back alive. They also made plans to have lunch and go shopping tomorrow.

CHAPTER 62
Lauren's Back

Carlos was reviewing some intel his teams had sent him from the field. They were still out interrogating, and they were getting closer to the source of the kidnapping. Carlos felt he knew who it was. He just needed the proof. His hacker was tearing through piles of code to try and trace the source of the kidnapping request. Always follow the money. Carlos was working out of his condo office tonight, and he was bone tired yet all he could think about was Ale. He loved being beside her at dinner and watching her eat—the girl had an appetite—and just seeing the overall love she had for and from her family. It was so endearing. Carlos never thought about shit like this, yet here he was dreaming of Ale, all the while, trying to keep her safe.

His phone beeped and he checked it—a text from Ramone confirming he dropped off Ale's momma and zia. Carlos smiled. Zia probably gave him a run for his money. He directed Ramone to stakeout at Ale's apartment for a while just to be close. He had two others nearby too; he wasn't taking any chances. Another text came in from Ale letting him know she was having lunch with her momma and zia tomorrow. After that, shopping therapy. Wonderful, Carlos thought, *he now had to send the team on a shopping spree.* He texted O'Malley to let his team know as well.

Carlos thought about what Gio and Sophia were going through

and the cousin willing to give away his child. Then he thought about his own father.

Another text came in from the control room. Apparently, Lauren was posting shit on her social media about him and Ale. *Fuuuuuck.* He needed to figure out a way to get rid of her. They sent him the links and he looked them over. Unbelievable. Someone had taken a photo of him and Ale going into the restaurant with her mother hugging them. and Lauren was not happy. Just what he needed.

Once again, the gutter called. He went downstairs to find his hacker.

CHAPTER 63
Shopping With Momma and Zia...

Ale started the day with sewing and more sewing. She finished the order for papa and texted Danny. Papa was super busy right now, so she was sure there was more coming. She jumped in the shower and put on a cute outfit to go pick up her momma and zia for lunch.

They settled at a cozy café in downtown LA called Lucy's and sat outside on the patio. There was never a lull in the conversation. Ale watched her momma and zia as she ate, sisters who barely spent any time apart. It was unbelievably beautiful. They loved and cared for each other so much, as they did her. They looked nothing alike, acted differently, yet they operated with one heart.

The day was beautiful, so they took their time at lunch, ordered appetizers to share. The food was delicious. Ale stuck with water and lemon, zia had a glass of red wine, and momma a glass of white. After lunch, they strolled the area window shopping in boutique stores versus mall shopping. They noticed a number of their favourite stores hadn't made it through the pandemic, but they shopped in the ones that did and found some cute items. They shopped for dresses and shoes—usually, they bought their shoes from Italy, but they wanted to help the small business economy and it felt good.

Ale was exhausted by the time she got home from dropping momma and zia off. She kicked off her shoes, grabbed her faux-fur blanket and took a nap on her bed. She loved being on vacation!

CHAPTER 64
There She Blows...

The first thing Ale noticed when she opened her eyes was a large body lying beside her, dressed all in black. She panicked until her eyes moved up and saw the face. He had a five o'clock shadow, which was very sexy. He saw that Ale was awake and turned to stared at her.

"Tough day?" he asked, smiling.

"Yup." She pulled the blanket up higher around her neck and buried herself into the mattress. She scooted over closer to Carlos because she felt his warmth. God the man gave off heat. *What is that? A Latino thing?* He pulled her closer, and Ale thought about her breath, but at this point it was a bit too late. He didn't seem to care, so she pulled the blanket over him too and climbed aboard. They rolled over on his back, and she started kissing his neck, his ear, and making her way to his mouth. He grabbed her sexy hair to guide her, and their tongues started fighting for control. They were both groaning, and Ale was writhing like a new puppy. She stopped and looked at him, putting her hands on his face. "I like this look." The hair on his face was soft, not like normal stubble.

"I love the way you look at me," he growled and brought her mouth to his.

His hands moved down to her ass as he rubbed her against him. Carlos was super hard. His hands moved up and one got under her tank to her nipple. *Dear God.* Ale had super sensitive nipples, beyond anything. They were large and puffy for her small breasts, and they seem to fascinate those who get to see or touch them. Carlos was no different. He started to thumb her nipple and she moved her head into the base of his neck because she knew she was about to go off. Her left hand pushed against his chest and her entire body went rigid. *"Oooooooooh," she moaned.* It had been far too long.

Carlos seemed pleasantly surprised that Ale could reach orgasm this easily. She moved her hand down between them and he rolled them over, so he was on top. His eyes were black in colour—the horny black, not the menacing black. She managed to get her small hand inside his pants, and she gently closed her fingers around him. He was rock hard. Oh, how the man moaned. He gasped and pushed against her; he wasn't pulling her hand away. Carlos thought he would die from the feel of her tiny hand on him. He thought about pushing her away, but he was too far gone. Instead, he started to use his mouth on her breasts, and that was all it took. With what he was doing to her and her stroking him, it was too much. She kept slowly moving her hand and lightly clasping. She could tell by the way he was responding that he was so close. He moved his mouth from her breasts and replaced it with his hands, claimed her mouth with his, and they were writhing, kissing, thumbing, and stroking each other into a frenzy. Ale arched to come again, and Carlos moaned as he covered her hand in warm liquid. She smiled. Finally! She continued softly stroking as he buried his head in the side of her neck. "Christ, Ale."

She knew that had to feel good, as he'd been carrying that around for a while! She continued to be slow and soft with him, and when he rolled over onto his back, she brought her hand out. She looked him in the eyes and licked it. He closed his eyes and shook his head. Ale's tank top was up around her neck and her nipples were still wide awake. She pulled her shirt down and got up to wash her hand. He followed her into the bathroom to clean up and she went back to the bed and waited for him.

When he returned, he laid down and pulled her into a snuggle. He looked almost embarrassed.

"You, OK?" she asked.

"I am now," he said, his eyes smiling.

"Sooo, you met my nipples."

He grinned. "I've been wanting to meet them for a while."

"Yeah, they have a mind of their own." He started rubbing them again through her tank and she pushed into him. "Carlos," she pleaded.

"I'm infatuated now. I can't stop. God, Ale, you are so soft."

She kissed him again and she really thought they were going to go for round two, but he stopped.

"I've a difficult time staying away from you," he said rolling over and staring at the ceiling fan.

She climbed on top again. "Why were you here when I woke up?" She had forgotten to ask before things got hot and heavy.

"I texted and you didn't answer, so I wanted to make sure you were OK."

Crap, her phone. She didn't even know where she had left it. She always hid the "Disney" phone in case Carlos snooped around when she wasn't in the apartment.

"Oh, sorry. I came home from shopping and needed a nap."

He smiled and rolled over to look at her, his eyes roaming south. "I see you bought a few things," nodding to the shopping bags on the chair. Ale also noticed Danny had made a visit and brought her more sewing, which meant there was an envelope of cash lying around somewhere.

He was staring at her and moving his hand over her breasts, completely fascinated. "I sure hope you managed to use up some of that cash you have lying around here," he said, not taking his eyes off her. She closed her eyes for a few reasons. Finally, she took his hand and moved it elsewhere because she couldn't concentrate. He grinned.

"Umm. So, about the cash. Papa and Leslie pay me in cash, and I make more than I spend." He rolled over on his back again and really laughed. She'd never seen or heard him laugh like that. It made her smile. She rolled over on him and looked at him. "You seem happy with me."

He patted her bum and said, "You are changing the subject. I don't know a single woman in LA who makes more than she can spend." He had a point.

"I worked a lot of overtime with COVID and it's all in my bank account. I don't have many bills or credit card debt, so I use the cash for the spa maintenance, hygiene necessities, groceries, or household items. Sometimes I splurge on material for sewing or fresh flowers. I pay my rent a year in advance." She shrugged, not knowing what he wanted her to say.

"Do you have any idea how unique you are?" he asked, playing with her hair, she shook her head. "I'm normal Carlos, I'm just, normal."

She continued. "Oh, I have cash in other places besides the safe. It's, everywhere in here." His eyes got big. "And I have a safety deposit box." Ale had no idea why she was telling him all this.

"Ale, you have a problem." He looked concerned.

She looked up at him. "I think it has something to do with having been in foster care."

He wrapped her in his arms, content to not ruin the moment. Carlos could not imagine how a little six-year-old-girl survived any of what she went through. It only made him love her more. She was the complete opposite of every woman he ever spent time with. She attached to his heart, and he couldn't shake her off if he tried. She had no idea how special she was.

"It could be worse," she interrupted the silence. "I could be in debt up to my ears," she added, thinking of so many of her cousins who spent money and didn't earn any income. Carlos just held her closer and kissed the top of her head. Ale felt so comfortable and safe with him wrapped around her, her entire body relaxed.

"To answer your question," Carlos said, "I AM happy around you, especially today."

She smiled and snuggled in closer to him. "Sooo... you enjoyed that?" she asked, her insecurities showing.

"Believe me, you have some mad skills. Jesus, Ale I love how excited you get, it's so damn refreshing." Ale had no clue what he was talking about. She figured any woman would get excited if Carlos was lying in her bed.

"When are we going to seal the deal?" she blurted out and she could hear him chuckling.

"Soon. We need to get this kidnapping thing resolved and I have some things I need to clean up before we can start," he said, exhaling.

"Can you tell me what *they* are?" she asked. "I told you, I understand the rules. I can handle it."

He just kissed the top of her head and said, "Patience, baby."

Grrrrr. She hated that patience word!

"OK, but I want a date now, not just the Striker sex. I want dinner and conversation, the whole deal. I want to make you work for it."

He laughed out loud at that one. Like he wasn't working for it already. "Deal."

He kissed her lips. Gosh he was an amazing kisser. She could eat him up. Matt, her ex, didn't kiss like that or pay any attention to her breasts. It's weird how certain people just heighten your senses and others just don't. Maybe zia was right about her being *RIPE!* Oh, and she had mad skills, too!

CHAPTER 65
Time to Get Out of Dodge...

The next day, Ale was driving up the highway to Santa Barbara. She felt free. Firstly, she attended an early session with Mac and a yoga class, then set off from there as she had her overnight bag in the back, along with her cowboy hat and boots. She couldn't wait to see her zia and zio. Their beautiful ranch was nestled near the Santa Ynez mountains among acres of rolling fields. It had a big and beautiful white farmhouse, several large barns, and a stream that ran through some of their riding trails. It was also just minutes from the ocean. Her zia's children, Ale's cousins, had grown and moved away and it was just the two of them and some ranch hands to run things. Ale loved staying there and couldn't wait to arrive.

Zia was on the porch when she pulled up the long, fenced driveway. She came bouncing down in her jeans and boots to run and hug her. It never got old! Ale had just seen them at her birthday party, but that didn't matter. Every time was like this. They always greeted everyone the same. They hugged and kissed, she grabbed Ale's bag, and held her hand to lead her up the stairs to the big wraparound porch. Gosh, the view was breathtaking; you could see for miles. The horses were in their different corals with the hands working and zio on the tractor. What a great life. Maybe Ale needed to get a job in Santa Barbara! Zia had freshly made lemonade ready, and they sat at the little table and chairs and caught up. She was so glad she made the decision to come here. She could hear Dr. Louise's voice in her little ear. *Ale, do something that doesn't involve making money.* Here she was.

After they caught up and had a lemonade, Ale changed into her boots and grabbed her hat. Time to go meet the horses. They had three mares that were pregnant and one very horny stallion. Those were zia's words, not hers. The stallion was way off in a different coral, and he was not happy. They had to watch him closely. Meanwhile, the mares were eating away quietly ignoring him. *Ale could relate!*

Ale found her beautiful Appaloosa mare, Maggie. She came right over to her, and they made up quickly. They headed into the barn and zia introduced her to the hands. One of them grabbed a saddle and they started getting the horses ready. Zia and Ale were going for a ride, and she couldn't wait!

They rode for hours and decided to dismount from the horses to let them have a drink in the stream. When they started to walk the horses back, they noticed another black SUV in the driveway, they looked at each other. Ale had put the kidnapping out of her mind since she'd been there, and seeing the SUV made her start to panic. Then, she noticed a man talking to the hands and they were all laughing. It was Carlos. Maybe he had news? They climbed back onto the horses and rode towards the house.

Carlos was smiling. "Ola!" Ale said and tipped her hat. He spoke in Spanish, thinking her zia wouldn't understand it. "Baby, you look sexy as hell on that horse." Her zia quickly replied, "Gracias." Everyone laughed! Ale introduced them and they got off the horses so the hands could take them back to the barn.

"Is everything OK?" Ale asked. "Have you figured out who's after me?" She badgered him as they walked up on to the porch and sat down. Zia poured them each a glass of lemonade. Ale's legs were killing her. Between her session with Mac, yoga, and riding, her body was screaming.

"What's going on?" Ale asked impatiently, "Why did you drive all the way out here?"

Carlos paused a bit, as if looking for the right words. "We caught a break last night tracing the kidnapping request and the responses. We've managed to mitigate almost ten different attempts." He stopped and looked at Ale. Ale wasn't sure what happened, but hearing that number of ten made her dizzy, she fainted and fell off her chair. She wasn't one to pass out; she was an ER nurse, so fainting was not an option. There she was, laid out on the porch with her zia putting a cold cloth on her head, repeating her name. Ale opened her eyes and leaned forward, they both pushed her back. *Helllooo … she's a nurse, remember?*

"I'm OK, sorry. Help me up." Carlos picked her up easily and set her on his lap while he sat on the chair. Really? Eye roll. He made her take a drink and Ale leaned into him.

"Did you say ten?" she asked.

"Yes." He replied, quietly, her zia was shaking her head.

"We managed to remove the initial request from the underground network and we have a trap set up in case another request appears, so we can quickly take it down. We don't believe the person organizing this is all that tech savvy." He paused. "We put a trace on them and it's leading back to Italy." He looked at Ale directly as he said it. Ale frowned. Who in Italy would want to kidnap her?

"Ale, we are very certain it's connected to Moss." He held on to her tightly to ensure she didn't faint again.

"No!" she said, standing up and facing him. "Carlos, you met him. Why would Moss kidnap me? He doesn't need money. This makes no sense. I am his *cousin!*" Ale had tears in her eyes and her voice was getting louder. "You have to be wrong about this." She felt sick. *Oh God, please don't throw up*, she thought.

"Ale," he said calmly, "please sit.

Carlos didn't want to drive up here with this news and ruin her visit. He looked at her zia as if to apologize and she put her hand on his arm as Ale sat back down.

"Do my parents know?" she asked, he nodded. Ale hadn't looked at her phone since she landed. *Jeezus her phone was probably blowing up.*

"Were you trying to reach me? God, I'm sorry, my phone is in my bag." She went into the house and brought it out. It was dinging like crazy. So much for a nice get away.

"I'm sorry, Ale," he started. "I just wanted to get to you before you heard it from someone else. The investigation is heating up right now and the authorities in Italy are being notified for when Mossimo lands."

Shit, he had flown out today. "What about Gio? Oh my gosh, he's there." She panicked.

"We contacted him, he's got security, and he's pissed. Moss should be nervous."

None of this made sense. Ale put her head between her hands and just breathed. She didn't know what else to do. Zia just soothed her and rubbed her neck.

OK, Ale. Enough. Get your Big girl panties on!

"Tell me. Everything," she demanded.

Just then her zio came over and Ale went down to hug and kiss him. He held on to her tight, whispering in Italian. Carlos stood up and went down to meet him and shake his hand. Her zia announced she was getting dinner ready, and Ale decided she needed some air.

"Let's go for a walk," she suggested, even though her legs were sore, she had nervous energy to burn off and she wanted to show Carlos around the ranch. Zio went in to get cleaned up and zia went to get dinner ready. Ale would do kitchen duty after; she just needed some time. She checked her phone and cleared the messages then called her momma as Carlos and her walked. They spoke in Italian and Ale assured her she was OK, and that Carlos was with her. Ale ignored the other messages, something about someone named Lauren.

"Who's Lauren?" she asked, thinking it had something to do with her kidnapping.

Carlos shook his head. "Don't worry about her. I'll explain later."

Carlos provided more details on Moss. Apparently, he was involved with some very dangerous people, and he owed a ton of money; they were using Ale as a way to get him to pay up. They weren't entirely sure if Moss set up the kidnapping to get money from the family, or if the dangerous people did it to force Moss to get the money and pay. Either way, he was involved, and it was hard to believe. Moss attended her birthday, sat across from her at lunch and dinner, and acted like a concerned family member. My God, who was this guy? *A fuckin' monster, that's who.* She remembered how insistent he was about her moving to Italy and it gave her chills. What happened to that sweet boy they all loved so much? While she was relieved the immediate threat to her was over, this presented a real mess for her family. She grabbed Carlos's hand as they walked back towards the house.

Carlos was doing his best to stay calm. He really wanted to get the hell out of there and fly to Italy. He would never say that to Ale, but he knew she needed him right now and he would be there for her. The soldier in him wanted to hunt and kill.

"Thank you, Carlos. I know I haven't exactly made it easy for you," Ale said, feeling guilty.

He laughed. "Ale, nothing is easy with you."

She pouted. Her zia came out and told them to wash up for dinner. Carlos was staying! They gathered around the small table in the kitchen; they seldom used the big formal dining room. Not sure why it was even in the house. Zia made her famous lasagna. *Thank you, Jesus!* Ale scoffed it down while Carlos just stared at her.

"Where in God's name do you put the food?" he asked.

Her zia and zio laughed. "You should have seen when we first got her, Carlos," zio said. "She was so little and frail, all curls and eyes. We spoon-fed her for the first year we had her and tried everything to get that child to eat. Now we can't fill her," he added, making Ale smile. She loved how they said, '*we got her*', like she was everyone's, not just momma and papa's. *Famiglia!*

Carlos filled zia and zio in with what he knew about Moss. Zio just shook his head. Moss was his side of the family as zio was momma's brother. It hurt him, as it hurt her. Moss was like a brother to Ale.

Ale's zio looked at her and said, "Alessandra, sometimes people get themselves in messes and they don't know how to get themselves out. This is not your fault. This is on Mossimo and he will need to be punished." It still didn't make her feel any better.

Carlos excused himself as his phone was buzzing and he went outside to answer. Normally he wouldn't have his phone at the table, but today was different. Ale helped zia clean up and they served up her zia's yummy carrot cake for dessert. There is always dessert at an

Italian dinner. If there isn't, leave! Zia made Carlos sit and eat the carrot cake. He didn't eat dessert, but he felt obligated. He also told Ale that O'Malley wanted to speak to her. She would call him after cake. *Bitch—PLEASE!*

Zia made it clear that Carlos would stay the night and Ale almost choked on her cake. He protested but she wouldn't hear of it. She would fix up the other spare bedroom so he would get a good night's sleep. Ale could tell Carlos wanted to get back, but she really liked having him here, so he caved. *YAY!*

Ale cleaned up the dessert dishes, while zia went upstairs to get the spare room ready. Carlos retrieved his overnight bag out his car. Apparently, he travelled with one. Always prepared. Afterwards, they walked over to meet the horses as they were sleeping in their stalls. They weren't allowed to see Zorro the stallion. Ale introduced Carlos to Maggie, and they snuggled. *The bond between humans and animals was so uncomplicated*, she thought. Maggie instantly welcomed her back and forgave her for being away so long. Humans would never do that.

Carlos just watched in awe as the horse bonded with Ale. He could relate. It was difficult to stay mad at Ale or stay angry with her. He knew that firsthand. If he decided to pursue this relationship thing with her, he would have his damn hands full and he would never be bored.

As they walked back, Ale smiled. The air was a bit cool tonight, which meant they could sleep with windows open*! Hallelujah!* Since the kidnapping threat, she had to have her windows and patio doors locked shut, even in her fifth-floor apartment. Tonight, they see the stars, smell the clean fresh air. Ohhh, and the beds were so comfy here. All farmhouse-like, with wrought-iron headboards and homemade quilts. It was heaven.

"What are you thinking?" Carlos asked her.

"Nothing," she smiled.

"Tell me." He said, grabbing her around the waist.

Ale was laughing now, trying to wiggle away from him but he was too strong. "I was thinking that I could sleep with my windows open. I like that."

He turned her around to face him and he held her close. "Can I ask you something? Now that this mess is almost over." He looked serious. "I need to know how you feel about O'Malley."

Jeezus, where did that come from? She thought he and O'Malley had gotten all chummy since the kidnapping. Ale pulled away and walked towards the house. Carlos followed and they sat on the porch swing. Gosh, she loved it here, so peaceful and quiet, with no pollution.

"I met him for lunch, and we cleared the air," she said. "It's all good."

"He has feelings for you, Ale. He's told me as much."

She sighed. "I told him we could be friends and that's it. I can't help how he feels." She was feeling a bit cornered.

Her zia came out to say good night and asked them to lock up. Ale stood up to hug her and thank her for everything.

Carlos interrupted the silence. "Can you at least tell me what happened all those years ago?" Ale's head spun around.

"No." She wasn't ready for that conversation, and she was tired.

"C'mon, let's go to bed." She smiled when he looked at her. "Separate beds, per usual."

She rolled her eyes as he caught her and whispered, "*No por mucho tiempo.*" More teasing! They locked up and Ale showed him his room. She loved this old farmhouse and wanted one just like it. They said good night, cleaned up, and she opened her windows wide. She put on her PJs, crawled into bed, and fell asleep instantly.

Carlos laid there in the strange room thinking only of her and wondering if she was sleeping naked.

CHAPTER 66
Now What?

The sounds of birds chirping, sun filling the room, a soft ocean breeze, the smell of cut grass—it all filled Ale as she woke up and cuddled under the quilted blankets. She could hear people moving and the smell of bacon. God, did she love bacon. She checked her fitbit. It was 10 a.m. *Holy Shit.*

She quickly showered, brushed her teeth, and headed downstairs. Only zia was in the kitchen and Carlos's SUV was gone. That made her sad. She walked over and hugged zia from behind.

"Good morning," zia said in Italian. "The only way to get Alessandra out of bed is to start frying bacon."

Ale laughed. "I am so sorry, zia. I never sleep this late. Unless, of course, I am on late shift."

Zia smiled at her. "You are on vacation and yesterday was quite the day." Zia was making Belgian waffles; momma makes the BEST Belgian waffles, and they are Ale's favourite.

"Is that momma's recipe?" Ale asked.

Zia smiled. "Yes, we all use it. Your momma is a good cook."

"So are you!" Ale said. She needed to move in; she loved this woman. She sat at the breakfast bar and watched her cook. Zia didn't like people in her kitchen, and Ale respected that.

"Carlos leave already?" Ale asked.

"Yes, he was gone when we got up. He's a busy guy. He left all of us a note." She handed it to Ale.

It read that he had to get back to LA as he had early meetings and a big thank you for the hospitality.

"What did you want to do today?" Zia asked. Ale thought about it as she piled her plate with blueberries, waffles, and bacon. She grabbed the syrup and butter and zia watched her inhale her breakfast.

"How about a hike?" Ale suggested, knowing Zia loved being active. "Or a walk on the beach?"

"How about both?" she asked, winking.

"Deal. I will need it after this meal."

Zia and Ale spent the day together, hiking and talking for hours. She told her zia about her man drama and about her COVID experiences. Zia always provided the right amount of advice. Ale felt the weight of the kidnapping attempt disappear as she inhaled the fresh mountain air and just breathed. Once again, the word "grateful" came to mind. This getaway was exactly what she needed. They rode the horses again, after they returned to the ranch. Her head was full of so many thoughts. Mossimo? What would happen to him? Was this really over? What does she do about O'Malley? And then there was Carlos.

CHAPTER 67
She Didn't Like to Be Ignored...

Lauren Mitchell stewed and fretted in her condo, which was probably going to be foreclosed on any day now. She constantly harassed her agent to find her new acting roles, but instead she had to use social media to peddle stupid products to bring in more cash. She had borrowed from everybody she knew and had even setup a Just for Fans account for people to pay monthly to see her pose naked. She didn't care; she was beautiful and sexy, and men wanted to see it. Why give it away for free?

She went on high-end dating sites to attract rich men. She didn't care if they were eligible, she just needed the cash and she'd gladly exchange nudity or sex for it.

The problem was it still wasn't enough. She couldn't make sufficient money through working, peddling, or posing or dating; she needed to marry rich. Pretty easy to do in LA and God knows she deserved it. She wanted a rich, beautiful man to treat her like the queen she was. Unfortunately, the rich, beautiful man she really wanted, wanted nothing to do with her.

Striker wanted her once and she was sure she could make him want her again. She just needed to get him alone and remind him of that incredible night seven years go. God, was it that long ago? She was twice the woman now and she would show him the time of his life.

First, she needed to find out about this mousy blonde. Jesus, did she even own a flat iron? That hair was nasty, and she dressed like she was going to church. Oh right, she was a nurse. *Dear God*, could it get any more boring? Striker deserved so much better. Maybe he was providing security? Apparently, she was a Ferretti. They had lots of money. He could be in it for the cash; Lauren could respect that.

Lauren had to get time with Striker. She had feelers out to text her when they saw him. She decided to go get her fake tan touched up and put on her favourite sexy dress. Lunch at Miguel's was just what she needed, plus she was hungry.

CHAPTER 68
May the Force Be with You...

Striker was at his office headquarters doing the one thing he hated the most, paperwork. He spent hours with his finance guy, they had to get the invoices out for all the work around the Ferretti kidnapping. His team performed flawlessly, and he knew this would provide his company with additional business with other authorities. His company would be off-the-charts busy, and he would need to work with his HR guy to hire more people.

The other thing on his mind was Ale. God he was more confused than ever. He seemed to gravitate towards her without even knowing it. He marveled at her strength. Getting through the last few days was hell and she just rose to the challenge. He'd never met anyone like her. He thought about that day laying on her bed, my God what she had done to him. He wanted to make love to her so bad, and yet he knew if he went down that path, he wasn't sure he could stop. Everything in his life would have to change. To her, it would just be a night of sex. Those were his rules, but he wasn't sure he could follow them.

And then there was O'Malley. She had a soft spot for him, and he wanted to know the story. O'Malley had a reputation with the ladies, but he wanted something different with Ale. Striker knew the feeling. If they shared a past, it would be easy for him to win her over. A pop up appeared on his screen, and it showed Ale was driving home from

Santa Barbara. He also received a text saying Lauren was at Miguels looking for him. *Jeezus.*

CHAPTER 69
Heading Home...

Ale hated leaving her zia and zio, but she had to get home. Her Momma was texting her constantly and she really needed to see her friends. She hadn't been able to tell them anything about the kidnapping, so they made a date to hook up at Miguel's tonight and she couldn't wait. She drove down the highway feeling lighter and a bit happier than she'd felt in weeks. She just happened to arrive at momma's at lunch time. *Coincidence?*

Momma met her at the door and went through the normal ritual of hugging, kissing, and crying. "Oh baby, you look so good. You got some sun." She was turning Ale around and checking her out. Ale wore a pair of jean overall shorts, a tank and low cowboy boots. Momma frowned at the outfit, but Ale was used to that.

"I had a fabulous time with zia; it was just what the doctor ordered." Ale sat down and started filling her plate. Oh wow, momma made her baked ziti. Yesssssss! Papa came through the door, and he received the same treatment from her. Seriously? She just saw him four hours ago. Then again, Ale thought, she would probably be like that with Carlos.

Papa gave her a kiss on the cheek and sat in his chair and momma served him. They had this dynamic that worked. Yes, he could serve himself, but he didn't have to. She wanted to do it, so he let her. Ale smiled at them as they talked quietly in Italian while she made him a plate. She thought about how close they were, how intimate their relationship was. They talked about everything and were so comfortable. It made her grateful to be part of it. So many friends' parents couldn't even stand to be in the same room. Her parents couldn't stand to be apart.

Ale snapped out of it when papa spoke. "How are you?" OK, papa hardly ever asked her a direct question, especially with food in front of him. This was his way of telling her he had been worried. That made Ale sad. The damage Mossimo had caused had ripple effects.

"Good, papa. I feel really good," she said, trying to reassure him; all of them. He nodded. It was all he needed to hear.

They ate and discussed the whole situation in Italian. It depressed all of them.

They both praised Carlos's efforts and Ale asked them to make sure his company was paid for the manpower they provided to keep her safe. Papa nodded. Man of few words, remember?

"You should use the money from my trust fund," Ale said, shovelling the ziti in her mouth.

Papa frowned, and momma spoke up, "Alessandra, please. That is your money; it's for your future."

"I wouldn't have a future, momma, if they had kidnapped me. I say, money well spent. Besides, I have money. I don't even need the trust fund." Ale hated the whole trust-fund thing. She had a large trust fund as part of her real parents' estate that hadn't been touched in 22 years. It grew to an obscene amount. Then papa and momma gave her one when she graduated. She's never used either of them and she didn't plan to.

Momma shook her head. "There is plenty of family money to pay for the help. Don't you worry about it." Papa nodded. OK then.

"Why don't we invite Carlos to dinner one night to thank him personally," momma suggested. Ale knew where this was going. She rolled her eyes and papa smiled at her.

"Momma, please," she said, buttering her bread.

"I just think it's the least we can do. He went above and beyond." Ale thought about their afternoon rolling around on her bed and smiled. He sure did!

She helped momma clean up and headed for her quiet apartment. She made a quick stop at Fortino's to pick up some items for her lunches. Back to work in two days, she had tons of laundry to do, and she needed to sew.

Once she settled into her apartment, she mixed up some dough and set it to rise. She put the whole chicken in the oven to cook and headed in to sew. She sewed for hours while doing the laundry as she wanted to get the pieces back to papa. She texted Danny and went out to the kitchen to remove the chicken and put the dough in pans. Ale texted Gio and Soph to see if they had any updates on the baby. They both replied with "not yet." She sent them the hearts and fingers-crossed emojis. God, she hoped this plan worked. Gio replied: *Glad you are safe.* Always the big brother.

The girls were texting her. Time for a quick shower, a cute sexy outfit, a bit of mascara, and she was out the door heading to Miguel;s. She and Amalia shared a Lyft and the others met them there. *Ole!*

Miguel's was packed as they walked up to the hostess stand and stared straight ahead at Carlos who was sitting in a large booth enjoying a lot of attention from the ladies. He saw Ale, and she turned her head and smiled at Miguel who was waving them towards him. They followed Miguel to their table where Liv and Katee were already waiting. They all hugged as they were all so happy to finally be together. Amalia kept looking at Ale. She saw Carlos too.

As they were absorbed in margaritas and nachos, talking over each other and laughing, it reminded them there is nothing like girlfriends. They just made everything better. Ale listened to their updates, very aware that the update she had to drop would be life changing.

Out of nowhere, a very curvy woman with way too much makeup, beautiful long hair, and a dress that was three sizes too small appeared at their table. She had on six-inch stilettos and carried a Prada knock-off. Her over-inflated breasts were pouring out of her dress. It was hard not to stare at them. Her lips had too much filler and the only thing that came to Ale's mind was Miss Piggy.

"Excuse me," she said, looking directly at Ale. "Are you Ale?"

Ale was sure Miss Piggy already knew she was. "Yup."

She did a fake smile. "I'm Lauren."

Ding, ding, ding. So, this was Lauren. Nothing to worry about, she believed Carlos had said.

"Nice to meet you, Lauren; how can I help?" Ale used her most pleasant voice.

"I thought I should introduce myself. I know you've been spending time with Striker, and I wanted you to know that he and I are in a relationship."

Ale almost burst out laughing. "Oh, congrats. That's great. He was just doing security work for my family," Ale replied.

Lauren cleared her throat. "I know. I just know how women can get other ideas with him and I wanted to just nip it before you got your feelings hurt or anything," she said in a very fake voice. Ale's girls were about to get up and bitch slap her, but she sensed Lauren wanted a scene.

"Good to know. I can assure you, Lauren, he is all yours," Ale said, smiling.

"Great," she said. "Glad we cleared the air. Enjoy your meal." And her big arse walked away.

"Holy butt implants!" Katee said. Katee would have taken Lauren down with a single swing, no contest.

"Anyone else think of Miss Piggy while she was standing there?" Ale asked. Amalia turned her head, trying to stifle her laugh. As a nurse, it pained Ale to see what lengths women would go to with plastic surgery. There was no going back. She applauded and supported those who did it for the right reasons. The others? She just felt sorry for them. Desperate was the word that came to mind.

Now everyone looked sorry for Ale.

"Guys, it's OK. Nothing happened between Carlos and I, and nothing will." Ale drank her margarita and tried to convince herself that she wasn't lying. Instead, she did what she always did and changed the subject by updating them on her kidnapping attempt. They all just stared at her.

Liv was the first to speak. "Jesus, your life is interesting." They all burst out laughing.

They finished up at Miguel's and decided they wanted to go dancing, so they piled into a Lyft and headed over to Gio's nightclub, Spirits. They had an area reserved for family. Ale hadn't been at a night-club in years, but she remembered to turn her phone off before she left so nobody could follow her. *Let's DANCE!*

CHAPTER 70
Moving On...

Ale stumbled home at some point in the middle of the night and could not wait for a shower. She pealed off her clothes and headed straight for the shower. After she cleaned up and dried off, she opened the bathroom door, Carlos was leaning against the door jamb. *Jeeeezus.*

"Christ, don't you knock?" she said, angrily.

"I tried texting you, but someone turned her phone off." He didn't move, just continued staring. Obviously, he was in a bad mood, too.

Shit! Forgot about the phone.

Ale let her towel drop and his eyes lowered. She quickly grabbed her robe and put it on. She started picking up her clothes when she noticed he had her underwear in his hands. "Looking for these?" he said, eyes smiling. She snatched them and threw everything into the hamper. She brushed her teeth and put her wet hair up. She stared at her hair and became emotional, Lauren had beautiful hair.

"Alessandra," he said quietly, "You're upset."

"Nope. All good. Had a great night with friends and now I need my beauty sleep. Would you mind locking up when you leave?" She headed for the bedroom, and he grabbed her arm, gently.

"Ale."

She fought the tears; she really didn't want to cry in front of him. *Jesus.*

"Can I explain?" he asked.

"Nothing to explain." Ale turned around. "We aren't in a relation-ship, like you and Lauren." His eyebrows raised. "She introduced herself to me tonight and basically told me to back off." Carlos looked both surprised and angry.

She continued, "Had I known you had a girlfriend, I wouldn't have had my hands down your pants the other day." Tears were coming, she could feel it.

"Lauren and I are not in any kind of relationship," he said, firmly. He still had her arm and slowly moved his hand down to hold hers. She tried to pull away, but he wouldn't let her. Ale was getting frus-trated, and she wanted him to leave.

"If I *was*, in any relationship, I wouldn't have *allowed* you to put your hand down my pants. And, I certainly wouldn't have been sticking my tongue down your throat or stroking your beautiful breasts." Ale's nipples wanted to say "*Hello.*" She could feel them. She hugged her robe together tighter.

"Carlos, I am very aware of who you are and how you live. I am OK with signing up and getting my night with you, but I am not OK if you have a girlfriend. I don't poach and I don't want the drama."

Ale was hurt, and he could tell. "Understood, I will take care of it," he said.

"OK, Great. Can I go to bed now?"

He looked at the opening of her robe. "Are you having dinner with O'Malley tomorrow?" *SHIT!*

"He asked me over to his place for a barbecue, and I said yes," Ale replied, thinking the two things were not the same.

"So, you can be in a relationship and have your hands down my pants, but I can't? Are those Ale's rules?"

Ale looked at Carlos and he was not happy. She forgot about the stupid phone. Was it the same? Was it a double standard??

"O'Malley is a friend. Can you please stop monitoring my phone? How would you like it if I did that to you?" He handed her his phone. *OK, that didn't work,* she half smiled.

"If you think O'Malley invited you to dinner to eat, you are even more naïve than I thought." He started to leave, and this time Ale grabbed his arm. He stopped and she saw hurt in his eyes.

"Come here," she said and led him into the bedroom. "Please sit." He sat on the bed, she sat on his lap and put his arms around her, then she cradled herself into him. "I'm sorry; I'm being childish."

His muscled arms pulled her closer, and he kissed her forehead. "I'm sorry about Lauren."

She looked at him. "Did we just have our first fight?" she asked, smiling. He took her chin and kissed her, slow and perfect. *Yum.*

"There," he said, "we just made up."

Ale was kind of hoping for more than that, but OK.

"Now, talk to me about O'Malley, please. I think I have the right to know."

Grrrrrr. She sighed. "We have a history. I've known him since school. I, umm, well…" she stalled. "He took my virginity." Carlos's whole body tensed. In one swift move he picked her up, set her on the bed, and headed towards the door. *Oh shit!*

"*CARLOS!*" Ale screamed, he stopped and turned. He was more than angry. He was in kill mode.

"Please, please listen to me," she begged. "He didn't rape me. He didn't do anything wrong. We were kids."

Before she could finish, he interrupted her. "How old were you?" She looked at him. Oh God, was he disgusted?? She felt that shame all over again and she just turned around, tears coming down her face.

He came up behind her so quiet. "Ale." She ran to the toilet, and everything came up. So much for her margaritas and nachos. When she was done and there was nothing left in her body, she cleaned up, brushed her teeth, gargled, and walked back out. He was sitting on the bed again, so she went and sat on his knee.

"I'm sorry," he said, "I didn't mean to upset you. Is this normal that you throw up every time you are upset?"

"Yes."

"Carlos, O'Malley and I didn't intend for it to happen. We were both young and it scared us to death. Up until last week, we'd never even discussed it. Losing my virginity was going to happen at some point. Just my luck it was him."

"I hate that it was him," he said as he held her tighter. "He wants you again, Ale. I know this as he's told me. I need to know if you feel the same. I understand you have a soft spot for him, because of this."

Ale sat up and turned to straddle him.

"I was 17," she said, as Carlos pulled her in and rocked her.

"I was curious. I was a shy, awkward teenager and overprotected. Boys didn't look at me or ask me out. They were terrified of Gio. O'Malley paid attention to me, flirted a bit. When he kissed me, teenage hormones took over and before we knew it." She put her arms up.

"Where?" he asked.

"Zia's bakery." Carlos stared at her. "Not my finest moment. I worked there after school, and he came in before closing. I would give him the stale cupcakes."

"Do you still have feelings for him?" he asked.

"I care about him, as a friend. I *WANT* and have feelings for you." She pulled his head in so she could kiss him again. She wanted to ditch the robe and show him just how much.

"Did he hurt you?" OK, he was still on it.

"It hurt. Obviously, there was blood."

He squeezed her. "Fuck, I want to kill him right now."

"OK ... no. You sound like Gio. Besides, that wasn't the worst part." She hung her head.

He used his finger to bring her chin up. "Finish."

"We, umm, we didn't use protection," she whispered; she couldn't look at him.

"Ale, did he get you pregnant?" he asked, concern all over him.

"Nooo!" God, she hated talking about this. It was 13 years ago. "I worried about being pregnant until my period arrived." She was playing with the belt on her robe, still feeling ashamed.

"Did he know?" The words were coming out as if he was gritting his teeth, attempting to control his anger.

"He knew he didn't wear a condom. My zia went after him, Gio went after him. I thought my family had done something to him. He disappeared after his dad passed and we never heard from him again."

"Jesus, you must have been terrified."

"Please, let's move on. This, is why, I didn't want to tell you." She was wishing to God they could talk about anything else. "It's been a long night and we're both tired. You should go get some sleep and I'll do the same. Deal?"

He nodded.

"Unless you want to stay?" she said, hopeful.

He smiled. "You know I want to stay."

"What's stopping you?"

"You wanted a date."

"Forget I said that." He laughed and pulled her close. "We will have our date and then I will have you naked."

Ale shivered. "OK, but I'm almost naked now!" She was close to begging.

"Be careful of O'Malley, please." He stood up and headed towards the door. "Sweet dreams," he said as he locked the door behind him.

More like wet dreams. *Jeeeezus!*

CHAPTER 71
A Barbecue with O'Malley

Sunday was church day and Ale had missed the last two weekends, so her attendance was expected. She put on her pretty church dress and the family picked her up. She was praying nobody would be shooting at their vehicle while they were driving. Afterwards they went to zia's for brunch.

Zia's home was breathtaking. Every room tastefully and elegantly decorated with no expense spared. It's open-concept floor plan with wall-to-wall windows, which displayed an extended outdoor area with a large pool. The kitchen was state-of-the-art, of course. The furnishings were top of the line. It was a showpiece. Not surprising, zia was a realtor, and she knew her stuff.

Ale's favourite part of being at zia's was cuddling with Pearle, their golden doodle. They usually spent the entire visit in each other's arms. The discussion of the day was Mossimo. Ale still didn't know if they had arrested him, or who the other people were. It was all being kept secret. She felt bad in a way as she couldn't imagine Moss in jail. She thought about Moss as she watched her zia Connie and zio Tony dance around each other in the kitchen laughing. They looked happy. There were rumours that they had an open marriage, and both slept with other people. Her zia had never said anything to her, and she wasn't one to keep secrets. They always looked happy, and they attended all the family functions together. Who really knew?

She chose to ignore it all and just pet Pearle. Plus, she had a barbecue date tonight with O'Malley.

Ale caught a ride home with momma after stopping at zia's café and buying some pastries for her dinner with O'Malley. She decided on a Sunday afternoon nap since she barely had any sleep after Carlos left the night before.

A few hours later, a text woke her up and it was O'Malley saying he was coming to pick her up. She could have driven herself as she still had the SUV Carlos loaned her, but she didn't feel right using it. She asked Carlos to take it back, but he refused.

Ale grabbed a quick shower to wake up and since it was a casual barbecue, she wore a pair of loose button fly jean shorts and oversized light blue long-sleeved T. She wore canvas flip flops and put her hair in a messy wet pony. She went downstairs and he was waiting for her in his cop car.

O'Malley lived on a quiet street in a residential part of LA. It was a two-bedroom Tudor-style house that had been renovated, yet still had some original charm. It was sparsely furnished but had the basics to make you feel comfortable.

They went through to the backyard after the two-cent tour and settled under an outdoor table with a big umbrella. O'Malley had the grill all set up and started lugging out food. O'Malley was long and lean, but he could eat! She asked if he needed help and he declined. He brought out two beers and some potato chips and Ale made herself comfortable. It was nice. Ale loved being outside.

They chatted about Moss. He couldn't really give her any update—ongoing investigation and such. She told him about Gio and Soph going to Italy to maybe adopt a baby. He updated her on his family. All very neutral topics. He had his back to her, showing her his quite lovely ass and his muscled back, as he had a very tight T-shirt on. Something about a man and a grill.

"How's Striker?" he asked, flipping the burgers.

"He's good," she replied, like it didn't matter.

"What's the deal with the two of you?" He turned around to look at her and walked over to sit down. He really had the most brilliant blue eyes, like his mom.

Ale shrugged. "Nothing to tell, really. He's protective of me."

O'Malley smiled that sexy smile and took a drink of his beer. "Ale Cat, he wants more than to protect you; he wants you for lunch."

He stood up to check on the meat. He was melting the cheese on the burgers and God it smelled good. Had it only been a few hours since brunch with zia??? He brought the food over and they dug in. For some strange reason, O'Malley felt comfortable to her. She didn't mind sitting and stuffing a giant burger in her mouth, talking, laughing. He had a sarcastic sense of humour. Truth be told, he and Carlos were night and day. And yet, they both made her nipples happy.

She tried to change the subject and he just smiled and swallowed his burger. She didn't think he even chewed. She was still eating her first one and he was piling on toppings for number two. She liked that he had a good appetite. So did her family. Carlos ate healthy all the time. Who does that?

O'Malley sucked back another beer. He was in his comfort zone, sitting in his back yard, eating his second burger. He loved having a back yard and a barbecue. He really loved that Ale sat across from him, looking so damn sexy in a pair of worn jean shorts and a baggy T-shirt. He could spend the entire day just looking at her. Actually, he'd been doing just that for the past few weeks as part of this kidnapping case. It damn near made him crazy.

She got up to help clean, but he told her to sit. He took the stuff back into the house and brought out the pastries and more beer. She rubbed her belly. "Jesus. O'Malley, even I couldn't shove a pastry in after that dinner. You're very good at barbecuing burgers; that was delicious!" O'Malley smiled, swallowed a chocolate éclair and opened another beer.

Ale tucked a leg under her and leaned back in the chair.

"Carlos thinks you have the hots for me," she said, feeling brave after two beers.

O'Malley grinned. "He'd be right. I've had the hots for you since I was 18 years old. Time hasn't changed a thing."

"Jason." She only used his first name when she was super serious. "I'm not that same scared girl from high school. We are both very different people."

"It doesn't change anything. I'm as horny for you as I was 13 years ago, probably more."

Ale rolled her eyes.

"Your timing sucks," she said.

"Because of Striker?" O'Malley was playing with the label on his beer. "Ale, you know how Striker operates. He makes it clear."

"I know. How do you operate?" she asked. Might as well get to the point.

He laughed. "You are better at this interrogation thing than I am."

"So, answer. You say you are horny for me, so would this be a one-night stand horny thing?"

"I would never do that to you again. I want you in my bed until you get sick of having me around and kick me out. Even then I might not leave." He looked her in the eyes the entire time, he wanted her to know he was sincere.

"Is it just sex you're looking for?" she asked, hanging her head, dreading the answer.

"Ale, I want whatever scrap you will give me. God knows I don't deserve any of it, but I want it. I want you 24/7. In bed and out. I want a real relationship. For the first time in my life, I can say I'm ready."

Ale stood up. Jesus this was too much. What the hell was happening? She walked around a bit and just breathed. When she turned back around, he was standing behind her with his arms crossed.

"How do I know you aren't just saying what you think I want to hear? She had doubts, at least with Carlos she knew the rules. O'Malley always had her on shaky ground.

He walked over and took her face with his hands and gently kissed her. *Mmmmm.* Memories came blooding back. She wanted to push him away but instead she put her hands on his very hard abs and kissed him back. O'Malley usually went from 0–60 when making out. She remembered that, however, this time he just kissed her. He dropped his hands and tucked a curl behind her ear. His eyes told her he was horny and wanted more, as did the large bulge in his jeans.

Ale exhaled. "We shouldn't do that." She rested her head on his chest, keeping her hands on his abs.

"If you want to be with Striker, you need to tell me now." His voice was tight.

"I don't know what I want. I need time. Can you give me that?" she asked.

He wrapped his arms around her and said yes. He felt confident he made some progress tonight.

CHAPTER 72
Back to Work...

It was Monday and Ale's shift started at 7 p.m. Night shift in an LA hospital was always entertaining. Ale and Lacey were there early as they had a meeting with Michael Bennett, chair of the hospital board, to discuss the fundraiser and their proposal for the nurses' calendar.

Ale dressed in a nice pale grey suit with a pencil skirt, a pink camisole underneath, and black pumps. She piled her lunch and all her necessities in her tote and headed to the hospital. She was thankful she had the SUV to drive and didn't have to take the bus in a suit and pumps.

Lacey was waiting for her in the staff lounge. Ale quickly put her stuff away, retrieved her tablet, and the two of them headed for the executive lounge on the top floor near the cafeteria.

Michael Bennett was a very busy man. He was a CEO of a large manufacturing company, as well as a board member for several other non-profits. He believed in giving back and he worked tirelessly to raise money for the Good Samaritan Hospital. It was where his beloved wife, Emma spent her last few hours.

Ale and Lacey were ushered into the large, yet comfortable office. They'd been here a few times, so they knew the drill. Mr. Bennett stood and greeted them, shaking their hands and asking them to sit. He was a handsome older gentleman. Kind and fair. Ale loved working with Mr.

Bennett, she'd spent a great deal of time with his now deceased wife, Emma when she was brought into the hospital years ago.

He started. "First, let me say, from the bottom of my heart, how thankful I am that you are both still here." They both teared up. "Your efforts during the pandemic did not go unnoticed, and your commitment to our patients and to this hospital are inspiring. I need you to hear these words. I want you to always believe that what you do is important and recognized." He stopped and leaned back in his chair, smiling.

Lacey and Ale grabbed tissues and thanked him for his kind, heartfelt words.

"Now, let's get down to business," he continued. "I reviewed your proposals, and I am impressed. You have every detail outlined along with estimated costs. Some days I wish you would both work for my company and manage my accountants." He smiled and looked up. "Talk to me about the calendar. We have some very uptight people on the board. I need to understand the concept."

Ale took him through their ideas and even provided some photos Amalia had taken of her and some of the other nurses just as proofs. She explained it was a view into the personal side of the nurses, seeing them in a new light. A hint of sexy, but not explicit, she also gave him the ROI numbers and he smiled again.

"OK, I want final approval on the photos and the layout. You have my permission to proceed with the calendar." Lacey and Ale were smiling ear to ear.

"Now, the fundraiser. You have three possible dates. We should decide now so we can start booking things. I am hearing the party and fundraising circuit is crazy this year after the pandemic. We need to get ourselves in the line-up." He circled the date he wanted. No discussion.

"I like all the suggestions. I love the idea of bringing back some of our success story patients and I love the idea of having the calendars there for people to buy. I would like when you return with the calendar—and I am assuming it will be for 2024—or...?" He stopped. Lacey explained it would be a twelve-month calendar from April to April, outlining all the hospital events, medical seminars, breast cancer month, all of the awareness programs.

He smiled. "Great thinking. People can put this up on their wall with a lovely photo of our nurses and track their appointments and such." He took notes.

"Before we finish," he said, "there has been an influx of cash donations coming through the anonymous donation box. Would either of you know anything about those? They both shook their heads and he smiled.

"OK then, ladies, you are approved to move forward. I will let Lorraine know to give you access to the allocated funds as you need it. Please ensure all the receipts are kept and let's try to stay on schedule. I will have her book us a review of the calendar layout for two weeks out. Enjoy your shifts." He shook their hands again and ushered them out.

Ale and Lacey giggled the entire way to the change room, Ale grabbed her cell out of her locker and saw a text from Carlos. He had to go out of town. *Please use the SUV,* he wrote. She replied with, *Safe travels and Yes, already using it.* Ale was a bit relieved he was going to be out of town. She needed some serious space from men right now.

She texted Amalia and told her she was hired to do the calendar photoshoot and that they had two weeks to get a layout ready. She had a group text distribution list setup for the nurses who agreed to be photographed. Ale texted them that they were a "go" and laid out next steps. Lacey scheduled a Zoom call for a time when everyone could participate. Ale started with booking the hotel, caterer (Leslie, of course), invitations, and the flowers. She also needed security, and sent another quick text to Carlos. He replied, *Yes, but only if I can be your date.* Ha, she asked if there was anything she could do to get his rates down and received the reply, *LOL. Smart-ass.*

They put their scrubs on and headed to the ER for what would most likely be a crazy night. They got all kinds in during the night shift, so they had to mentally prepare for anything.

The turnover went smooth, and they settled in to take care of existing and new patients. After a few hours, Ale was paged to go to the main desk at the same time as they were notified an ambulance was coming with an elderly lady with congestive heart failure. She paged Dr. Foster who was on-call and took the phone call. It was Pepe. The woman coming in was Diego's mom, Ana. *SHIT.* Ale ran down the hall to receive the gurney and get the room prepped.

CHAPTER 73
La Hermosa Madre de Diego...

Ana Torres was so frail and ill, it made Ale want to weep. She hated when people came in who she knew or cared about. Lacey was hooking up the IVs as they did the transfer from the EMTs. Ana's pulse was weak, she wheezed when she attempted to breathe, her blood pressure was low, and she was very dehydrated. Ale tried talking to her in Spanish, but she wasn't responding. Diego came through the curtain and Ale rushed over to hug him hard. He wrapped his arms around her, and she just held him.

"We are going to take good care of her, OK?" She was looking him in the eyes, forcing him to see her. "We are giving her fluids and we need to be careful as she's already congested. The doctor is on his way. He will most likely prescribe an antibiotic drip."

Diego was nodding, the entire time watching his beautiful mom. Ale looked at Lacey, who gave Ale the OK to take Diego somewhere private. She would continue helping Mrs. Torres. They already increased the security at the hospital. When a gang leader has a family member in the hospital, rival gangs can use that to their advantage. They changed her name in the paperwork and once Dr. Foster did his initial assessment, they'd move her to the VIP floor.

Ale pulled Diego into a consultation room to give him news he didn't want to hear.

"Diego, your mom's in good hands, but I need to be honest with you. Congestive heart failure is typical and sometimes very easy to treat. It can easily return and is sometimes related to organ failure." He glared at her. "We will do a full scan on her, trust me. But I need you to hear me right now. This will be difficult on all of you." He nodded. "You should call your sisters; we are going to move her to the VIP floor where it's more secure and private."

He grabbed her hand and just held it. "She means more to me than anything or anyone. I will provide security," he said. Ale understood what that meant. He opened his jacket and handed her a very heavy and large envelope. "This will take care of everything." Ale thanked him and walked him back to her ER room. Pepe was on guard.

She went in the room to talk to Dr. Foster, explaining the sensitivity around who the patient really was. He understood and gave them their directions. They moved her into a private room up to the VIP floor and took care of all the paperwork. Ale dumped the bag of money off to the finance office and headed back to VIP. It was slow in ER, so Lacey told her to go to VIP and she would page her if things got crazy.

Ale knocked lightly and went into the room. Diego had his rosary out and was praying. It would seem odd to anyone who didn't know him. Ana's color was returning, but she had yet to open her eyes. Her pulse was better, and her blood pressure was improving. She would get through this episode, but Ale was very concerned about what would come next. Dr. Foster had ordered multiple tests on her, including bloodwork. They will do scans tomorrow if or when she woke up.

Ale went over and wrapped her arms around Diego's neck from behind and hugged him and he kissed her arm. Ana Torres looked like an angel sleeping. She was a petite lady with a beautiful smile. She adored her family. She had lost a husband, brother and two sons to gang violence. She was more than rugged. His sisters arrived and Ale escorted them in quietly. Everything and everyone who came to VIP came in a different entrance. Good Samaritan Hospital had the VIP floor for just that reason. Because it was LA, they had patients that required privacy for whatever reason. People were stupid and would take photos and sell them, paparazzi will be all over, gang riots would break out. They had to be extra careful. The VIP floor also provided the patients with "anything" they wanted. The rooms were like hotel rooms, but you paid for it.

Ale let Diego and his family know she was going up for something to eat and told him to have her paged if he needed her. She had left the Disney phone home. She met Lacey in the cafeteria and had herself a little cry. Seeing a tough-as-nails gang leader break down over his ill mother was more than the heart could take. They ate together and continued with the fundraising. It was a nice distraction.

Before heading back to VIP, Ale made a call to Carlos. She never called him, so he picked it up quickly. "Ale? What's wrong?"

She tried hard not to break down. "Hey, sorry to bother you. I, umm have to tell you something, but you have to keep it private."

"OK" he said, waiting, worrying. It was 2 a.m. What could be this important?

"Diego's mom is here, congestive heart failure," she said, crying. Carlos knew about her strange relationship with Diego and Pepe, and he had kind of made peace with it.

"Shit," he said, "How can I help?"

Ale smiled. "You're helping by listening."

This news worried Carlos. Gangs with ill family members were always a target, so the hospital could be a target, too. There was silence and finally he said, "Take good care of them. They need you, Ale."

YES, exactly what she needed. "Yes, I will do that. Thanks for listening."

"Anytime baby. Be careful." They hung up and Carlos texted some of his team to have them watch Ale, just in case.

The VIP floor was quiet as Ale headed to Ana's room. She knocked and entered. Ana was awake and sitting up with a big smile. She put her arms out to Ale and she wanted to run into them. "Alessandra!" Ale had nursed Ana a few times in the past and they bonded over her son.

Ale smiled. "Well, look who's awake." Ale walked over and gave her a kiss. She checked her vitals and reconnected a new fluid bag. Diego and his sisters were at the other side of the room that had a couch and some chairs. Pepe stood by the door. Ale checked her heart rate and her pulse.

"You gave us a scare, Ana," Ale said in Spanish, of course. Ana smiled and patted her hand.

"I like to keep them guessing." She winked at Ale. God, she loved this lady.

Ale excused herself and went to get Dr. Foster. He came in and did his assessment. He was very, pleased with her progress and felt she could eat real food, so Ale went to get some Boost and a straw. They set the tests up for the morning and Ale was supposed to be off shift at 7 a.m. Dr Foster requested she work a double as she had the relationship with the family. Ale gave the good news to Diego and his siblings that she would be staying on to help with their mom and assist with getting her heart tests completed. She also advised them that they will need full-time nursing care at home. Both of his sisters, Sonya and Ana Paula said they would do it, but Ale shook her head.

"Sonya, this is far too much. She will need around-the-clock care. Trust me when I tell you that you will want a nurse there if anything goes wrong." Ale understood the need for a family to want to care for their elders. She respected it. There comes a time, though, when it's too much.

"Diego, I have names of some Spanish-speaking nurses who are discreet. I've worked with them before, and they would welcome the income. I will text their names them to you." He nodded.

Ale went back to the main desk and grabbed her phone. You could have your phone on the VIP level. She texted her nurse friends to see if they were available. They had had fabulous nurses here at Good Samaritan, but they just couldn't deal with the shifts. A number of them went to work for private companies who did at-home care. The concern with this job was the security. Nobody knew where Diego lived. A driver will pick you up, blindfold you and take you to his home. You visit or work and they blindfold you again and take you back. Some people might not be OK with that.

Ale continued to monitor Ana. She drank some Boost but she wasn't very interested in real food. At 9 a.m. she got Ana ready. She sponge bathed her tiny body, reassuring her and soothing her. She checked for bed sores and put lots of lotion on her. She tied on her gown, and they wheeled her down to have the dye test. Ale was fairly certain Dr. Foster suspected something; however she was not prepared when Dr. DeAngelo, chief of Cardiac Care, came out with the results. Ale had to keep it together. Ana had two blockages and needed a valve replacement. She would never survive either of those procedures.

They took Ana back and got her settled in the bed while the family fussed. Ale needed a minute to compose herself. She asked Diego and his sisters to come out and she took them to a meeting room. Ale called it the Bad News Room. Dr. DeAngelo came in, introduced himself, and turned the lights off so he could show them the photo of her heart. They all sobbed. Ale grabbed Diego and just held on to him. They asked questions in Spanish and Ale translated. They knew they had a long and difficult journey ahead of them.

At times like this, they had to suggest palliative care, however the family was adamant they would hire people and care for Ana at home, unless, of course, she was suffering. Sadly, that time would come. Ale gave them time to be alone and advised them to try and stay positive for their mom's sake.

Additional nurses were called in to help in ER as Ale was staying in VIP for a while. She had an idea to help with Ana's refusal to eat. She went down and grabbed what was left of her original lunch and brought it upstairs. She heated up her homemade soup and pulled out a piece of homemade bread, buttered it, and took it in to see if Ana would try it.

At first, Ana made a face that told Ale she wasn't interested, but then she picked up the spoon and explored what was in the bowl and decided to take a small taste. She smiled. Ohhhhhh... she liked it!

"You make this??" Ana asked in Spanish.

"Si."

"And the bread too?" She was eating the bread as well.

"Si."

"Am I eating your lunch, Alessandra?" she asked, smiling.

"Si," Ale said, and everyone laughed.

"Diego, you should marry this one; she can cook. The wives you have only know how to have babies." Ana kept spooning the soup into her mouth and Diego shook his head.

Now that they had her eating food, they would keep her a bit longer to make sure her other bodily functions were operating before sending Ana home. Ale worked through until the morning of the next day and did a turnover with another VIP nurse who was also fluent in Spanish. VIP floor patients could be very picky. Ale told them she would bring in some more soup and bread later that day, and Diego asked if he could place orders so she could have it at home. Of course! She gave them all hugs and left.

When she walked out to her SUV, all the tires were slashed. *WTF?*

CHAPTER 74
What Now??

Ale always sensed that even though they told her they have the people responsible for her potential kidnapping, it was too good to be true. Ramone and company rescued her from work that day and gave her a new SUV. The camera footage of the parking lot just showed someone in the night with a hoodie. It was deliberate vandalism only to her vehicle.

Ale kept rolling. She made batches of soup and bread and Pepe picked them up discreetly, of course. Ana was home and they had full-time care hired to take care of her. Ale promised she would visit on her days off.

She worked through her next set of shifts which were midnight to noon. Again, her tires had been slashed. The StrikeForce team gave up and Ramone became her chauffeur again. Carlos was still out of town. He had texted her, but he was very busy. That's OK. So was she. When she wasn't working, she was cooking, baking, and getting a calendar ready, along with a fundraiser.

Amalia loved doing the photo shoots for the calendar and they asked Katee to help as she has done a few. Ale loved the photos, and she couldn't wait to do the layout and show Mr. Bennett. All the photos were tasteful and interesting. Ale's photos had been taken at the beach near a rocky shore. Mal had her dressed in jean shorts, a silk camisole, cowboy boots, and a straw cowboy hat. She had her leaning back against the rock as the sun was setting. It was the most beautiful photo Ale had ever seen. Mal's talent was wasted on accounting. Eye roll.

Ale was putting the calendar layout together on her kitchen table when she heard her locks click, along with her heart. Carlos peeked in and she jumped up and ran to him. She kissed him like she meant it. Gosh, she really missed him, and apparently, he missed her too.

"Babe, you feel good." He kept rubbing her against him. *Yup, so did he.*

"I missed you." He just kept kissing her neck and feeling her up through her shirt.

"It's been crazy. Fucking criminals," he said finally releasing her and heading to the fridge. This time he took a beer. "You want one?" he asked while opening the bottle.

"No, I'm good." She went back to the table to start cleaning up. Carlos spotted the photo.

"What's this?" his eyes darkened. "Who took these?" He wasn't happy.

"Amalia, my friend. We're putting a nurses' calendar together to raise money for the hospital." He just kept staring at the photo. "Do you like it?" Ale asked, hoping he liked it as much as she did.

"I can see your nipples," he said. *OK... seriously?*

Ale loved the photo and her nipples were barely showing. "Sooo... that means you don't like it?"

He sat down. "So, every guy in LA is going to buy this calendar and stare at my girl's nipples all through the month of February?" he asked.

Ale started to laugh. Not a good move, but she couldn't help it. He wasn't laughing. "Carlos, it's a beautiful photo. I'm proud of it and Amalia did a great job."

He shook his head. "I didn't think my week could get worse," he said, staring at the photo.

"OK. How about we photoshop the nipples? Are you OK with the rest of it?"

Jesus, this was really upsetting him. She knew a large number of women, especially in LA, who enjoyed posting almost nude or nude photos on the internet. Ale didn't use social media but her friends and family did. She actually thought this was classy and tasteful, but if you looked really close you saw nipples and he would only ever see nipples. Story of her life.

"It's beautiful, Ale. YOU are beautiful. My God, I'd have to be dead not to love this. In fact, I want one, a big one for my wall, with the nipples. But only ME. The photoshopped one can go into the calendar." He wasn't negotiating and she wasn't pushing the issue.

"OK, that's fair. Thanks babe." She bent down to kiss him, and he pulled her on his lap and stuck his tongue down her throat. He has mentioned on occasion that he doesn't share, and that Latinos are very territorial. Ale was sure she got a taste.

Ale texted Amalia and she LOL'd her and sent them an updated photo right back.

"Better?" Ale asked. Carlos nodded, all the while staring at the nippled one. She was some glad she showed it to him before they made the calendar. She cleaned up the table and took his hand and led him to her couch. "Tell me what's got you so worked up, besides my nipples."

"Any idea who is slashing your tires? Ale asked. He shook his head.

"Tell me about your date with O'Malley," he said, continuing to admire her PJs. .

"It was nice. Great food and conversation."

He just stared at her.

"We are not discussing O'Malley," she said. "You're picking fights. What's going on?"

"I don't feel like talking." He rested his head on her shoulder.

"You hungry? I have enough soup and bread to feed the neighbourhood. It's the only thing keeping Mrs. Torres alive."

He looked at her, confused. "How is she?"

"Not good. She has two blockages and needs a valve replacement, and she's too frail for the procedures. We couldn't get her to eat, so I fed her my soup and bread and she loved it. So now Diego is paying me to make her food. She has fulltime care at home, but she won't get better."

"I'm sorry," he said, kissing her neck. "I'm shocked Diego didn't convince you to be her private nurse."

"He tried," she said, moving her head to the side so he had better access.

"It's no wonder he's in love with you—now you are making his mom food."

Ale wasn't biting. She looked at him. "Babe, do you need me to take the edge off? Because I am happy to do that."

He finally smiled. "Yeah, that would be nice. I'd rather we get naked and just fuck our brains out."

SHIT! Yes please!

"OK." She grabbed his arm to pull him up and pulled her back down. "Are you seriously teasing me again? I don't give two shits about the date. Come on, you need this, and God knows I do. I will beg if you want."

He kissed her deep and hard. Her toes curled. He really needed a release. She reached down to stroke him, and he groaned.

"Babe, let me help," she said, kissing his neck and rubbing against him.

He stopped. "What plans do you have tomorrow?"

"Mac, yoga, momma lunch, meeting at hospital, visit with Mrs. Torres." *SHIT.* She should have left that last one off.

"Excuse me?" he said.

"She perks up when I visit, Carlos. I have to. She won't be here long."

"No. Ale. Fuck, it's dangerous, you know this. Are you trying to piss me off?" He looked so tired and stressed.

"No, I'm sorry." She hugged him and thought, *I need to get him out of here.*

"She stood up. You have three options, 1. Go home and get some sleep. 2. Stay and sleep with me, no sex. 3. And my personal favourite, sleep here AND have sex with me. What's it going to be?"

He smiled. "I want to stay with you."

Great, option two; this will be fun.

"OK, let's go to bed. You're tired." They headed towards the bedroom. She didn't even want sex at this point. *Jesus.*

"OK, if I shower?" he asked.

"Of course." She showed him where everything was. He went into the bedroom, opened a drawer in the bottom of her platform bed, and pulled out a toiletry bag with some underwear. *Seriously?? When did he put stuff in there???*

Ale brushed her teeth and went to bed. Carlos crawled in, smelling yummy and was asleep immediately. Go figure.

CHAPTER 75
Fundraising...

Waking up with a sexy Latino in her bed was the best thing ever. Of course, it would have been, if Carlos was still *in her bed*. Carlos was gone, and her heart dropped. Ale had abandonment issues, having lost her parents so young and being put into Foster care. She struggled.

When Ale first moved in with her momma and papa, she screamed every morning when she woke up. They were beside themselves, trying to figure out why. Her momma would hold her tight and rock her and Ale just sobbed. Finally, they solved the mystery. It happened when Ale woke up and papa was gone to work. The days he didn't work, Ale was fine. From that point on, papa would gently wake her up, kiss her, and tell her he was going to work. Then he'd reassure her and tell her he would be home for dinner. He did this every damn day.

Ale was OK if you had to leave, she just liked to know that you're going and would rather be woken up.

She put it behind her as she had a crazy busy day ahead. She met Mac for her workout and did her yoga. Then, it was on to pick up momma and take her to the hospital with her for their meeting with Mr. Bennett as well as go to the hotel to solidify some of the plans for the fund raiser. Ramone was still chauffeuring her around.

Mr. Bennet approved the nurses' calendar layout. Out of spite, Ale almost replaced her photoshopped picture with the nippled one. They reviewed the fundraiser plans and Lacey updated them with staggering numbers as 75 per cent of the tickets for the fundraiser had already been sold online. Their tickets were $500 each. It sounded like a lot of money, however they were in LA. They were also organizing a silent auction as they always brought in large amounts of money. Lacey updated them with the amazing donations they received for bidding. NBA, MLS, NHL and NFL tickets for local teams. Hotel stays, spa sessions, restaurant coupons, golfing, airline coupons. Seriously, Lacey was kickass at this stuff. She and Ale couldn't contain their excitement.

After their meeting, they drove to print shop to drop off the calendar layout and then headed over to the hotel to discuss and agree on the plans. Lacey had other errands to do, so momma and Ale went to the hotel and decided to stay and have lunch. Momma was very experienced in fundraising, so Ale loved having her tag along. They met with Ashley, the event planner for the Hoxton where they had her birthday party. They reviewed the numbers and toured the ballroom going over Ashley's proposed setup. They needed a separate secure room for the auction, a dance floor, and a stage with associated audio and separate round tables. Leslie and her team would coordinate with the hotel restaurant, like they did for her party. They signed off and Ale gave Ashley a deposit cheque.

Momma and Ale found a table near the window and sat down to have lunch. They were both dressed up today. Ale was in a navy-blue fitted dress with a square neck and momma was in an emerald-green dress that hugged her body and made her big brown eyes even brighter. Her beautiful ginger hair was down today and, as usual, everyone turned to smile at momma when she walked into the restaurant. It happened all the time!

They placed their order and she smiled at Ale. "Thank you, honey, for including me in your errands today. It was nice to get out and spend time with you." She reached across the table and grabbed Ale's hand.

"No problem. I love having you around. We need to do this more often." Ale was looking out the window feeling a bit off. They accomplished a lot today, so why was she feeling so restless?

"Something's bothering you. What's going on in that head of yours?" Momma asked, taking a drink of her water and pushing back a curl from Ale's face. Ale's phone was beeping in her bag and being annoying. She took it out, just in case it was an emergency, and looked at the screen. Leslie needed a server for tonight for a posh party in Beverly Hills. She replied yes. The rest were people sending her links of photos of Lauren and Carlos together. Ale had no idea when they were taken, but Lauren was saying it was last week. Well, that explained a lot. OK, she shut the phone off and apologized to momma.

"Did you like the photo of me in the calendar, momma?" she asked, feeling very insecure. "Oh Ale, it's stunning. Amalia did an amazing job. All the photos are so beautiful and natural. It's a fabulous concept." Ale smiled and waited while the waiter brought their lunch and left.

"We had to photoshop mine. Apparently, my nipples were obvious on the original," Ale said, whispering.

Momma broke out laughing. "Oh, those damn nipples. I've been taping and hiding them since you were eleven." Ale started to laugh. It was true. Nipples had ruled her life, especially when she started to develop. Poor momma didn't know what to do. They sewed pieces of fabric into every bra and top she owned.

They talked about Gio and Soph, as they were both worried. It must be hard for Gio as he had the business to run as well. They had lawyers involved and the Italian and American governments to deal with. Ale couldn't imagine that they are just going to show up with the baby. They would probably have to go back and forth for a while to finalize things. Would it take years? It was daunting.

They finished lunch and dropped momma off at the apartment. Ramone drove Ale back to her place and she told him she would be heading out again to serve at a party. She remembered to turn her phone back on, changed out of her dress, and put her serving uniform on. Tonight, it was a white buttoned up long-sleeved shirt, a burgundy tie, and a black pencil skirt. She would put on a burgundy apron once she arrived. She put her hair up in a tight bun, changed out her jewellery, and headed back out the door. Sometimes it was good to stay busy.

CHAPTER 76
Party in Beverly Hills, Baby...

The party tonight was at the Griffin Club in Beverly Hills. Ramone dropped Ale off and told him she would text when she was done. Ale headed towards the kitchen area where they received their orders for the night. Seriously rich assholes would be here tonight, so they were all warned on how to behave. Leslie would be keeping an eye on everything. The security was provided by the club itself.

They started with the usual, circling with champagne and appetizers. Tonight, however, there would be a formal sit-down dinner, too. Lots of big heavy trays and loads of food. After dinner, they would remove the dishes from the tables and bus boys would hike them back to the kitchen. The kitchen staff would take it from there. Everything went off without a hitch, the crowd enjoyed the food, nobody dropped anything. Aside from a few fussy eaters, for the most part it went very well.

The large dance floor had a DJ setting up. They cleared all the dishes, and Ale was circling with a tray to do a double check. The bar was opened so people could get their own drinks, or they could use the wait staff to order. She was only serving, so she could leave after this last walk around.

She walked outside the event room towards the kitchen so she wouldn't be in the way and an arm grabbed her and spun her around.

"Ale? Is that you?" Lauren burst out laughing. "Serving fucking meals at a country club? Are you fuckin' serious? You're the goddamn help?" It was Miss Piggy. Wearing another too small sequin halter dress with her gross breasts swinging freely. She took out her phone and snapped Ale's photo. "Cannot wait to post this," she said laughing.

"Oh, hi Lauren, nice to see you again," Ale said, chewing her tongue off. She turned to leave and get the fuck out of there when Lauren grabbed her again. This time Ale shook her off and Lauren stumbled. Ale took self defense, so she could lay this chick out in a flash, but she didn't want trouble for Leslie.

"Woah." Lauren put her arms up. "Easy there, working girl. Does Striker know you wait on tables? I thought you were a nurse or something?" Ale wanted to wipe that stupid smile off her face. "Striker and I had a great time last week in Miami," she said, looking for a reaction.

"Good, I'm glad. If you'll excuse me, Lauren, my shift is over." Ale walked to the kitchen, pushed open the door, and grabbed a bottle of water from the fridge. She really wanted tequila. Leslie came over to give her an envelope.

"Hey, you OK? Oh jeeze, Ale, was someone rude or inappropriate to you?" Leslie asked, grabbing her into a hug. She must have looked a bit off.

Ale hugged her back. "No, I'm OK, honey. All good, everything is cleared up out there." Ale said, reassuring her.

"Thanks so much, I know it was last minute." Leslie gave her a kiss and stuffed the envelope into her hand.

"No problem. Sorry I haven't been available much. That should change now. Oh, I sent you the details for the fundraiser dinner! Thanks again. I will talk to you later." Ale grabbed her bag, shoved the money in and found her phone to text Ramone. It was almost midnight, and she was ready for a shower and her comfy bed.

They drove home in silence and Ale told him she wasn't going anywhere the next day, thanked him, and said good night. She hoped to God nobody was in her apartment because she was NOT in the fuckin' mood. She had a nice long hot shower and climbed into bed. She knew why she hasn't had a date in years: men were assholes. How did she forget that??

CHAPTER 77
Rebel with a Cause...

Ale slept well, despite her Miss Piggy encounter. She walked into the kitchen and made a batch of dough to get bread started. She did a whack of sewing for papa and texted Danny to let him know it was ready for pick up. She grabbed her Disney phone and texted Pepe to pick her up in the back of her building, as she wanted a visit with Ana. She didn't care what Carlos thought. She would leave her other phone home so they wouldn't track her. Afterwards, she would have Pepe drop her off at the beach and she could take the bus home.

Seeing Ana was difficult as Ale could already see what others could not. She was slowly deteriorating. Ale kept up her smile and held her hand for a bit. She checked her over and spoke to the nurse. Diego was not home, but she spoke with his sisters and told them what she was seeing. She wanted and needed them to be prepared. Pepe drove her back. After a certain point, she could remove her blindfold.

"*Hermosa*, you seem sad, is the big guy giving you trouble?" Pepe asked smiling that devilish smile.

Ale had to be careful. One word and Striker would be on a hit list. She thought it funny that they called Striker "the big guy" since Pepe was much larger.

She sighed. "You could say that." She was looking out at the traffic as they headed towards the beach.

"You need help?" he asked.

"No, I just need some time to think about stuff. Lots going on with the kidnapping, fundraising, worrying about Ana. I don't have room for the male drama."

"You know the deal with Striker, right?" Pepe was strangely easy to talk to. It made Ale miss Soph.

"Yeah, I know, I'm OK with that. I've told him. But I think he has other interests. I need to let it go and move on." Ale sounded and felt defeated.

"You referring to that *puta* posting naked photos all over the place?" He was watching the cars in front of him with ease.

"Yeah." Ale looked over at him. He always wore sunglasses, but he had the kindest eyes she'd ever seen. When she first met him, she could not believe he was the infamous Pepe.

"Hermosa, you are a beautiful and kind lady with class. Don't go into the gutter with that. She's desperate. I'm sure Striker is not interested. He might have tapped it years ago, but he is private, and he is selective. This one is *loco*. You want some advice from Pepe?" he smiled, and she smiled back.

"Sure."

"Make whoever it is work for it. My guess is Striker is interested in you because you are discreet. There are beautiful and sexy women all over LA. Problem is, they like attention. You don't like attention. You don't need it. A man like Striker doesn't have time for needy. He runs a tight ship, and he needs to stay focused. You are a nice distraction, believe me. Diego and I adore you because you are discreet, and you are kind. You don't find a lot of kind these days." He parked near the beach and turned to her.

"Thank you, Pepe." She leaned over and kissed him on the cheek. "I adore you, too. Thank you for always looking out for me." She meant it, she knew she could always count on them, no matter what. It was a weird friendship that nobody would ever understand, but they did.

"If he hurts you hermosa, I will kill him," he said firmly. Ale believed him. She thanked him for the drive and the advice and headed to beach. She needed the sun and sand.

CHAPTER 78
Out of His Mind...

Carlos sat in his mom's kitchen listening to her go off on him for the third time. Make no mistake, Rosa Montoya had opinions and they were strong. All the while, she was making him lunch. He thought he would stop by for a nice quiet visit, but she had other plans. Thank God Justina wasn't here. He wasn't in the mood. He had to take it from his ma; he didn't have to take it from his sister.

He nodded and listened. She wasn't happy with him. Somehow, she knew about the posts from Lauren, she knew that nothing had moved forward with Ale. She couldn't understand him. What did she do wrong? How could he get her hopes up and then let her down? Fuck, if he was a drinker, he would be halfway through the bottle by now.

"Ma, sit, *por favor.* You're giving me a headache," he said, pulling the chair out. He was afraid she was going to have a stroke.

She sat down and stared at him. "Carlos, what are you doing? You found a nice girl and you told us, right here in this kitchen that you thought she was the '*one.*' And now this? What is wrong with you?" Her arms were moving the entire time.

"Please don't believe all you see on social media, ma. I am doing nothing with Lauren, I promise you."

She held her hand to her heart. "What about Ale? That sweet girl.

Carlos, please tell me she isn't going to be a conquest for you. It's time for you to grow up. Don't you dare mess with that girl. She deserves to be treated special." She was pleading.

"I know this, and I'm trying to figure it out. There is a lot you don't know, and I cannot tell you," Carlos said, rubbing his forehead.

"She can't be happy about this stuff all over the internet about you. Have you spoken to her?" she asked, taking his hand.

"Not today. Actually, I'm thinking of walking away from her and leaving her alone. I'm not able to give her what she deserves or needs." Carlos had been feeling this way for a while. He wasn't relationship material. He knew that. He knew Ale agreed to his rules, but he would never forgive himself if he hurt her or made her feel differently about herself.

His mom started to cry. *Jesus.* This visit was a mistake.

"Carlos, is this about your father? This behaviour of yours, it's self-destructive. I hear nothing but wonderful things about this girl. A good family, she has a great career, works hard, she's beautiful. What are you looking for? Why are they never enough?" She was getting more upset.

"It's never about them, ma. It's me. I'm a busy guy, and I like my life the way it is. I don't want or need drama. I have physical needs and I don't want to use Ale that way." At least he was being honest.

"Then, you should move on without her and leave her alone. She does deserve better." She got up and went over to counter to finish making lunch.

He knew what he had to do and would do it. For both their sakes.

CHAPTER 79
Money & Pizza...

Ale took the bus home from the beach and felt more like herself than she had in weeks. She showered and grabbed her phone. She'd missed a ton of texts and calls but didn't care. She threw the phone on the counter. Danny had been there and dropped off more sewing and cash. The cash. *Shit*. She had it everywhere. Envelopes from Leslie last night and several from papa. Ale quickly bundled it up and stuffed it into the safe. She really needed to count it all and do something with it. It reminded her that she needed to check her bank account. She'd been operating on the cash and had no idea what her balance was. Her pay went into her accounts automatically, and during COVID she worked so much overtime. Not to mention that she hadn't spent any money as she couldn't go anywhere.

She grabbed her tablet and signed in. *SHIT*. She had over $300,000 in her bank account alone. She needed to talk to Gio. He would know what to do with it. Her phone beeped and she looked at it: O'Malley. He was downstairs with a Vito's pizza. *YUM*. She gave him the apartment number and buzzed him up.

She opened the door when he knocked and smiled. She was very happy to see him. Oh, and he had beer. He strolled in with the goodies, and she gave him a hug. He was dressed in jeans and a T-shirt and had a big smile on his face.

"This is a nice surprise." She meant it.

"I took a chance you'd be home. Nice place, Ale." He walked around and made himself at home. He stared at her diplomas and then looked at her with his eyebrows raised. "Seriously? Over-achiever. That is impressive." He walked into the bedroom, and she reluctantly followed him. "Is this where the magic happens?" he asked, looking at the bed.

"Yes, but not on the bed—with the sewing machines." He turned around and saw the sewing corner.

"Wow, you're sewing for Vito?" he asked.

"Yeah, and I sew for me, too." She walked back out to the kitchen, and he followed.

"Thanks for bringing pizza and beer. I was getting hungry." She started putting out plates and cutlery.

"Ale, you don't need to be fancy with me."

Momma raised her well, you always set the table!

They sat at her little round dining table, and she couldn't wait to dig in; she loved Vito's pizza.

"How was your day?" she asked.

"Quiet. Ran some errands, visited with Meg, and went to my nephew's soccer game. You?" he was on his second slice and Ale was still on her first.

"Good. Went to the beach." She sucked back the cold Corona and it tasted incredible.

He looked up at her and smiled that sexy smile. "You should have called me."

She gave him a look. "I have carrot cake," she said, changing the subject. Just then they heard the locks on her door unlock. O'Malley reached for his gun that wasn't there, and Ale just rolled her eyes. "It's Striker," she said, calmly.

Carlos stuck his head in and stared at O'Malley.

"Hi," she said, getting up to get another plate. "You want some pizza?"

"Sure." He nodded to O'Malley and sat down. Ale put a plate and some cutlery down in front of him and brought him a beer. This wasn't awkward at all. O'Malley rolled his eyes and Ale smiled.

"What brings you here?" she asked innocently. Ale knew it was because she hadn't answered any of his texts or calls or probably that someone saw O'Malley show up.

"I have an update for you on the kidnapping case." He said looking right at her. Her body tensed and O'Malley straightened as well.

"They released Mossimo," he said, reaching for her hand. She just stared at him. *What?* she thought, *Please tell me she heard wrong.*

"Why?" She just lost her appetite. O'Malley kept shovelling it in.

"No proof he initiated the kidnapping. He claims he was just a victim." Carlos finished chewing and wiped his face. He took a drink and never took his eyes off her.

"A victim?" she said, trying to understand.

"So, what now?" Jesus, she thought this shit was over.

"My guess is 'the family' will take care of it." Carlos looked at O'Malley and then back to her.

Ale stood up and ran to the bathroom. Yup, it was coming up, all of it. Carlos and O'Malley were right behind her, but she slammed the door and locked it.

"You had to tell her while she was eating?" O'Malley said, disgusted.

"She needed to know." Carlos was in no mood for O'Malley.

"Ale, you OK?" O'Malley talked through the door.

God, she wished they would both leave. So much for her great day; she should have checked her phone. That would teach her. She cleaned herself up and walked out towards the sink, brushed her teeth, and wiped her face. They were both standing there looking at her.

"I'm OK." She looked at Carlos. "How did you find out about this?" she asked.

"I went there last week."

Ale had a confused look on her face. "You went to Italy?" she asked with a frown. *What about Miami with Lauren?* she wondered.

"Yes, I wanted to look the fucker in the eyes," he said walking back to the table and finishing his beer.

Carlos turned and handed Ale his keys. "I am giving you your keys back. I've stopped monitoring your phone and I've removed Ramone from driving you around. You have your life back." He turned and walked out the door.

Ale just stood there. *What the hell was going on?* Tears streamed down her face and O'Malley grabbed her and wrapped her in a hug as she started to sob. "Fuckin' asshole," he whispered, kissing the top of her head. "It's OK, shhhh." Ale just hung on.

"You mentioned carrot cake?" he said, and she broke out laughing. She could always rely on him to find the humour in anything. She cut him a large piece of cake and she took a small one to see if she could keep it down. She stuck to water, and he took another beer. They sat in the living room where it was more comfortable. Ale pulled her knees up and covered them in a blanket.

"Thanks O'Malley. I don't know what just happened. He's been acting weird lately and I was told he was in Miami last week; I had no idea he went to Italy. I have too many questions," she said, slowly eating her cake.

"I'm glad he's staying away from you; you deserve better, Ale," he said, putting the empty plate down. She guessed he liked the cake. Her heart hurt. She was being strong in front of him, but she was really, really upset. O'Malley stayed a bit longer and helped her clean up. When he left, he gave her a hug and a kiss on the cheek. She shut out the lights and went to bed, crying herself to sleep.

CHAPTER 80
Life Goes On, Until It Doesn't...

Ale managed to put Carlos behind her. She had so much to do to prepare for the fundraiser and the last thing she wanted was to pine over a guy who obviously didn't want her. They had to interact on security details and events where she served for Leslie, however they were both civil and professional. Her heart always skipped a beat when she saw him, but she figured that would disappear in time. She worked her shifts and went back into her normal, single routine. She had the occasional meal with O'Malley but kept him at a distance. She just wasn't ready or willing to do anything more in the relationship.

Gio returned without Soph as she was staying with the baby. They had a few more hurdles to get through before they could bring the baby home, however Gio had business dealings that required his attention. Ale never asked about Moss; she was afraid to. She figured they would never hear from him again.

A week before the fundraiser, Ale was busy sewing Lacey's dress when her Disney phone beeped. She ran over and received the news she never wanted to hear; beautiful Ana Torres was gone. Peacefully and at home. Ale wept. *Dios te bendiga, Ana.*

The funeral would be private, as expected, and all Ale could do was send messages via Pepe.

CHAPTER 81
The Fundraiser...

Ale was super excited the Good Samaritan Annual Fundraiser and Auction was finally here! The entire crew did an amazing job of organizing, this night would be like no other.

Ale's dress was a black sheer sexy number, sewed with her own hands. It was a halter dress with a deep V in the front and back, revealing a lot of skin. The skirt had a sheer cover, which floated as she walked, and it draped all the way to the floor. The rose gold necklace from zia and the matching earrings from momma finished off her look. Her hair was pinned back at the nape of her neck, in a messy, curly bun.

Lacey's dress was very much the opposite. Ale made her a beautiful deep purple sequined dress with a sweetheart bodice and a flair skirt that suited her figure perfectly. She also wore her hair up and borrowed Ale's diamond string earrings. The two of them spent the morning together at the Sunflower Spa getting pampered and ready.

The fundraiser was completely sold out, which meant 200 people had paid $500 apiece just to attend. The silent auction was set up and secure, and Ale let Lacey deal with Striker on the logistics. A booth was on display near the front so people could buy the nurses' calendar as they entered. The stage where Mr. Bennett would say a few words had been audio tested and the DJ area was directly beside it. The guest tables and flowers completed the elegant look.

Ale checked in with Leslie regarding the food and gave her a big hug. This fundraiser was a huge deal for both of them. Leslie promised her she would take a few minutes to enjoy the event, however Ale knew her friend would work herself to the bone to ensure everything food related was perfect. The servers were starting to mingle with champagne and appetizers, the bar was open and staffed. *It was Show Time!*

Ale and Lacey greeted the guests as they entered. Attendees included nurses, doctors, actors, politicians, athletes, you name it. *Thus, the need for security.* Oh, and they had the Ferretti's, an entire table of them: Momma and zia Connie never missed a fundraiser. Some of the non-paying guests included nurses and some former patients, specifically children, who had been born with addiction and were able to thrive and be adopted. They were the hospital's true success stories. These beautiful little souls represented the hope they wanted to share with their contributors. Ale couldn't wait to see some of the former patients again.

The excitement in the air was exhilarating. People loved being social again, even at $500 a pop. It made Ale want to put the price up for the next fundraiser. Mr. Bennett was their MC and he always did a great job. He made everyone feel comfortable, while promoting the hospital and telling pathetic dad jokes. Everyone still laughed. They were the luckiest hospital in the world to have him at the helm.

Everyone was enjoying the six-course meal, talking and laughing. Wine was being poured, dishes were either being presented or removed in a timely fashion. Ale roamed around, speaking to some familiar people. She watched the auction room and noticed several bids being placed, along with a Latino in a tux. She kept moving. At the front she could see all the calendars were sold out and people were asking her to sign the month of February. She was a calendar girl!

Part way through the evening, a male nurse approached with a large paper bag. "Ale, a very large Mexican man dropped this off for you. He said you would understand." He handed her the bag and walked away. Ale went out into the lobby and asked the front desk for a small meeting room for privacy. He directed her down the hall and she opened one of the doors and closed the blinds. She opened the bag: inside was a large sum of cash with a note, as well as a small, beautifully wrapped box.

She read the note, written in Spanish. *Dear, Alessandra. A donation for your fundraiser. In loving memory of our beautiful mother, Ana Francisca Gomez Torres.* Ale wept. The amount of cash was staggering. She would need the hotel safe. She also had other donations attendees had handed her that required safeguarding. Ale unwrapped and opened the tiny box and her breath stopped. It was Ana's rosary. She took it out, made the sign of the cross, and just held it in her hand. The tears were rolling down her face now as she read the attached card. *She would want you to have this, Thank you, Ale.* Ale was overwhelmed, not just with grief, but love. The love and thoughtfulness that went in to giving her this beautiful and special gift. She would cherish this rosary forever. She kissed it and placed it back into the box with the money. She wiped her face delicately, trying not to ruin her make up, and opened the door. Carlos was standing there waiting for her.

Carlos could tell she was crying. At first, he had followed her thinking she was meeting up with someone and he was extremely jealous. He had no right to be, but that didn't stop him. He was going to break into that little office and beat the shit out of whoever the guy was and probably kill him. Then he saw her face and his heart just stopped. Why was she crying? He walked over and folded her into his arms.

Ale wished he wasn't at every corner. Prior to a couple of months ago they had never even seen each other, now he was everywhere. *WTF?*

"Ale, what happened? Why are you crying?" he asked, taking out a handkerchief and handing it to her. She wiped under eyes.

"Thank you, I'm OK. Sorry. I have to take this to the hotel safe." She walked away from him and headed to the lobby to talk to the manager.

Carlos watched her and couldn't take his eyes off her. That dress was nothing short of the sexiest thing he'd ever seen. Her bare back and chest, just a hint of cleavage, with her skin glowing. The sheer fabric teasing and flowing as she walked. God, he thought he could walk away, but look at him. He was more in love than ever. She headed to the ladies' room and he reluctantly went back to do his job.

The music was rocking, and people were up having a great time. Ale's momma came over and hugged her. "Oh Ale, what a great job, this party is incredible. Everyone is really enjoying themselves." She looked at Ale, her momma signals going off. She knew something was up. "What's wrong, honey?"

Ale smiled. "Nothing momma, just a bit tired," she lied, and momma knew it.

"C'mon, lets grab zia and dance." Momma pulled her to the dance floor, and they joined the others.

A bit later, Ale was in need of a drink and heading towards the bar when a beautiful Latino lady lightly grabbed her arm. "Ale?" she asked, then gently moved her hand to her necklace, like she was nervous.

"Hi! Yes, I'm Ale. Can I help you?' Ale said, curious and hoping it wasn't another Striker girlfriend.

"My name is Justina. I am Carlos's sister," she half smiled.

"Oh. Hi!" Ale said grabbing her into a hug.

She hugged her back. "It's so great to meet you."

"You too. I've heard so much about you, Ale. Would you mind coming over to our table? My mom would love to meet you." Ale was stunned. Firstly, she didn't know Carlos's family was here and second, she didn't know they knew about her.

"Of course, I would love to. Shall I speak in Spanish?" Ale asked.

"She'd love that." She grabbed Ale's hand and led her to their table. Justina introduced her to her mother, Rosa, and wow, did Ale know where this family got their beauty. She was a stunner, my gosh.

"Ale, it's a pleasure." She took Rosa's soft hand in hers. Ale sat down beside her, and they proceeded to have a great conversation. Ale was introduced to Carlos's other sister, Mariella and Justina's daughter, Vanessa—all beautiful women. They sat and chatted; Ale immediately fell in love with them. Her heart ached for what could have been. They exchanged numbers and promised to stay in touch.

The winners for the auction were posted outside the locked room and people were starting to clear out. Everyone was congratulating and thanking each other. Ale knew the evening was a great success and she had great hopes to expand on this for the next fundraiser. She was super-excited to find out how much the total amount raised was, but that would be for another day.

CHAPTER 82
The Date...

Ale sent Lacey home and she stayed to ensure everything was tidied up and the associated payments were distributed. She ordered a Lyft, put her long black velvet cape over her shoulders, and headed out with the giant bag of money, her gift, and a slew of unopened envelopes. She was checking her phone for the Lyft info when she looked ahead.

Carlos was standing beside his car, his bow tie hanging loose, jacket opened, arms crossed, waiting. *Jesus.* Not now. She walked towards him. "Hey, I ordered a Lyft," Ale said, trying to sound flippant.

"I cancelled it," he said, not moving, just looking at her. She recognized that look and she was sure she was done with him. Just that look made her second guess everything.

"Why? A new threat?" She stared back.

He unfolded his arms and reached out to pull her in and she let him. He pulled the cape over her shoulders so she wouldn't get cold. "The only threat you have is me. You look beautiful, Alessandra."

Here comes the sweet talk. God, she knew the pattern now, he needed a new line!

"Thank you."

"Can I take you home?" he asked, looking hopeful.

"Sure, why not?"

He smiled, opened the door and helped her in. He walked around the front and got into the driver's seat and started the vehicle. They buckled up and pulled out of the hotel lot. She leaned back and closed her eyes. He put his hand in hers and she let him. She loved his hands.

"You did great tonight, Ale. The fundraiser was a huge success. Everyone was complimentary," he said, looking over at her in serious Carlos mode.

"Thanks, but it wasn't just me. It was a team effort. I met your family tonight." Once again, she was changing the subject.

"So, I heard. They loved you. I think my ma is already planning our wedding." He was paying attention to the road now and she noticed they weren't heading towards her apartment.

"Where are we going?"

He ignored her. "What's in the bag?' he asked.

She ignored him. Obviously, they still had trust issues.

They pulled into the underground garage where they had picked up Ramone after their rendezvous up the coast that day. Maybe he was dumping her off to Ramone? He parked the car and went around and opened her door. She took his hand and he ushered her to the building door and into an elevator. She just kept looking at him, saying nothing. The elevator doors opened to a hallway and a single door. He used a key fob and unlocked it, holding it open for her as she walked in. It was an apartment that looked like a showroom. The floors were marble. The décor was masculine and dark, with expensive furnishings and exquisite details. They walked straight ahead, past a small bathroom on the left and towards the kitchen with a giant island. Straight ahead was a large dining table in front of wall-to-wall glass doors overlooking a balcony. To the right was the living area with a large sectional dark leather couch and a giant flat screen on the wall above a modern gas fireplace.

Ale stopped in her tracks and just took it all in. *WOW*. She noticed a door to the right, one straight ahead that looked like another bathroom and a small office to the left, past the fireplace. He took off her cape and she rubbed her shoulders. Her arm was getting sore holding her leather tote which also had the giant bag of money in it. He reached out to take it, but she held on to it, he smiled.

"Is this your place?" she asked. He walked over to the kitchen, opened the wine fridge, and took out her favourite bottle of white wine.

"Yes, I also have a house, but I spend most of my time here." He poured them each a glass of wine. Ale realized she had barely drank or eaten anything tonight. She took a drink and it felt nice and cold.

"It's beautiful, Carlos," she said, holding on to her tote.

"Ale, are you going to set your bag down? I promise you; nobody will take it from here," he smiled.

"Why am I here?"

"Do you want to sit?" She shook her head.

"OK, I brought you here because I wanted to apologize, and I want to spend the night with you." He was looking down at the floor.

Wow, OK.

"Why now? I thought you moved on?" He wasn't getting off easy, he hurt her. She knew and accepted his rules and he played dirty.

Carlos leaned against the island and took a drink. His night was uneventful, his company made a great deal of money, and here was this feisty little blonde challenging him on all angles.

"I thought it better that I leave you alone. You have had nothing but trouble since I came into your life." He said it as if he really didn't believe it either.

"And now?" she asked, still holding the bag and drinking all the wine in her glass.

Carlos raised his eyebrows and came over and filled up the glass again. "Thank you," she said politely.

"Ale. I am out of my element when it comes to you. I have been since the day we met. I am breaking every rule I put into place with regards to women. I can't stop thinking about you, and every time I see you it just gets worse. I want you—badly. I'm sorry that I hurt you and left suddenly. The Mossimo incident and then seeing O'Malley... I just felt like you needed better people around you." He sat on the arm of the couch.

He looked tired, she thought.

"You're going to have to explain, 'out of your element' and what rules you broke for me."

"Well, for starters, you are here, in my apartment. You are the first and only woman I've ever brought here. You are the only woman who's met my family." He looked like he could have kept going, but she interrupted him.

"What about Lauren?" She finally set the bag down and walked towards him. He shook his head and looked up at her.

"I'm sorry about her, as well. She's out of control, and I've done nothing to encourage it. She's stuck in the past and cannot move on. What she did to you is unforgiveable. I have a restraining order against her, and I would like you to do the same. She's unstable." He looked embarrassed.

"Did you go to Miami with her?" Ale asked, confused.

"NO. Jesus, Ale I wouldn't go across the street with her. She's crazy. I slept with her seven years ago and this has been going on since. She's relentless." He rubbed his head.

Ale set her wine down and reached to run her fingers through his beautiful dark thick hair. "You must be *REAL* good if she's still pining after seven years," she said, hoping to lighten the mood. His shoulders started to shake with laughter, and he looked up smiling. He wrapped his arms around her waist, and they leaned against each other.

"So, are you going to take me into the bedroom, or how does it work?" she teased.

He immediately stood up, lifted her chin for a kiss, soft and sweet. He took her hand and led her into a room on the right. *OK, WOW.* The bed to the left was gigantic. Her parents had a California King, but this was larger. Above it was a long narrow window that went the width of the wall. Luxurious bedding with two night tables and wall sconces. To the right was a sitting area with two comfy chairs and two doors. One door led to a very large walk-in closet with built-in everything and the other door to an even larger ensuite bathroom in marble with a double vanity, sunken tub, and a shower the size of her kitchen.

"This place is a dump. Jesus, Carlos, how do you stand living here?" she asked.

He put his arms around her and kissed her with all he had. Something else was introducing himself to her and God her nipples were singing with joy. Oh man, this was finally going to happen and now she was terrified.

She pulled back from the kiss. "Would it totally ruin the mood if I showered?" she asked. "I want to smell and feel good when I'm with you, and right now I am neither."

He smiled and extended his arm out to the bathroom. "Towels are on the shelf, but don't take too long." HA! She thought, *I shower at work all the time and I know how to do it fast!* She dragged her bag with toiletries, undies, and extra clothes—oh, and a ton of money in with her—and he laughed.

She showered and cleaned everything, especially the *purpose*. Oh my, the *purpose* was going to be so happy and sore after this. She dried off, put on some moisturizer, and tied her wet hair up. Hmm… no jammies… OK. She looked around for a robe or something and noticed he had some freshly dry-cleaned dress shirts hanging on the back of the door. She grabbed a white one and put it on. Guys think that is sexy! She brushed her teeth and felt both horny and human again. Please God, don't let him be sleeping.

Ale opened the door and *MY GOD* the sight. He was naked on the bed with the sheet just sitting at his waist. She'd never seen him without his shirt. He was beautiful and he had tattoos! She had to explore those! One arm was behind his head, and he looked very relaxed. Her?? Shaking in her non-existent boots! Ale turned off the light and walked over, climbing up on the bed so she straddled him. His arm came down to caress her thigh and the other hand went right for the nipple. *Damn him.*

She moved his arm away from her nipple because she wanted to take it all in. She put her hands on his chest and his abs and moved them over his nipples, over a large tattoo on his left pec. She couldn't make out it almost looked like initials. He had several scars. Being a nurse, she was trained to look for things on bodies. She touched each one, recognizing bullet wounds and knife scars. She lowered her head to kiss them, and he grabbed her hair to take it out of the elastic. He liked her hair down. She trailed slow kisses down his abdomen towards his bulge. *Sweet Jesus.* How was this going inside her? She started to panic.

Carlos was trying hard to control himself, but Ale was not making it easy. When she appeared in the doorway with just his shirt on, he had to count to twenty. She was perfect and she was his. Now she was touching him, exploring with her soft hands, kissing and, God, he had to remain cool and be easy with her. He had no idea how to do that. Normally he could take his time and be in control. Not tonight. Not now.

He pulled her up so she laid on top of him and he could kiss her. He was such a great kisser! His hands were under the shirt and rubbing her butt. He gently rolled her over and positioned himself between her legs. He was looking at her as he slowly unbuttoned the shirt and slid his hands up to massage her breasts. Her nipples were in agony. He was rubbing himself below and her *purpose* was so very wet. *Dear God.* He moved up and started kissing and sucking her nipples. That was it, she went off. Her breathing was heavy, her pulse quickening, her limbs felt like Jell-o, she arched and pushed on him.

"Oh Carlos," she hung on until it subsided. He wasn't even inside her yet.

Carlos knew that Ale had super-sensitive breasts. He relished in watching her come. She surrendered beautifully, so innocent and natural. He was dying to be inside her, but he knew he had to get her ready. If she hadn't had sex in a while, he couldn't just shove it in.

Ale opened her eyes, and his dark beautiful horny eyes were watching her. "Carlos, do you have condoms?" she asked, half dazed. She had no clue how she remembered that. Without missing a beat or a suck on her nipple, he reached for the side table drawer and opened it to bring out a condom. Then he trailed his lips down, down, and before he could dive in, he smiled and looked up at her.

God, she was mortified, what? Did it look different?

"Nice landing strip, babe. Did you think I wouldn't find it?" She laughed and put her hand over her eyes.

Ale had had issues in the past with men going down on her. *If you aren't good at it, leave it the hell alone!* Otherwise, you are just going to annoy the fuck out of her. Seriously, don't bother. Some people are just good at certain things. Stay in your damn lane. She was praying to God that Carlos was good at this. It could be a deal breaker. If you don't go at it like it's a giant, juicy peach, don't go. She would rather they moved on.

Needless, to say, the man did not disappoint. Ale was writhing and moaning, grabbing his hair, as she called his name a million times. She rubbed herself up to meet him, his poor face must have been covered because she was sooo very wet. He was also moaning, "Jesus" she heard a few times, lots of sexy Spanish words and she lost count of the orgasms.

When he finally pulled away smiling, he pulled himself up on his knees. He licked all the way up to her mouth and kissed her so she could taste herself. Guys love that. "Ale, my God, you taste incredible."

Carlos was rubbing his large weapon against her, and it was trying desperately to get inside. Things were getting crazy. "Carlos, the condom."

"Mmmmmm, te quiero, Ale."

She heard that between kisses and rubbing. He gently slipped inside, and she froze. He went back to her nipples, and she became distracted again. He pushed in a little and wow, this was not going to be easy. She felt him testing the waters as he removed it and kept it there with his full body on her.

"Let me touch you," Ale pleaded as he kept kissing her neck and her breasts.

"Baby, I am really close."

"Put the condom on please, Carlos. I want you inside me. Now!" He reluctantly put the condom on.

Normally he was a stickler about condoms. He had to be. With Ale, he desperately wanted to know how it felt to be natural with her. Only her. He knew how good she would feel. He rolled over on his back and pulled her on top of him as he guided himself in, slowly. It took every ounce of his strength. She opened slowly but she was so goddamn tight. He held his breath, slowly inching inside her. She was kissing him and moaning. He bent his knees to push a bit more and she tightened. *SHIT.*

Ale could feel him inching in and she knew it was killing him, but damn she was small, and he was *NOT*. She moved his hands to her breasts, and she rocked on him. It seemed to help open her up and eventually he pushed all the way in. *OH MY GOD*. She felt pinned.

"That's it, baby," he whispered over and over in Spanish and then they got into this rhythm. She lost it. The sensual stroking was more than she could take. She came and came. He just kept moving her up and down in a steady motion, his breathing was faster, her head was down near his neck, and his arm was across her, moving her slowly. She was lost, and surrendered with the intensity. Finally, the pace picked up and he pushed her down on him and held her there. His body tensed and he groaned. "*Fuuuuck.*" He stayed inside and they just laid there, breathing. Completely satisfied and yet wanting more at the same time.

CHAPTER 83
So... This Is What Heaven Feels Like.

Ale lost track of how many times and how many condoms. Eventually she fell asleep on top of him and slept there most the night. In the morning she felt someone touching her arm. "Ale, honey, wake up." She opened an eye, she was in a ball on one side of the bed. Carlos was fully dressed and sitting on the bed looking at her. "God, you're beautiful in the morning," he said, pushing her hair from her face.

She grabbed his hand and said, "Babe, you got laid; you don't have to sweet talk anymore."

His eyes smiled. "I have to go downstairs for a bit. I didn't want to leave you here to wake up alone."

Her eyes narrowed on his... hmm... where did he get that tidbit?

"Momma?" she asked, and he smiled.

"She's fierce, that one."

Ale covered her eyes. Knowing momma, she even told him about her nipples. Jesus.

"So, I owe you another apology for leaving you the other morning. I didn't want to wake you."

Ale rubbed his hand. "It's OK. You didn't know."

He pointed to a fresh glass of orange juice and told her breakfast was in the kitchen whenever she got up. He started to get up.

"Carlos."

He turned.

"Umm, thanks for everything." It felt weird, but she knew the rules and she wasn't going to make a scene. "I will be out of here as soon as I shower. I'm sure you aren't used to having a woman here. No clean get away."

He kissed her hand. "Take your time. Ramone will take you home when you are ready."

Ale smiled and he left. She walked delicately to the shower to hose herself down.

CHAPTER 84
Let's Bake...

Ale quickly showered and grabbed some food, which was delivered by Leslie's catering service and just happened to have all her favourites. *Momma*! Ale was half out of her mind starving! She texted Ramone and he told her to take the elevator to B1 and he would meet her there. He had a sly smile on his face when the doors opened. She bet they all knew what happened and she blushed.

"*Como estas, Alessandra?*" he said happily. She smiled and put her sunglasses on. God, what had she done?

Carlos was in his office reviewing a security system with his lead tech. He was completely distracted with what had just occurred in his bed. Apparently, his team was thrilled that he got laid because he'd been a real asshole to work for lately. *Hmm. Go figure.*

Carlos knew making love to Ale would be special, but nothing prepared him for what had happened last night. He couldn't get enough of her; they explored every inch of each other. He probably had an hour of sleep the entire night, but he wasn't complaining. It was the best night he's ever had, and he wished it could have lasted for days. He couldn't stop smiling at the very vivid memories. Normally, he would satisfy his needs and never think about it again. Not Ale. He had no idea how to move on and he was already wanting more. He was going to break all his rules, but he kind of knew that would happen.

Ale asked Ramone to stop at Fortino's so she could pick up some items. She had so much energy, *Thank you, Carlos!* She needed to cook and bake. Also, her nipples were raw. She needed some nipple cream. Thank God her zio wasn't working today!

Ramone helped her bring the bags up and of course she still had the giant bag of money and her dress to lug home. He checked out the apartment and kissed her on the cheek. She thanked him and he left. She had a tiny crush on that guy, kind of hard not to. She changed into a comfy pair of fleece shorts and a tube top after applying the nipple cream. Put her hair up and washed her hands. She put on her nona's apron and got busy. Roast beef cooked with baby carrots and baby potatoes, her favourite. Easy and delicious. She started up the dough for bread, covered it in plastic wrap, and set it to rise.

Her phone was buzzing. She scanned it—nobody important—and kept baking. Cinnamon rolls first. Since she was making a carrot cake, she would make double of the cream cheese frosting and use it on both. She also made four dozen chocolate chunk cookies. She could always freeze them. She deboned the already cooked chicken and made herself a sandwich. She drank two Diet Pepsis. *Man did she have energy!*

Her phone buzzed again, and she looked at the screen. A delivery was at her door downstairs. Ale never let anyone come up with deliveries, so she went down to retrieve it. Well, she wasn't sure she could carry it. The vase of flowers was gigantic and weighed more than she did. She courageously carried it back to her apartment and unveiled it. WOW! Beautiful soft pink and soft yellow baby roses, lilies, and orchids. It was stunning. Ale opened the card, and it just had the letter C. on it. Hmmmmm. They looked lovely on her coffee table. She texted Carlos and thanked him It made her wonder if he did this for all his "dates." Could get expensive.

Ale continued baking, listening to music with her earbuds in and enjoying her day. She loved days when she had zero responsibilities and could do whatever she wanted. This was her day! Plus, she got laid! She was a happy girl. She removed the perfectly cooked roast beef and veggies, let it sit on top of the stove, started making the yummy gravy, and put the cinnamon rolls and cake in the oven. The smell was killing her. Her phone kept dinging through her music, which was annoying. While the cake and rolls were baking, Ale decided she would deal with all the money that she brought home from the fundraiser. She would take it to the hospital tomorrow. Today was Sunday and she had totally blown off church. She was sure momma was the one blowing up her phone and she better text her back, or momma would send Danny to fetch her. Ale replied telling her she was tired from the gala, never mind the Striker sex fest, and she would text her later. She gave brief replies to her friends asking how everything went last night. Nobody knew about her, and Carlos and she wasn't really in the mood to share. It was her choice to sleep with him, even though she was upset and angry at him, and some people wouldn't understand her decision.

Ale counted $100,000 in cash from Diego's family and dug out the Disney phone and sent a message: *Thank you for the donation & gift.*

You are welcome hermosa, how did it go with the big guy last night?

Seriously?

Oh, it was OK. Laughing emoji.

I love my new calendar. February is my new favourite month.

Ale blushed. It was nice to see him flirting again. Imagine how much he'd like February if he had seen the nipples!

She continued opening envelopes to find another $100,000 in donations. My gosh. People were over the top generous, especially Diego and his family. The hospital would have to do something super special in memory of Ana. She updated her spreadsheet app and added the line items of $$ by donator. They had to include the ticket sales, calendar sales and auction sales. Of, course costs would need to be deducted. They were well on target and especially after a pandemic. So many people thanked them last night for being so brave during COVID, this is how they show their gratitude, it was all so humbling.

CHAPTER 85
Seconds!

Carlos was at his desk working on a new security design when a knock came at the door.

"Boss." It was Zeus.

"Come in," he said.

Zeus had a giant four-by-four-foot flat package wrapped in brown paper. "This was delivered for you and it's not ticking."

Carlos had no idea what it was. He began unwrapping it and started to smile. There was his girl, in a beautiful black and white photo leaning back over a giant rock with the water and sunset behind her. Her arm was holding her hat down and there were those nipples. *Jesus.* He started to laugh.

"Get me a hammer and some fasteners. I need to put thing this up," he said to Zeus who was smiling too! Carlos decided he would hang it on the wall he stared at all day. That way, people who came into his office wouldn't be staring at her, but he would. This made his day. He texted Ale to thank her and she sent back the winking emoji. God, he was hard again. He needed to see her.

Ale was dancing around her kitchen, spreading frosting on her carrot cake when someone tapped her on the shoulder, and she jumped. *WTF?* She turned around and Carlos was leaning casually against her fridge. *SHIT.* She didn't even hear him come in. Ale smiled and took out her earbuds.

"Hey, Jesus, you scared the crap out of me."

He had a smirk on his face. What was he up to? He was dressed casually, in jeans and a white T-shirt. She took her finger covered with icing and put it next to his lips and he sucked her finger into his mouth. She laughed and he grabbed her into a toe curling, knee buckling kiss. *Yum.* Carlos and cream cheese frosting. She wrapped her arms and legs around him, and he carried her, spatula and all into the bedroom and laid her on the bed.

God, he thought, *she looked adorable.* Little shorts and a sheer white top with no sleeves, an apron, and UGGs. She was always wearing those little boots. He just stared at her, smiling. He took the spatula back to the kitchen and she raised herself up on her elbows. When he returned to the bedroom, the spatula was gone and so was his shirt. *DAMNNNN!* Ale just stared at his beautiful body. Nothing was sexier than a good-looking fit man in just a pair of button-fly jeans. Her mouth just hung open.

"What's going on?" she finally asked.

"What's it look like?" he said, removing her UGGs and edging her legs apart.

"Am I getting seconds???" Ale asked excitedly.

He grinned that beautiful grin and she was like a kid at Christmas. Actually, this was more like Christmas, birthday, and New Year's all in one. "Are you breaking your own rules??" she asked, teasing.

He smiled and laid on top of her. She moaned. God, she loved the weight of him. He started kissing her slowly and perfectly, and she wrapped her little legs around him so he couldn't escape. It was like they hadn't seen each other in months. Clothes came off and they were both breathless and moaning.

Things were moving way too fast, and Ale stopped in a panic. *Shit. Condoms.* "Carlos." She pushed him off, he was ready to slip in, *Jesus.* He pointed to a box on her nightstand. *Where did they come from?* Carlos focused on her poor nipples, and she was losing her ability to think. He kept just rubbing the head of his weapon against her and with the nipple attention, she *came* so hard. She pushed on his chest and her whole body just went tense. "Oh God, Carlos."

Carlos was completely out of control, he kept whispering, "That's it, baby, that's it."

Ale was drowning. He slowly pushed all the way in and the sensations, along with the passion, were more than either of them could handle. The pace quickened and the frenzy of what they were doing to each other took them both over the edge.

He collapsed on Ale, and she didn't have an ounce of energy to give him an atta boy. *Holy Hell.* What just happened? OK, realization was kicking in and she realized the condom did not get on. NOOOOOOOO! She wasn't worried about a pregnancy; she had been on the pill for a while. She was worried about STDs, which were rampant in LA and probably everywhere. Ale had to be tested every month in order to work for the hospital, but Carlos was a different story. Her afterglow was fading. He slowly removed himself and rolled over.

Ale could feel stuff running down her leg. *Good GOD.* There was a LOT! She glared at him, and he smiled. *NOT FUNNY.* She slowly got up and ran to the bathroom to clean up. This is why she liked condoms; the men got cleanup duty. Jesus, it was everywhere. She took out a clean facecloth and rinsed with warm water, then went back into the bedroom. He had a surprised look on his face.

"Relax, Tarzan. I'm just giving you a much-needed sponge bath. I happen to be an expert in this field." He laid back with his arm above his head and let her clean him with the nice warm cloth. "Just part of the Gold service we provide here," she said sarcastically. He smacked her butt as she put the cloth in the hamper.

Ale crawled under the covers and on top of him because he was so friggin warm and she loved it.

"We need to talk about what just happened," he said caressing her butt and back slowly.

"Yeah, we do. I'm on birth control, so you don't have to worry about pregnancy."

"I know," he said.

She sat up and stared at him with squinty eyes. "How?"

He smiled. "They're in your medicine cabinet, and I do my research on ladies I'm interested in. Plus, you are responsible, very responsible." He was now distracted by her nipples, so she tried to cover them with her hands, but he batted them away.

"Carlos, I'm serious. STDs are everywhere and you are more active than I am. It concerns me." She needed him to hear her. "Wait. Research?" OK... She needed to understand this.

He grinned. "Ale, contrary to popular belief I don't screw everything that walks. I am very selective and lately I have been extremely selective."

Her nipples were really enjoying the attention, and she was losing her concentration. She tried to wiggle away but he caught her and rolled her under him. *OH OH... to be continued.* Every time she'd try to get conversation out of him, this happened. He was already inside her and she had to admit, it felt way better without the condom, but they were being irresponsible, and they both knew better.

CHAPTER 86
Thirds or Fourths???

It was well into the night when they finally decided they needed a shower and food. Ale also changed the sheets. She warmed up the roast beef dinner and set the table. When he walked out with just his jeans on, she almost forgot about dinner again. What was wrong with her??? God, he must be used to this. He smiled. Yeah, he was.

"This looks incredible, Ale, thank you." He sat down and dug in. She cut up some of her homemade bread that was already made as the other batch was still rising.

"You're welcome. I'm starved." She was shovelling it in, and he just stared at her. He shook his head and continued to eat normally.

"Can you please tell me about this meeting with momma?" This disturbed her. Momma had no filter or boundaries.

Carlos took a drink of water, wiped his mouth, and laughed. "Your mother is a trip!" He looked at her. "She adores you Ale."

Ale's eyes started to water. She knew that. She felt it every single day. "I know she does, and she means well; she just gets overly involved sometimes and there is no controlling her. Papa just walks away and lets her get away with everything."

He looked up at her and his eyes were smiling. "He's crazy about her. Anyone can see that. They both care about you and want what's best for you. It's quite lovely."

"Carlos, what did momma tell you? You're stalling." Ale got up for seconds. The food was delicious.

"How about we address the condom issue first? That way, we can crawl back in bed and not have to worry." He brought his plate to the counter.

"You're staying?" she asked, surprised.

"Unless you have plans."

She thought about that. "Well, my *other* boyfriend is stopping..." She didn't get to finish the sentence, as he picked her up, put her over his shoulder, and took her to the bedroom. "Wait! I wasn't finished dinner," she said, still holding her fork.

"You can eat later," he growled.

"OK, but we didn't have the condom talk." She was removing what little clothes she had put on after the shower and he was already naked, she could only stare. "And I also want to know about the four bullet wounds and 11 stab wounds on you. And can we please talk about your tattoos?" He just shook his head and pushed her back on the bed. *Here we go again!*

She had to hang on for dear life as he was *HUNGRY.* Clean up, Aisle 6. So much for clean sheets and bodies. Ale was like a rag doll on top of him. How did this keep happening? Can people actually die from too much sex? She was a nurse, and she didn't know these things? She needed to do research.

"So, who's the other boyfriend?" he asked while running his hand up and down her back, she snorted.

"I can't even remember his name."

He chuckled. "Good. Latino men don't share well and are very territorial, Ale."

"Really? Huh. Would never have guessed." He pinched her and she squirmed.

"For the record, you're the first and only woman I've been with in over a year."

WHAT?? Ale sat up. OK, again the nipples, but seriously, she had to look him in the eyes. "Carlos, c'mon, you cannot be serious. I can handle it."

"I'm being very honest with you. The whole pandemic happened and then I met you New Year's Eve and I've been obsessed ever since." He was staring right at her.

"Carlos," she whispered and bent down to kiss him like her life depended on it. She rubbed herself all over him. She had no idea what came over her.

"Oh God, baby." His hands were roaming. She sat up, took his hands and put them over his head as she leaned her breasts into his mouth. All of a sudden, she was beyond horny, even he seemed surprised. She adjusted herself to move in just the right direction, and he was inside her, moving slowly. She set the pace. He was gasping. She moved so that just the tip was inside, and she rocked there. *OH. MY. GOD*, she came! He was crazy now, muttering in Spanish He untangled his hands from her grip and grabbed her hips. He shoved her down so deep, she could only arch and cry out. *Sweet Jesus*. He took control and never let go. Nothing in her life had ever felt this good. Nothing.

"Jesus Christ, Ale," he sighed.

She was barely breathing. "Mmmmmm," she moaned. "You should have started with the '*I haven't been with anyone in a year.*'"

He laughed out loud. "You didn't even let me finish," he said. Ale laughed and rolled off him to go clean up—AGAIN.

"Oh baby. I think you finished just fine!" She strutted to the bathroom.

CHAPTER 87
The Future...

Ale crawled back in bed and snuggled up to Carlos. He looked at her and said, "I get tested monthly on STDs, and so do my staff. I emailed you the report."

OK, that was surprising. She was a nurse, so she can tell if tests were doctored. "Fair enough, what happens now?" she asked.

He kept playing with her hair, "Would you like to continue doing this?"

She frowned, "Like in a couple of minutes or tomorrow or what do you mean?" Her nipples were paying attention.

Carlos sat up and turned towards her. "I would like us to continue doing this on a regular basis."

Hmmm... how romantic.

"Like just having sex?"

He nodded.

"Exclusively?" He nodded.

"Would it be like a secret or what are you thinking?" Ale was both aroused and troubled by this.

"No, we'd be a couple."

WHAT?????

"Carlos, you don't do relationships, remember? You do this!" She pointed to her *purpose*.

He took her hand and kissed it. "I only want to be with you, Ale, and I want us to be together."

She just stared at him. He looked serious. Was this really happening? How did she not see this coming? Ale rolled over on her back. "Are you sure about this? Maybe all this fantastic sex has messed with your brain?"

He cuddled beside her. "I've never been more, sure of anything in my life. In fact, that is why it's taken me so long to get you here. I wanted to be sure. What about you?" he asked, putting his arm across her stomach and bringing her closer to his warmth.

"I don't know. I just always thought we'd have a good time, and we'd move on. Everyone told me the rules and I was OK with that." She turned to snuggle again.

"Is that a yes or a no?" he asked, looking down at her. "I promise it will only be you." He sensed her doubts.

"I believe you, Carlos. I trust you, obviously. I just worry that neither of us has really done this before and what if we screw it up. I would hate to not have you in my life, even if it was just friends."

He hugged her close and said, "I will always be in your life, Ale. That is a guarantee." She smiled and well, things started happening again. The man has some serious stamina.

CHAPTER 88
Things Just Got Real...

Ale went back to work the next day. Carlos had loaned her another vehicle to use. She brought in the donation loot, as did Lacey and with the auction donations. They were well over $500,000. They were super-excited. She updated all the files with the details, and sent them to Mr. Bennett, and finance. She also requested that a special thought be given to Ana, as her contribution was one-fifth of the donated amount.

Ale's shifts went by like the wind. It was work, eat, sleep for three days. A few intense surgeries. Rainy season was producing mudslides and, as a result, additional patients. She hadn't seen Carlos as he was busy, and she was sleeping. They texted and stayed in touch.

After her last night shift, she was sound asleep when she woke up to someone with their hands on her breasts. It took her a while to open her eyes and see that handsome face smiling at her. She had no idea what time it was or how long she slept, but she liked what he was doing. His hand drifted south, and she curled into him and wondered why his clothes were still on. She moved her hand down and found his weapon and slowly massaged it through his pants. "Babe," he said. He was kissing her neck and *OH BOY*. What that man did to her. After several minutes of ecstasy, Ale was feeling extra good and, of course, hungry. He rolled off her and traced his finger over her lips.

"I love watching you sleep," he said.

"Hmph... I kind of thought you liked what just happened."

He laughed. "I LOVE that." Sucker!

She slowly got up and cleaned them both off. He was accustomed to the ritual now; hygiene was important. It was 6 p.m. No wonder she was hungry. She put her robe on and he was still laying in bed naked. "You hungry?" she asked.

"Yes. How about I take you out for a meal?" he said.

Hmm... they'd never had the date. "Where would this meal take place?" She had to think of wardrobe.

"Antonio's?" he suggested. Mmmmm... great steakhouse.

"Deal."

She quickly dressed in a nice denim dress. Sexy but appropriate as momma would say. She put on strappy beige high heels, put her hair up, and off they went to eat some meat.

Carlos had a table reserved and they were quickly ushered in. The sexy hostess gave her a glare and the waiter was tripping over himself to make them happy. People knew Carlos and you knew the gossip was going to start, the social media posts, the crazy Laurens. Ale would have preferred to order in.

Carlos ordered wine and Ale ordered escargot for an appetizer. Full of garlic butter, of course, hot rolls.... she was hungry! They talked about work, and she asked him to spill the beans on his big, beautiful tattoo that covered his shoulders and some of his back. He told her about his time in the military, but he seemed reluctant to talk about his past, so Ale let it go. She loved that they always had something to talk about. Everyone said he barely spoke, but they always had conversation, and not just when they were naked.

She mentioned going to the gym tomorrow and he gave her a strange look. "Problem?" she asked, taking a sip of the yummy wine. She could feel her body relaxing after one sip. She reached and took his hand. "Carlos, you know Mac and I've been working out for years now. What's the deal with you two?" She could sense tension whenever Mac asked about him. Mac was protective of her, as was Diego, but Mac was intense, and she would not want to get on his bad side.

"I talked to O'Malley today," he said. Her fork dropped. *Shit.* She thought they were talking about Mac??? "Let's just say it didn't go well." He moved back in his chair while the waiter put their plates down. He did the pepper thing and cleared her escargot dish, after she licked it. *JOKING.*

"Oh man. Carlos, why didn't you let me do it?" she asked. This was not good. She felt sorry for O'Malley. She did have feelings for him, but they were nothing like her feelings for Carlos. Also, she thought Carlos would be a one-night stand, so it wasn't even supposed to be an issue.

"He's in love with you Ale, and he thinks I will get tired of you and break your heart, so he said he'd just wait."

Ale chewed and swallowed her steak, then looked at him. That was optimistic. *Jesus.*

"He's hurt, I need to talk to him," she said, a bit annoyed. Men were idiots. Everything was a competition.

"Ale," he said, like a father would to his kid.

"Carlos, he is my friend, and I will talk to him. If this is going to work, we need to trust each other. I have a handful of admirers, and you have a whole city! I will talk to him. I owe him that much." She continued eating her incredible meal.

Carlos loved being out in public with Ale. She was sweetly unaware of how beautiful she looked and of how many heads she turned when she walked into a room. But he was. *He was very aware.* He also loved watching her eat! The O'Malley thing was a thorn in his side, but he would back off and let her deal with it. She always saw the good in people, one of her best qualities, well, maybe second or third best, thinking of their lovemaking. She was definitely not shy in bed. He smiled thinking about it, and she smiled back. It took a long time to get here but she was worth every minute of it.

"After you're finished with yoga, are you heading to your momma's for lunch?" he asked her.

"Yup, I was going to tell her about us, unless you think I shouldn't?" Ale wasn't sure of the rules anymore.

"Yes, I'll pick you up after yoga and we'll go together to tell her."

Ale just looked at him. "Umm OK."

"Then we will head to my mom's place and update that side. That should keep the families happy." He said it like he was telling them he found a new job or had a wart removed.

"Gosh I hope momma doesn't start on weddings and babies. Just ignore her, OK? She gets crazy about this stuff. It's the Italian in her. I should call zia and ask her to be there. She calms momma down, plus she thinks your hot," she said winking. Carlos shook his head. Crazy zia.

"Sounds like a plan."

Brave man, she thought. Brave man. "Carlos, you never mention your dad." She knew it was taboo, but she was raised by momma. She had some of her nosiness.

"He left when we were young, and nobody knows where he is." He looked away.

Hmmm… OK, Carlos is paid to find people who don't want to be found. She was sure he knew exactly where his father was. He just didn't want to talk about it.

She took his hand and said, "I'm sorry."

After the lovely meal, which included dessert, another favourite of hers, bread pudding, they went back to his place and well, you know what happened. Luckily, she packed a bag so she could drive directly to Mac's and yoga in the morning. Then they had to deal with momma.

CHAPTER 89
Dealing With Mac, Papa and Momma…

Ale arrived at Mac's happy and ready to get her arse kicked. Mac wasn't his usual self. Some would say Mac was a bit moody, but she just thought he was male. They were all moody—at least the ones in her life were.

"Hey, Mac!" she said, walking in with her towel and water bottle.

"Ale Cat. Good to see you," he said lamely.

Hmmmm. "Everything OK?" she asked him, concerned.

"Yeah, yeah. All good." He faked a smile and they got to it.

OK, here is the other thing about having a moody personal trainer. They take their moods out on their clients. Holy crap. After an hour, where she almost threw up three times, she was lying on the floor sweating and ready to call an ambulance. He had put her through the wringer.

"Good job," he said and walked towards the desk.

She gave him a thumbs up. *JESUS*. Ale slowly stood up and wiped the sweat off. "Mac, what's going on? Did I do something or say something that bothers you?" she asked, he seemed extra moody today.

"You tell me." He said in that very deep rough voice. Mac was strikingly handsome, and she had a thing for redheads. He was more ginger, covered in beautiful freckles and muscles. His blue eyes were off the charts.

"I don't know," she said softly. He turned to look at her. She must have had a hurt look on her face.

"Striker?" he asked.

Ahhhh. OK. She sighed. "You don't approve."

"Ale, I think the world of you, you know that. You are smart, brave, and beautiful. You don't need guys like Striker in your life."

He wanted to go on, but she put her hand on his chest and said, "Please do not say I deserve better. I hate that. I appreciate you, Mac. You are important to me in so many ways." She started to cry. "Please don't make me choose between you and Striker. We are just seeing where this goes and if I screw up, I need to screw up on my own. I'm going to make mistakes." He hugged her hard, sweat and all.

"I worry for your safety Ale. He has a lot of enemies," he whispered in her ear holding her tight.

She understood. "I know, I'm careful, always."

Mac and Ale made up, so she headed to yoga where she was able to focus and find her balance. She quickly showered and changed into a cute outfit as she was seeing momma AND Carlo's family today. She really needed tequila. Carlos was waiting outside the SUV when she came down the stairs. Her hair was still wet but she left it loose so it would dry faster. She smiled and he opened his arms, he kissed her neck and said, "Mmmm, you smell good." She brought her head back and he kissed her like he meant it. It never got old. She threw her bag into the back and off they went to face the Maria music. God help them.

They went in through the back and Ale noticed papa's light wasn't on, so he was probably upstairs. She hit the button for the elevator when her papa came out of his office and motioned for her to go see him. Ale looked at Carlos. "OK, this can't be good." She gave Carlos her bag and pushed him on the elevator to go handle momma while she walked in the store to see what papa wanted.

"Hi papa." She walked over and hugged him hard and kissed him. He was a great hugger.

"Hi baby, how are you?" he asked. Papa was not one for small talk, ever. This was all confusing to her and she wondered if it was a stall tactic so momma could grill Carlos? Not sure.

Ale looked around the store with mannequins dressed in exquisitely detailed suits stood in the old-fashioned windows. It had rows and rows of shirts, ties, socks, Italian leather shoes and private dressing rooms were to one side with an office and a washroom on the other. In the back was the large sewing area with five sewing machines, large presses, with great lighting. Sewing mannequins were everywhere with bits and pieces of fabric. Shelves of beautiful fabrics lined the walls. Ale loved this place. She loved everything about it.

"I'll be finishing up the sewing tonight," she said, in case he was worried.

"Yes, of course. Sit, please, Alessandra." He never called her Alessandra. She sat.

"Papa, what's wrong?" All her medical fears started to bubble up along with her tears.

"Ale, no, honey. Nothing is wrong. I want to talk to you about Carlos." *SHIT*. She'd rather a health scare??? OK, no she wouldn't.

"OK." She said, wiping her eyes.

He handed her a tissue. "You happy?" he asked.

"Yeah, papa, I'm happy." This is the most he's ever said to her in 22 years.

"Does Carlos make you happy?"

If only he knew how much, she thought to herself. "Yes, he makes me happy, and I like being with him,"

"OK," he said. "You are a grown woman, but you are still my little girl. If things change with regards to your happiness, Ale, I will be watching."

She felt immense pressure. "Papa, we just started dating. We don't even know where it's going, or if it's going." She knew momma had put him up to this.

"Understand." He continued, "Your happiness means everything to your momma and me. There isn't anything we wouldn't do to keep you happy." He was driving home a point and she was hearing it loud and clear.

"Thank you, papa." She stood up, hugged him and thought, *Sweet Jesus, what had she gotten Carlos into? This family was crazy.*

They rode up together in the elevator and they could hear momma entertaining Carlos as they came through the door. "Ahhhhh, there's my baby girl!" the normal retriever greeting. Hugs, kisses and more kisses.

"Hi momma. Sorry I was downstairs talking to papa," Ale said giving her the death stare. Momma smiled a fake smile.

The table looked like something at a wedding. *Jesus*, nothing like going overboard, momma. Carlos was quietly sitting and smiling.

"Ale, I already have your workout clothes in the washer." Of course, she did. Ale looked at Carlos and rolled her eyes.

"Thanks, momma."

"Sit, honey." She kissed papa and he and Carlos shook hands. Papa went to his normal seat at the table.

"Zia is on her way and so is Gio." She said smiling, Ale had forgotten about Gio. She looked at Carlos and then scrambled to find the wine. She poured a big glass for both of them.

"Momma, do you need help?" Ale asked, heading to the kitchen.

"No, no. Everything is ready Ale. Please start with the bread and help yourselves to the wine," she said puttering and moving stuff on the counters. Momma had a huge kitchen. It took up most of the apartment. Most Italians have huge kitchens, even the ones who don't cook.

Ale went back to the dining area and poured papa some wine, then they heard the door slam and people clomping up the stairs. Only zia and Gio could be that noisy.

"We're here!" Zia announced as she busted through the door, smiling. She was always smiling. Ale ran over to hug her and Gio.

"Gio, zia, you remember Carlos."

Gio shook his hand. "Striker." Then he went to the other side of the table to sit.

Zia held out her hand. "Carlos, so good to see you again." She kissed both his cheeks too. "Oh my, you smell good. I love when a man smells good!" My zia. Always flirting. He smiled and thanked her.

Momma cooked pasta primavera, for Carlos, no doubt. She had a beautiful garden salad with homemade Italian dressing, and garlic bread with cheese. It was delicious. After the morning she had, Ale dove in, and Carlos smiled. She seriously loved her momma's cooking. Everyone was eating. Momma was making small talk. Talking about how great the fundraiser was and Ale updated them with how much they raised.

"Gio, what's the scoop on the baby?" Ale asked. He looked up from his plate.

"It's moving along, slowly. All the papers have been signed. The family has been cooperative. Soph has pretty much moved in and is taking care of the baby full-time. It's sad really." He stopped and looked at Ale. Everyone was looking at her.

"Ale, I'm sorry." Hmmm. Gio doesn't apologize.

"Gio, don't. I am fine. This is a totally different situation than mine. Please, feel free to tell me stuff. I am truly happy for you guys. This little girl will have the best life, just like I did."

Momma was crying. "It's all so emotional, isn't it? I remember going to get Ale like it was yesterday. I remember every single thing." She grabbed a tissue. Papa was nodding and eating. Poor Carlos looked lost. Zia was crying. *Jesus.*

"What's her name?" Ale asked, trying to distract everyone.

"They named her Isabella," he said, passing her his phone with all the photos.

"Gio, she's beautiful." Then Ale got teary. This was such a BIG deal for her family.

"She's a great baby. She's completely smitten with Soph. Soph is already in love with her. We just have to get through the fuckin' red tape. I think another two weeks tops and she will be here."

Ale stood up, went over to Gio and hugged him hard. "I am so happy for you, *fratello.*"

He grabbed her arm and said, *"Ti amo, Ale."* She loved Gio like crazy and this was going to change his life for the better. They couldn't wait to meet her. It made her think of how excited everyone was when she had arrived here. They would be the same with Isabella. They would surround her with Italian love like she's never seen, with hopes that she will *ONLY* remember being loved. Ale had to excuse herself and go to the bathroom and get her shit together, but she could hear them all whispering.

When she came out, momma was asking Carlos about his family. They had moved on. Ale knew they purposely didn't talk about the baby in front of her, but she wanted to know. She needed to know.

"I met your family at the fund raiser gala, Carlos. They are lovely. And what beauties! I know where you get your looks," Momma said, winking at him. Was momma flirting?

"Thank, you Mrs. Ferretti," he said, taking a drink of water. He barely touched his wine.

"Please, you must call me Maria," she smiled.

"Soo, Carlos and I are kind of dating," Ale blurted out. She drank ALL her wine. They all laughed.

"Yeah, I think we know that." Gio said sarcastically, giving her the hairy eyeball.

"I think it's wonderful," said momma.

"So do I," said zia, already on glass number two. She held it up. "To Ale and Carlos." Everyone repeated it and clinked. That went almost too easy.

"Dessert?" Ale asked, knowing full well what they were having. It had gotten her through two hours of workout.

Zia smiled. "Of, course baby; has zia ever let you down?"

Ale smiled and rubbed her hands together. She helped momma collect the plates while zia and Carlos made small talk and they served up the beautiful lemon and coconut cream cake that Ale adored.

Everyone was served a piece. Ale was served a LARGE piece! Zia proceeded to tell Carlos the story of how Ale came to love her cake and he just looked at her as she was cramming it all in her mouth. She probably had the same look when they were making love. Yup, he smiled a dirty smile.

Lunch went off without a hitch, and they stayed a bit longer. She helped momma tidy up, the men talked business and politics. Ale grabbed her workout gear out of the dryer and put it in her bag.

Zia came over and hugged her in the kitchen, away from everyone. "You look VERY happy," she said.

Ale laughed. "I am, zia. He's good to me."

Zia hugged her harder. "Good. If he isn't, I will kill him." She laughed and went back to the table.

Wow. You can't buy love like that.

They said thank you and did their hugging and headed to the car. Ale buckled her seatbelt and let out a huge sigh. Carlos took her hand and kissed it. "That wasn't so bad," he said, smiling. He drove her back to his place as they had a few hours before going to his mom's.

Carlos gave Ale a tour of his facilities. It held a huge command centre on one floor with monitors everywhere and staff watching, lights flashing, screens hanging everywhere. The command centre was surrounded by glass walls and the hallway was setup to surround it.

On the outside of the hallway were small offices which had windows on both sides. Carlos had large corner office at the end that also had a small washroom and closet. On one floor there was a gym, a pool and sauna, and a soundproof shooting range, which Ale was sure was illegal. She pretended to ignore that.

He showed her a small office that had a bathroom and a large storage room. She just looked at him.

"I thought you might be able to use this as your sewing room." He must have noticed the shocked look on her face.

"What do you mean?" He took her hand as they walked to his office, and he shut the door. Ale saw her photo on his wall and smiled. "Wow, she's gorgeous. You're a lucky man, Carlos."

He sat in his chair so he could look at it and she sat on his lap. "I get to stare at this every day." He paused. "But it's not enough. I want to see you more, Ale. I want you to move in."

WOAH. WHAT??? Her head turned so fast, and she stood up and paced the floor. "Carlos, seriously? This is a lot. We just started this and neither of us has ever lived with anyone before. Wait—have you?" she asked. Christ, she didn't know anything about this guy, really. Only what he felt like telling her.

"No," he said, looking at her. He stood up and walked towards her and she backed up to the door, he had a devilish smile. "I don't want to be with anyone else but you. The more I am around you, the worse it gets. I'm falling in love with you, Ale."

HOLY HELL. This was not happening. "Carlos, this is huge." What was happening? He was Striker, he didn't do relationships, remember??

If she was honest, she probably fell in love with him months ago, but she just didn't admit it. She assumed he didn't do love.

"Let's do this," he said, excitedly. "I hate sleeping in that bed without you and I hate waking up without you." *Jesus, he had it bad.*

"Can we get through your mom's dinner first?"

He smiled. He knew he would get his way. But damn, she didn't want to move into this fortress. She liked her apartment. Oh, and momma! *She will lose her shit!*

CHAPTER 90
Big Next Steps...

Carlos laid in bed watching her sleep. She always fell asleep on top of him and God how he loved it. He played with her hair and stroked her back. He felt like the luckiest man alive.

Dinner with his family was special. Ale fit right in. It helped that she spoke Spanish, so the conversation flowed. Even his brother, Milo, enjoyed himself and seemed to really like Ale. He hasn't seen his mom that happy in years. Carlos knew he had made the right decision.

Having her move in would be the next task. Naturally, he wanted her there, next to him, naked. He loved her company, with or without clothes. He also needed to keep her safe. If she lived with him, he could easily keep her safe. He had enemies and a past, and she would be a prime target. Of course, she didn't need to know any of that.

Ale stirred a bit. He noticed after spending nights with her that she had nightmares, probably from childhood. Her journey wasn't an easy one and there were always scars. She rarely talked about her real parents or her adoption. He got a sense of it at the dinner with her family. It was obviously still very raw.

He soothed her again and she settled. Now he had to convince her to move in and make this permanent. One thing is for sure, he loved her, and the idea of losing her was not an option.

CHAPTER 91
Letting the Secret Out...

Ale had the day off and headed back to her apartment to get some sewing done and sort through her thoughts. She started some bread and got it ready for rising. She had stopped at Fortino's for a chicken and started making soup. She loved her little apartment and her kitchen. The thought of moving in with Carlos was daunting. It was a huge step for him to even ask or tell her his feelings, but man things were moving very fast.

She had a lunch date at Miguel's with her girls to update them on her latest adventures. Carlos would make sure there wasn't any trouble. Even though he had put a restraining order on Lauren, she seemed to ignore it. Ale wanted to look extra nice as she was sure people would be watching. It was a bit overcast today, so she opted for a grey ribbed long-sleeved fitted short dress with ruffled edges on the sleeves and neck. She added her thigh-high black leather boots and grabbed her black Chanel bag. She brought her white and black plaid overcoat and headed to meet her girls.

Miguel greeted her per usual with a big smile and kisses. He led her to the table and Olivia was already there. "Hey!" They both hugged, while Miguel went to get their margaritas. "How are you?" Olivia grabbed her hand and smiled. God, Ale loved her. She made everything great.

"Good, how about you?" Ale said, getting her coat off and settling into the booth.

"I love those boots!" she said rubbing the nice leather.

Ale smiled. "Thanks, it felt like a boot day. Who's coming?" she asked, looking at the menu but knowing exactly what she wanted to order.

"Both Katee and Amalia said yes." Liv was also looking at the menu.

"How's Joe?" Ale asked, thinking of Liv's dreamy boyfriend.

"Joe's fine and he says hi. He's been in Washington for weeks now." She took off her Lawyer glasses and looked at Ale. "How's Striker?" She smiled that sweet smile.

Ale laughed. "How do you think? Intense. Sexy. Sweet. Did I mention sexy?" She asked laughing.

Katee and Amalia arrived together, and they snuggled in with hugs. Gosh, Ale had the best girlfriends.

The waiter brought their drinks and took their order. Their table was tucked in the corner so people couldn't really hear them. It was busy but Ale thought they put her in the reserved section—probably Carlos's idea. The salsa and chips arrived, and they dove in. Everyone gabbing and laughing.

Ale quietly announced. "Carlos and I finally did it." They all stared at her. Then they looked around to make sure nobody heard.

"Are you freakin' kidding me?? Jeezus Ale!" Katee was fanning herself.

"OK, spill." Amalia was the shy, conservative one. The fact that she wanted details made Ale laugh.

"He took me to his place after the gala," she said, sipping her margarita.

"Wait. His place? Striker never does that," Olivia said.

"Yup. Stayed all night, too. Then he came to my place the next day and we continued into the next morning." Ale smiled.

"*HOLY JESUS.* You had two straight days of nailing Striker and you are still walking?" Liv asked. Ale just kept smiling. "Dear God, I bow to you, sister. I bow to you. Tell us mere mortals, was it as good as everyone says?"

Ale replied. "Better. There are no words for how good it is."

They all sighed. Food came and they dug in. Ale always ordered the beef burritos, they were incredible. Katee ordered chicken fajitas, the sizzling pan sending off smells that made them all moan. Amalia and Liv shared a giant pan of pulled pork nachos, covered in guacamole and sour cream. God, she loved the food here. Ale decided to wait until after they finished eating to drop the other bombs.

"Striker wants to have a real relationship with me. He's asked me to move in with him," she said sheepishly, trying to gauge their reactions.

"Are you serious?" Katee asked.

"Yeah, he told me loved me."

"Ale, are you messing with us? Not that I don't believe someone could fall in love with you, but Jesus, this is *Striker*," said Mal, sucking back her marg.

"I hear you. I'm as shocked as you all are. I thought I was just going to get the one night and it would be over. Ladies, we have been inseparable AND we've both met each other's families."

"*HOLY SHIT!*" Oliva said. "I knew something was up with him. He took his time with you. Normally he just strikes, thus the name. Ale, how do you feel about this?"

"Honestly, overwhelmed. I just wanted to get laid."

They all laughed out loud.

"Now I have a boyfriend who loves me and wants me to move in with him," she shrugged.

"Damn girl, I have no good advice for you. It's a really great problem to have, especially if you like him and enjoy being with him," Katee said, shaking her head.

They continued to bombard her with questions. What was his apartment like, his body, his stamina? Obviously, Ale didn't give all the details as both she and Carlos were very private. The intimate stuff was just that, intimate. She did notice a few women giving her the hairy eyeball as they walked by. Apparently, the word is out. She also noticed a few of Carlos's security walking around, probably watching out for Lauren.

They caught up on each other's lives. Amalia was receiving a ton of extra work with her photography due to the nurses' calendar and was seriously rethinking her career choice. Katee was starting a new TV series for Netflix and would be filming again in Vancouver, Canada. Olivia waited until the very last minute to announce that she and Joe had decided to get married. *WHAT???*

Liv showed off her beautiful diamond engagement ring.

"Olivia! My God, that is the best news!" Liv was the ultimate independent woman. Joe had to wrestle her in order to get her to move in with him.

"I thought you were OK with status quo?" Katee asked.

"I love him, he loves me. We survived the damn pandemic and didn't kill each other. I want this. Nothing big and fancy, but intimate and beautiful. Maybe Greece," she said smiling.

"Oh my gosh." Ale hugged her like crazy. "I love that idea, Liv. And don't think we won't be there. You already have a photographer and God knows Leslie would find a way to cater the food! Do you have a time frame in mind?" Ale asked, hoping it was soon so they could all go to Greece and have some fun.

"No, but we are discussing it. Joe is even more excited than I am. He's been wanting to get married for a while and he wants it done before I change my mind." They all started to tear up.

"You will have the best marriage, Liv. That man would walk the earth for you. The way he looks at you is the way we should all be looked at." Ale gave her another hug and wiped her eyes.

"This is better than therapy!" Katee said and they all laughed and toasted the happy couple. *Amore!*

CHAPTER 92
These Boots Are Made For...

Lauren was in her car on the other side of the street from Miguel's when she saw that bitch Ale come out and get into the SUV that Striker owned. *Money-grabbing whore*, she thought. *Who does she think she is? And what was she wearing? Fucking restraining order.* Lauren pulled out behind Ale; nothing on the restraining order about being close to this bitch.

Ale received a text as she was leaving Miguel's that Carlos wanted her to stop by his place. She really wanted to get home and get some things done, but duty called. She headed to his complex and parked in the private underground. She had a key fob now; it was official. She took the elevator, which had a camera up to the top floor and went into the apartment.

"Hellooo, anyone here?" she asked taking her coat off and dropping her purse on the counter.

"In here," Carlos said from his office.

Ale walked towards the office and stood in the doorway. His eyes zeroed in on the small strip of thigh between her boots and her dress. Shocking! He smiled and his eyes were that dark black horny color. He stood up, walked over and kissed her, slow and deep.

"Alessandra, those boots," he said, with a heavy accent. Ale was blushing. He was turning her and checking her out from every angle. His hands touched that strip of skin above the boots, and he slowly started moving the dress up. She had a sexy grey lace one piece on underneath that she was sure he would love, especially with the boots. He started to moan.

OK, we all know what happened next. Obviously, the boots were a good choice!

After several rounds with Don Juan, Ale pried herself away and showered. Luckily, she had a few pieces of clothing that she kept there to change into, along with a pair of flip flops. *That man needed a hobby!*

Carlos was still laying in bed when she came out with her yoga pants and T-shirt on. He smiled at her.

"Those boots are staying here," he said.

"OK, you can have them." She crawled up the bed and sat on him, her hair was still wet, and she smelled like his soap. "Was this the reason you asked me to stop by?" she asked, kissing his neck.

"Yeah, why don't you stay longer? We'll have dinner." He had a sulky look in his eyes.

"Babe, I need to get back. I have soup in a crock pot and bread rising. Why don't you come have dinner at my place?" she suggested.

"OK. I have a few things to do here, and I will come over." It wasn't his favourite option, but sometimes you need to compromise.

"Great, I gotta run. Thanks for the great sex, by the way!" She winked and ran out before he could catch her.

Carlos laid in bed thinking life just couldn't get any better than this.

CHAPTER 93
Or Could It???

Ale drove to work after three glorious days off and could not wait to see what her patients had in store for her tonight. She and Lacey were working the 7 p.m. to 7 a.m. shift. Not their favourite shift; they always get the crazies, especially during a full moon. They dove into their shift, analyzing the patients that were already in rooms, looking for ways to free up beds to get things moving. They always had to be prepared.

Ale was busy tending to an ear infection on an adorable four-year-old old girl when she, heard some screaming in the waiting room. She ran out to the main ER desk and stopped in her tracks.

Mossimo had Lacey by the neck with a knife at her throat. The normal Ale would have found the bathroom and thrown up. The nurse Ale went into Mac mode. All the training he gave her, all the discussions... she was ready and she was pissed!

Innocent people were cowering in their waiting room chairs. Some were trying to escape through the exit doors. Ale's first priority was to get the patients out and get Lacey away from him. Simple, right?

She took deep breaths and could hear Mac's voice in her head, calming her.

Moss was waving the knife around with his eyes bugging out of his head. Obviously, he was on something. He looked like hell. He hadn't showered in months. Moss's hair was dirty and long, and his beard was long and shaggy. He had on a grey hoodie and jeans. Moss never wore jeans or hoodies. Ale couldn't believe the man she saw before her. *FOCUS ALE!*

"Moss, what's going on? Please put the knife down and we'll go somewhere to talk," Ale said, in Italian. Nya probably already hit the emergency alert button under the desk to notify police. Code White would be announced to all other areas of hospital, lock down procedures would be initiated, and hospital security would be on their way. *Jesus!*

"You are a fuckin bitch!" he screamed, holding the knife. "I'm in charge, you'll do what I say, or I will slit her throat right now." He wanted to converse in English, so everyone understood. Lacey's eyes were full of tears, but she was staying calm and watching Ale's every move.

"Can we let the patients go? Please, Moss, you don't need them. Lacey and I will stay with you," Ale pleaded.

"Where are the drugs, you stupid cunt? Fuck, you think I am here to spend time with you or attend a fucking party? You ruined my goddamned life. Fuckin' stupid bitch. You are pathetic. You've always been pathetic and weak."

OK, Ale thought, *she could take cunt, bitch, pathetic. But, don't ever call her weak.* Something came over her and she started walking towards him. *SLOWLY.*

"Let her go, then. You want the cunt. She's right in front of you. You are so fuckin' tough, let her go and come at me. I'm weak; you should be able to gut me in no time," Ale said, taunting the bastard. She could hear the sirens. She had to keep distracting him.

He threw Lacey to the side and lunged toward Ale, she moved to the right and he missed. She brought up her leg in a high kick and caught him under the chin. He fell backwards.

"Fuckin whore!" Moss jumped up and punched her in the face.

HOLY FUCK, that hurt. She staggered back, and when he moved forward, she hit him right back, just like Mac taught her. Black eye for you, asshole. She went at his arm to get the knife. He stabbed her leg and her abdomen.

"Fucking whore!"

Shit. OK, bleeding. She grabbed his arm, turned around and threw him over her back. She jumped on him and wrestled the damn knife out of his arm. It slid across the floor and Lacey grabbed it. She was watching in horror.

"Get the cuffs!" Ale yelled. The security guards were watching with guns aimed and Ale punched and kicked this motherfucker like the rubber man at the gym. He tried to roll her over, but she wasn't having it. She kneed him in the balls, punched him again in the face, and fell off him. He got up and went after her. The security guard tased his ass and he fell on top of her. *Fuck, Ale, what the hell were you thinking?* She pulled herself from under him and leaned against a wall. She was bleeding *bad*.

Lacey was trying to stop the bleeding, while other nurses were running around trying to get things organized. Dr. Walker was running towards her, Nya was helping patients get relocated, and security had Moss on a stretcher and handcuffed. Ale saw cops everywhere, flashing lights, O'Malley? Then she blacked out.

CHAPTER 94
What Were You Thinking??

Carlos, O'Malley, Gio, Mac, Diego, and Pepe were all pacing the halls of the Good Samaritan Hospital waiting to hear how Ale was. She had lost a lot of blood, had several knife wounds, a black eye, cut lip, cracked ribs, maybe a concussion, and maybe a sprained or broken wrist. They had all seen the video and none of them could believe it.

Carlos wanted to find where they were keeping Mossimo and end it. He was sure they were all thinking the same. God, what was she thinking? His heart just stopped when O'Malley texted him. His whole team rushed over. They were all pacing and worrying.

Gio was trying to fight off his mom, but they all knew Maria Ferretti would be flying in here any minute, telling them to get out of her way.

Lacey came out of the surgery area, and they all walked towards her. She had tears in her eyes and Carlos thought he was going to throw up for the first time ever. She smiled. "She's OK. Sorry, I am still emotional. She's my best friend and she saved my life. She's the strongest person I know." She wiped her tears. "She's in recovery, but she will be in intensive care for a while. They are monitoring for concussion, and she has some stitches. Dr. Walker was insistent that she would want them versus staples. Her face is badly bruised and cut, so don't be surprised when you see her. It's swelling. Her arm is in a sling; it's just sprained.

And of course, she is bruised all over. Dr. Walker will come out in a bit and let you know when you can see her, she's still under."

Gio hugged her and thanked her. O'Malley went over to talk to some other cops and give the update. Carlos did the same with his team. They all heard a bunch of hysterics and knew Maria Ferretti was in the house! She and zia Connie were running towards them. Gio caught them and pulled them aside. Maria was crying, but zia was very calm. Carlos hugged them and he introduced them to the others as they all waited. Vito, Danny, and Zio Tony arrived. Fuck, it was getting crowded. Lacey moved them into a large meeting room, which had a coffee dispenser and a water jug. Carlos ordered two of his guys to go get decent coffee and muffins. He also texted Ale's friends. He had them all as contacts on his phone now.

Within minutes, Liv, Mal and Katee were busting through the doors. Leslie showed up with a helper and loads of food. Normally the hospital didn't allow that, but everyone was so damn grateful for Ale, they let it go. The hospital brought in extra staff to deal with the other patients and to relieve the nurses who just went through the ordeal. They had HR people, counsellors, and union people on site.

Dr. Walker walked into the room, and everyone stopped talking. He smiled. He had kind brown eyes and adored Ale as much as they did. "Ale is doing great," he said. "She just woke up, she's in a lot of pain, we are managing that. And, well, to be frank, she looks like shit."

They all smiled through their tears. "Ale's big concern was her arm. As a nurse, she wanted to be sure she could still work. It's just a sprain, but she will need some PT once it heals. We are keeping her in intensive care for various reasons. She did hit her head a few times and we want to monitor for a concussion. She asked for her momma." Maria started to sob and got up to go with Dr. Walker.

Gio spoke "It's best to get the Maria visit over with first, trust me." Those that knew Maria, knew it to be true. Carlos took a look around at the people here. His mom, Justina, and Vanessa had also shown up. This beautiful, strong woman touched so many. Diego and Pepe and even some of their gang members were here. She'd probably stitched all of them at one time or the other.

After a few minutes, Maria came back in. "Well, she does look like shit," she said smiling and everyone burst out laughing. "It was so hard to see my baby's face all beat up like that, but she's strong and she will mend. I am going to the chapel." She grabbed zia's hand and they headed towards the chapel. Carlos's mom followed, as did Vito and Tony. Gio went in to see Ale next.

When Carlos walked into the room and saw the love of his life laying on a bed, hooked up to machines, he had no words. He had to be strong for her, but he wasn't feeling strong. She was so little and yet so mighty. He must remember to thank Mac: her training had paid off. It most likely saved Ale and Lacey's lives.

Ale looked up at Carlos. Well, one eye was still closed. She couldn't even smile as her lip was cut and had stitches. She slowly reached her hand towards him, and he took it and kissed it.

"Ale, I'm so glad you're OK." He wasn't going to scold or ask her what she had been thinking fighting Moss. He just wanted her better.

"You should see the other guy," she said, trying to smile.

"I have. He's lucky he's even breathing."

She tightened her grip on his hand. "He needs help Carlos. He's an addict."

Carlos's look changed quickly. "Don't defend that animal." Then her painkillers kicked in.

He went out and updated everyone, Ale needed her rest. Carlos talked to his team giving them their orders for the day. The Ferretti's had gone home but would be back in a few hours, especially Maria. O'Malley was sticking around as this was a police matter and they had a ton of work to do while keeping the ER open.

CHAPTER 95
Recovery

It was 6 a.m., the nurses' station was getting busy and noisy. Ale woke up a little dazed and confused. Oh, and in a lot of pain. She had finally been moved out of intensive care and was off a few of the pain meds. She asked to be removed from the normal pain pump and just wanted to take ibuprofen. She's a nurse, they had to listen to her!

The nurses had her up a few times through the night to go to the bathroom and see how dizzy she was. Using the bathroom hurt like hell. Her ribs were cracked. She asked Mal to bring her some clothes and toiletries.

Ale wanted to get up and go to the mirror. Mal appeared, as if on cue.

"Ale, what the hell?" She ran over to Ale who batted her away.

"I'm OK. I want to look at the big mirror on the back of the bathroom door." The drugs had worn off and now she could assess all the damage. Mal helped Ale get out of her gown, and they stood looking at her naked. OK, maybe that wasn't a great thing to do. *Jesus.* She was covered in bruises of all colours. Mal brought in her bag of stuff, closed the door, and they proceeded to do a sponge bath and get her in a tank with a shelf bra and a pair of plaid pyjama pants. She topped it off with a grey zip-up hospital hoodie, which they had to maneuver around her wrist as it needed to be in a sling. Ale pulled the tank up so she could examine her ribs. She would need to get those babies taped.

They put her hair up, gently. Moss had pulled her hair a few times and it hurt. She finally brushed her teeth, carefully as her lip had a few stitches. Her eye was still black, swollen and closed. It hurt like hell. She took a face cloth and Mal went to get some ice to help ease the pain and reduce the swelling. She put on a pair of slippy socks as her feet were cold and she slowly got into the bed after bringing the front up so she could sit up. Mal returned with facecloth and ice for her eye, plus some ice water and a straw since drinking was tricky with her injured lip.

Just then, the food and beverage Goddess, Jennifer, arrived with Ale's breakfast of scrambled eggs, toast and OJ. Ale really wasn't hungry, which was not a good sign, but she drank the OJ.

O'Malley poked his head in. *God, what time did he get up?* "Up for a visitor?" he asked, smiling that sweet smile.

Mal got up from the chair. "That's my cue. Hey O'Malley." She kissed Ale, and she left.

"You look a bit better today." He stood there looking nervous.

Ale looked at him with her one good eye. "Can't really look much worse. Want my breakfast?" He was staring at it.

"I believe that's for you to eat, so you can get better and get out of here," he said. O'Malley had a way of looking at you that made you feel like you were a criminal. He must be very good at his job.

"I'm not hungry. Please eat it, sit, and talk to me." Ale put her hand out and he took it.

He grabbed the plate and sat down to eat. "Fuck, Ale. You had us all scared to death. My God. I've been sick with worry about you. We all have." His eyes teared up, as did hers. Reality was sinking in… shock, disbelief, whatever you want to call it. O'Malley wolfed down the breakfast and watched her. His heart was in pieces. First the Carlos scenario, now this. God, the feelings he had for this woman were intense.

"Tell me about Moss," she said, not sure if she wanted to know.

"He's going through detox now, so it's not pretty. We'll be sending him to a rehab facility where he can get the help he needs. He's under arrest of course, but we want him 'sane' first. That way he gets the proper sentence." Ale stared at him. She knew with Pepe, Diego and Striker in the mix, Moss would never make it to trial.

"Was anyone else hurt?" she asked, scared for the answer.

"No. Lacey had a little cut on her neck and some bruising."

Ale started to cry, and he reached over to wipe her tears. "Ale, he's not the guy you thought he was. He changed. You only have to watch the video." Video. *SHIT. OMG* She bet they had all seen it. Oh man, she needed drugs. As if on cue, her nurse, Shelly, appeared with a cup and she helped Ale with the water.

"Ale, Dr. Walker will be around in a few minutes to check you over."

She nodded. This would be weird, having your peer seeing you mostly naked. Then again, he sewed her up, so chances are he'd seen it all anyways.

O'Malley spoke. "You need your rest. Thanks for breakfast. He leaned over and kissed her head. "I'm not giving up on us, Ale," he whispered and left.

GREAT. What man looks at someone in this condition and says that?

Dr. Walker appeared and did his checking. They re-bandaged her knife wounds and checked her vitals.

"You realize I have to give you a lecture, right?" he said smiling. She nodded.

Attacking Moss, Smart? No. Necessary? YES!

"You would have done the same thing."

He was checking her eyes for concussion. "Probably. Ale, he had a good 70 pounds on you."

She shrugged. "He didn't win, did he?"

He smiled. "I'm worried about your eye. Please keep the ice on it. Where do you hurt the most?" he asked.

"Ribs."

He nodded and took notes on his tablet. "On a scale of one to ten"

"Eight" she replied.

"I am going to send you for X-rays." He grabbed her hand. "You did great, kid!"

"Thanks. Can I leave today?" she asked, knowing the answer.

"One more day, please. I need to see improvement in your eating and that eye." He was being stern now.

Just then, momma blew through the door like a fresh breeze, speaking in Italian. Dr. Walker just stared at her. She did her retriever 'light' with Ale and grabbed Dr. Walker's hands.

"Thank you so much for taking care of Ale, we are so very grateful to you."

He looked like a schoolboy with a crush. "You are most welcome, Mrs. Ferretti. It was an honor to work on someone so brave."

Momma put her hand to her heart. "Bless you. Yes, she is brave. However, not so smart." *Another lecture coming.* Dr. Walker excused himself.

Momma was in a blue V-neck cashmere sweater that showed her bosom, tastefully of course, and navy dress slacks. Her hair was up, and she had brought a huge bouquet of flowers and a bag of food.

Hmmm…Ale needed to eat something.

Momma fussed with the flowers, all the while jabbering in Italian and releasing her nervous energy.

"Momma, please sit. You are giving me an even worse headache," Ale said, extending her left hand as the other one was in the sling. Momma grabbed her hand and fussed with her hair. She was upset and Ale needed to reassure her. Ale knew the drill.

"Momma, I am OK. I know it wasn't a smart thing to do, but I had to help Lacey, and I was concerned for the other patients." Tears ran down her face.

"Ale, you and Gio are my heart. Losing you would destroy me. You bring so much joy and love into our family—"

"Momma, I am right here. I am banged up, but I am going to recover and be as good as new, maybe better. I will be annoying you in no time." She took a tissue and wiped her eyes.

"Ale, I have guilt over Mossimo," she whispered.

"NO!" Ale said firmly. "Not anyone's fault but his. Let's get that straight." Momma put the ice pack on Ale's eye and played with her hair.

"Momma, the flowers are beautiful, thank you. What's in the bag?"

Ale needed to distract her.

"OHH, I almost forgot. I stopped by zia's bakery and picked up some of your favourites." She proceeded to pull the tray over and set it like a formal table. "Zia will be over later; we are going to tag team."

Oh great, Ale thought.

"Blueberry muffin and a chocolate croissant." She presented it like a game show host.

Ale smiled. Oh, and a large orange juice, Ale loved her OJ.

Momma helped with the straw and the OJ and Ale ripped apart the giant blueberry muffin with a sugar glaze. Ale had no idea how zia got her muffins to rise, Ale was not a good muffin maker. She ate a few pieces and that was it.

"Your appetite is not back. Do you think it's the pills?" Momma asked, cleaning up the crumbs.

"Might be. I think they have me on a blood thinner due to the bruising. I will ask Shelley. Oh, they are taking me to X-ray for my ribs." Ale pulled the blanket down to show her the bruising and momma put her hand to her mouth. OK, maybe that wasn't a good idea.

"Jesus, Ale. He did that to you? He's a monster!" She sat in the chair, shaking her head.

Nurse Shelley appeared, with a wheelchair to take Ale for X-rays. Momma needed a few minutes to get herself together.

CHAPTER 96
Moving In?...

Carlos hadn't slept. He wanted his investigation teams looking into where Mossimo had been and what he'd been up to. He was obsessed with this motherfucker. He quickly showered, changed and headed over to the hospital. He had two of his guys guarding Ale's hospital room. The hospital agreed, especially considering Ale's heroics. When he walked into her room, the bed was empty, however Maria was there looking out the window.

"Morning," he said solemnly. She turned around and walked towards him for a hug.

"Oh, Carlos. She's just down for X-rays. They think her ribs are cracked. They've been focused on the stuff that was obvious." She offered him a muffin or croissant and he shook his head.

"How is she feeling?" he asked, pacing the room.

"I think her ribs are bothering her the most and she doesn't have an appetite, which is worrisome." She was checking her phone and probably updating all the family members.

"Ale's not eating?" This was NOT good. She was a good eater and hungry all the time. He loved that about her.

"I brought her in some of her favourites and she picked at it. Drank some OJ, of course. Her mouth is sore too, so I am sure that is part of it. I am going to ask if any of the drugs they have her on might be contributing to her lack of appetite. They won't release her if she isn't eating. She's so little, she can't afford to lose weight." She rambled on. Carlos could tell she was very worried.

"Maria, Ale is a nurse, and she knows the rules. She will get there. Let's let her heal and feel better before we start to panic."

He put his hand on her shoulder and she leaned into him. "I think she should come stay with Vito and me once she's released. She cannot stay by herself."

Carlos had to be very careful here.

"Maria, I want to take care of her. I want her to stay with me. I have been asking her to move in with me anyway." He treaded lightly. Maria's head turned and she had a serious look on her face.

"You want Ale to move in with you? Permanently?" She put the phone down and stood up. *Momma bear!*

"I would, yes. First, I would like to take care of her as she recovers, so she can get comfortable with the idea. Then, with your blessing of course, she could move in, and we can be a real couple." He couldn't believe the words were coming out of his mouth and he knew Ale was going to kill him when she found out.

"How does Ale feel about this?" she asked.

"She's scared and worried that you'll be upset," he said honestly.

"Well, of course I'm upset. She is an independent, capable woman and moving in together is not a commitment. It's a cop out, to me. If you love her and you want a future with her, then you should do it properly." She was getting upset.

"Agreed. How about we try out the recovery at my place, after you've seen it and approve with the set up?"

She gave him a bit of a glare. "We'll see." She was tough. Jesus, no wonder Ale was terrified of her.

Just then Ale was wheeled in, and his heart skipped a beat. She was dressed and her colour was back, but her face was a mess.

"Hi beautiful," he said going over to help her out of the chair.

"Hey. I need to use the washroom before I get back into bed." She slowly walked over and both Carlos and Maria walked with her. "Seriously, you guys need to stop," she said and closed the door.

Maria and Carlos looked at each other and smiled. This was not going to be easy.

FUCK... Ale stayed in the bathroom just to get some peace and privacy. Getting up and down on the toilet was so bloody painful, not to mention the wiping. Fuck. Men had it so damn easy: just whip it out. She kept her moans quiet as she looked in the mirror and shook her head. She had three cracked ribs, Christ, she didn't even remember them getting hit. She washed her hands and splashed water on her face.

Of course, they were both standing where she left them. Ale walked slowly to the bed, and they came over quickly. She put her hand up and got in on her own. She laid back and sighed. Carlos noticed the tape on her belly and touched it. "Cracked?" he asked, she nodded.

Shelley came in and checked her blood pressure. It was high. She went out for meds, no doubt. The pain was bad now.

Carlos took her one hand and noticed all the bruising and cuts on her knuckles. His look said everything. She really didn't need a fourth lecture today. She turned away, and he kissed her hand as if to say he understood, and they'd talk about it later. Momma excused herself to go up and visit the babies. Her and zia loved volunteering in the neonatal unit and she knew Carlos and Ale needed some privacy.

Shelley returned with a cup of fresh ice water and straw. Ale reluctantly took the pills and thanked her.

"Ale, there are loads of flowers being delivered and people calling, asking about you. Do you want the flowers in here?" she asked, closing the blinds a bit as she knew it would be bothering Ale's eye and head.

"Maybe just bring the cards in. The flowers can go maybe to Peds or Palliative?" she suggested. Somewhere that needed a pick-me-up. Shelley smiled and closed the door.

Carlos leaned in and kissed her head.

"I want to kiss you, but that lip looks like it hurts," he said, smiling.

"I want to do more than kiss you, but my body is a fuckin' mess."

He burst out laughing. "Only you would be thinking of that right now." He finally sat in the chair, leaning back and observing.

"I love the beard, babe. Jesus, you are smoking hot!" He just gave her the sexy smile.

Seriously, this man needed to keep the beard, he rocked it. It was really soft, too.

"Drugs kicking in?" he asked, big grin. *Oh man, she could stare at him all day. How lucky was she?*

Ale started to dose off and he kissed her hand and said he'd be back. He no doubt left instructions at the nurses' station that she was not to be disturbed.

Epilogue

Ale was a few more days in the hospital and reluctantly moved in with Carlos at least until she was fully recovered—much to the displeasure of momma. Her body was starting to heal, Lacey was making daily visits, and Mac was starting to do PT with her in Striker's gym. She was starting to feel a bit more normal each day.

She had become a local celebrity once word got out, with the local news and social media as some jackass had his cellphone going the entire time, she was kicking Moss's arse. It was the one-time Ale was glad she was locked up in Carlos's fortress.

Gio and Soph returned with baby Bella and momma had a new focus. Praise God.

Moss was arrested for several offences. It was sad, really. He had a huge drug and gambling habit, which none of them had known about. He was involved with unsavoury characters that had loaned him money, money he couldn't pay back. Thank God the company was saved; the family would see to that.

Moss was a disgrace and yet Ale still felt so very sorry for him. She was a nurse, a healer. Ale never understood what drove people to intentionally hurt themselves or others. It always amazed her the lengths at which people will and do go. Yet, she would always try to remain hopeful that she could save at least one.

Ale and Carlos were doing well as a couple. He was handling her with kid gloves due to her injuries, trying to stuff food into her. She had lost some weight and that bothered him. Carlos could be intense, but somehow their weird relationship was working, and he was slowly moving her stuff in. He had her sewing room set up and had his guys move some of her personal things to his place, too. They still had so many things to discuss and to be honest, Ale still wasn't sure this is what she wanted for a relationship. She really missed her apartment.

There was no question this beautiful man loved her. He showed it constantly. She hated that she was getting used to him and was starting to depend on him. But, that's *amore*, right?

After a crazy pandemic and an adventurous year of sex, violence, and love, they all had so much to look forward to. Marriage? Carlos and Ale? Joe and Liv? O'Malley? Oh, and let's not forget about crazy Lauren!

To be continued...

CPSIA information can be obtained
at www.ICGtesting.com
Printed in the USA
BVHW070102031121
620550BV00005B/69